DISCRETION

DISCRETION

ELIZABETH NUNEZ

BALLANTINE BOOKS · NEW YORK

A Ballantine Book
Published by The Ballantine Publishing Group

Copyright © 2002 by Elizabeth Nunez

www.ballantinebooks.com

Library of Congress Cataloging-in-Publication Data is available upon request.

ISBN 0-345-44731-X

Manufactured in the United States of America

First Edition: March 2002

10 9 8 7 6 5 4 3 2 1

The better part of valor is discretion.
—*William Shakespeare,* Henry IV, Part I

For my father, Waldo Everett Nunez, who stayed, and for my mother, Una Magdalen Arneaud Nunez, whom he loves

ACKNOWLEDGMENTS

I was fortunate to have an insightful editor, Anita Diggs, and a supportive agent, Ivy Fischer Stone. I had friends who offered encouragement and advice, among them Anne-Marie Stewart, Patricia Ramdeen Anderson, Norman Loftis, Arthur Flowers, and Francis Carling. Daveida Daniel typed my first draft from longhand. The Paden Institute, run by two generous philanthropists, Alice Green and her husband, Charles Touhey, and The Yaddo Corporation gave me space to write away from the distractions of my daily life. To all these good people I am eternally grateful, but none more so than to my son, Jason Harrell, who continues to be the bright light in my life.

1

When I was a child no one envied me. I was born the son of a
mannish woman and a womanish man. Who in Africa would envy
me such a fate?

My mother, I was told, was so beautiful that men traveled far
distances for a glimpse of her face. I do not know if this is true, but
I have heard that when she obeyed the wishes of her father and
consented to marry the man who would become my father, her
suitors began a fast that lasted days. And there was one, who, unable to conceive of life without her, put a razor to his throat.

My mother never loved my father. But love was not a prerequi-
site for marriage in my mother's time. That she may have been in
love with the man who killed himself because he could not bear to
live one more day with the knowledge that she shared another
man's bed was of no consequence to her family, and, thus, it was
required to be of no consequence to her. I was just five years old
when she left my father for good. No one said she left him because
she did not love him, but the women whispered among themselves
that my mother wept in secret uncontrollably on the days when it
was her turn to sleep in my father's hut.

My mother had left my father once before. It was on the eve of her wedding. Her brothers found her, hours later, a mile away from the village where the man, ten years her senior, whom it was rumored she knew (and that word was used maliciously in its biblical sense), was discovered that morning sprawled across the floor of his hut, his clothes stinking of stale palm wine, the cut on his throat so fine, so miniscule, that one would have missed it entirely if not for the stream of blood that had since thickened near his neck and formed a dark red pool, almost black, around his head like a halo.

He was a surgeon, perhaps not called so by doctors in the West, for he was not trained in the ways of Western medicine, but a scientist nonetheless. A specialist in the art of slicing and stitching: repairing the human body. There was no doubt that he knew when he put his razor to the vein in his neck carrying his lifeblood freshly pumped from his heart that one movement of his hand, expertly applied, would stop the breath in his body.

It was a deliberate act, a suicide. The wonder of it was its cause: that love could have such power, that it could lead a man to his finality!

To the villagers' way of thinking, any man, supposing he was not sick or lame or disinterested in women, could easily replace one woman with another. A surgeon of the reputation of the dead man would simply have had to make his desires known and he could have had any woman of his choice, perhaps not one more beautiful than my mother, but certainly one with a dowry far richer than any her parents could have afforded.

In the first five years of my life I heard this story a hundred times, so it seemed to my budding imagination, which, when it blossomed later, would be the cause of much of my anguish. The women would tell each other the story about this man and my mother as if the mere retelling could shed light on a mystery that baffled them, the most puzzling part of which was that my mother, who was to be married the next day, would jeopardize her future and that of her family for a dead man. For my father was a wealthy and powerful man, far wealthier and more powerful than the sur-

geon who lived in one of the six villages that had been won in wars
by my father's ancestors, fierce warriors known for their brutality,
and, paradoxically, their compassion. When they conquered a village, they took for themselves everything of worth: the beautiful
women whether married or not, wood carvings that pleased them
and the artists as well, whom they would commission to sculpt
likenesses of themselves.

I remember seeing these carvings when I was a child. My
mother took me one day to a discarded hut at the back of my father's compound. Before we entered it, she made me take off my
shoes and bow my head, and she put her fingers to her lips, signal-
ing me to be silent. I knew immediately that we were in a sacred
place. Rows upon rows of wood carvings entwined with cobwebs
lay one on top the other, dead men, though strangely animated,
their faces expressing every emotion I had already witnessed in my
young life: joy, sadness, anger, disappointment, fear, hope, pain.
My mother told me afterwards they were copies of my father's people. Holy objects.

My father had not put them there. His father had, for he had no
appreciation for art and had long ago released the artists in bondage to his family. My father saw no reason to reverse his decision,
and by the time I was old enough and knowledgeable enough to
convince my father of the value of the treasures he possessed, he
had already sold them to some French traders for twenty grotesquely
ornate brass pots that within weeks lost the shiny golden luster that
had attracted him.

But, of course, what my warrior ancestors principally took from
their enemies was land, and it was in the seizure of this most valuable of assets to the people of my country that they showed their
compassion. So long as the villagers gave them a percentage of
their crops, they were free to return to their former way of life. Yet
there was no uncertainty about the penalty to be exacted for a single infraction, one iota less of the amount of dates, sorghum, or
millet than had been agreed upon, whether the cause was due to
laziness on the part of the villager or to the unpredictability of

nature, drought, or incessant rains. The punishment was swift and irreversible: immediate exile and the appropriation of that person's land, which would then be given to whomever my ancestors favored.

My father was not at all like his warrior ancestors, neither in brutality nor in compassion. He was a mild man who conducted his life by the code of live and let live. If the villagers did not trouble him, he did not trouble them. If they gave him enough so he could continue to live in the biggest house, have the largest retinue of servants, all the food and comforts he needed, he did not keep account of who owed him what or who should be punished for what.

He had acquired the lands he owned without struggle and so had not had inbred in him what he believed to be a false notion: that there is virtue in work, value inherent in the act itself. To him work was a means to an end, not an end itself. He saw no purpose in labor unless it was necessary, and when it became necessary for him, as it did after long stretches of droughts devastated his land for miles around and he was forced to join the farmers to make the soil yield the crops he depended upon for the maintenance of his lifestyle, he married again, taking three more wives whose extended families could relieve him of his labor.

It was not a difficult achievement. My father was still a valuable prize for the most desirable of women. Fathers brought their daughters to him; he did not go seeking wives. They knew he could provide for their daughters and employ their families on his farm. And the women were not burdened with my mother's tragic sensibilities. They did not need the pretext of love to consent to his offer of marriage. They were practical, cognizant of their dependence on him, and so were grateful. When my mother left my father for the second and last time, they, like the women in our village, pondered no more on the reason for her flight that first time, on the night before her marriage: Someone had put a curse on her years ago and it had not worn off.

My father did not seem to care when my mother left, so I was told. He shrugged his shoulders, opened up the palms of his hands and, with an insouciance bred from a laziness that comes from having little to desire, he said, "Let her go. She'll return."

I knew, although I was a boy, that it would not have mattered to him, either, had she taken me with her, and for years I carried a deep resentment toward my mother for abandoning me. This anger I harbored released such poison in me that I refused to allow myself to feel any tenderness toward her even on those nights when the natural desire of a child for its mother brought me dangerously close to tears.

Sometimes, though, when missing my mother caused me such pain I could not sleep for days on end, I allowed myself to find relief in the fantasy that my mother's decision to leave without me was not hers to make. I thought then, on those dark nights, that it was her brothers who had forced her to come to this conclusion, convincing her that they would have been left to the mercy of a man whose forefathers had been known for their brutality. My father, they would have told her, would not have rested until he found me.

But in the light of day I faced the truth. I knew my mother's family laughed at my father behind his back. I knew they called him the worst of names: a womanish man, a man who had lost the will to fight.

Yes, he would have let my mother go. He would not have hunted her down, even if she had taken his son with her, his eldest of three male children, a direct descendant from a long line of warriors. But it was also true that my mother's family would have been relieved that she had left me behind. Even though he was a womanish man, my father still owned the land they lived on, and I, given the natural course of inheritance, would one day own it all.

I did not see my mother again when she left my father's compound that fateful evening. She was dead within weeks, and it would take me years after that, when I was a man, already with a wife and children, to understand why the decision she made to leave my father was no decision at all, no deliberate act dictated by the brain. I would come to know she had no choice. I would discover how the loss of one's love could defeat the will to live, how it could eradicate all joy, all purpose to existence, how life could become unbearable if one could no longer touch the skin of the person you loved, hear her voice, kiss her lips; if one no longer had the happiness that came from those inexpressible moments, those intimacies of sharing one's soul with one's beloved, knowing one was understood, believed.

My mother, I am convinced, died when her lover died. She lived a living death with my father until she could live no more. I believe that when she left, she left to die. She left without clothes or money or food or water. She woke up one morning, handed me to my father without a word, turned her back on him, and walked steadily out of his compound, not once hesitating, not once looking back, though I was told I screamed and begged her not to leave me.

Those who saw her said she had put a spell on them so that they would not be able to stop her. But I believe they did not want to, or they were afraid to. They said she looked like a woman who had already become a spirit. She was walking to that other world where the man she loved was waiting for her.

Years later I would know well what they meant. For I, too, one day would walk that road, my spirit parched for a woman who was not my wife, for Marguerite, my passion burning my heart to ashes. I, too, would become a ghost though I wore the trappings of a man: skin covering bones, flesh containing blood.

My mother was a skeleton when they found her, her flesh glued to her bones from starvation, her eyes bulging from their sockets. People came from far and wide to watch her die.

Naturally, I was not embraced by my relatives in my father's compound. My mother had dishonored her people. She was a mannish woman, a woman who took it upon herself to follow her mind. (No one stopped to consider it was her heart, not her mind, that she had followed.) Most of all I was not embraced because it was believed that my mother had been cursed and that that curse could be passed on to anyone who sympathized with her. When the Canadian missionaries offered to take me to their boarding school in the part of our country the French had colonized, my mother's people advised my father to let me go. Once again my father shrugged his shoulders, opened the palms of his hands, and said: "Take him. He'll return."

When I was twelve and had been with them for five years, the missionaries decided I was bright enough to go to high school, and so they sent me to their main school in the English colony. My father did not protest. My mother's family did not protest. They believed that if I spent more years in a city, I would turn my back on the hardships of farming on an unyielding land. They had already ingratiated themselves with the mother of my father's second son, who was next in the line of inheritance, and had made themselves indispensable on my father's farm.

I, too, did not protest. I did not want to return to my father's farm. My mother's suicide and her abandonment of me still lay heavy on my heart, and because I had now learned from the missionaries that taking one's life is an abomination to God, I was also filled with shame for my mother and for myself. I thought myself the most unfortunate child in the world. Not only did I not have a mother, but the mother I once had had sinned against God and was condemned to burn for eternity in the fires of Hell. And why? Because of love. It was for me, then, when I was young, when life had not yet schooled me, had not yet humbled me, the most shameful, the most dishonorable, the most incomprehensible reason for taking one's life.

And yet I was not the most unfortunate child. Even friends who know my story, my beginnings as the son of a mannish woman and womanish man, say the silver spoon was still firmly planted in my mouth. "That Oufoula Sindede," they say, "nobody can take his silver spoon out."

Perhaps that is true, for the missionaries arranged for me to go to the University of London, where I earned a bachelor's degree in English literature. When I graduated, I was not only fluent in my native tongue but also in two of the most important languages of European diplomacy. I spoke, read, and wrote French and English.

I knew the writings of the most important men and women of letters from England and France. This knowledge of their literature and their language would serve me well, for I was destined for a career in the diplomatic service. Though no one envied me when I was a child, I would be envied then by men older than me, wiser, and, perhaps, more worthy of the prestigious positions I would hold in my lifetime.

2

I am told that I am a handsome man. My skin is the color of black plums. It is pitch black, but my blood shows through it and gives it a richness many admire. At fifty-five I still have a young man's physique and vigor though my back is bowed slightly at my shoulders. It is a habit I developed from talking to men shorter than me. An instinct for diplomacy I had even as a teenager when I had already reached a height few in my part of the world ever attain. Though at first I bent merely to hear more clearly, it soon became evident to me that others saw this simple act of lowering my body toward theirs as an indication of my generosity. For in my country, as in Western countries, physical height is often mistaken as a sign of virility. My seeming modesty, my willingness not to flaunt an advantage that could bring into greater relief this particular area of sensitivity in others, gave me a reputation for kindness before I had done anything to earn it.

My hair is beginning to turn gray now, but it is doing so slowly, powdering my thick nap of tight curls sparingly, but more densely along my temples. I consider myself fortunate that my hair did not gray early, for, like many of my colleagues, I could have been persuaded to dye it. Like physical height, black hair reassures a man of his masculinity. But had I dyed my hair, I would have regretted it. I perspired profusely when I played tennis, soaking the collars of my shirts with my sweat. On more occasions than I care to remember, I have been witness to the embarrassment of my partners who discovered too late, when we were off court, having cocktails or engaged in some diplomatic social activity, that the rinse they had used to dye their hair had stained the back of their collars.

Tennis, it did not take me long to discover, is the game of the diplomatic world, a world in which I have spent most of my adult life. The tennis we diplomats played, not the gladiatorial spectacles one sees on tennis courts today, requires *sprezzatura*, an ability to make the game seem easy, to mask the effort needed to achieve that ease, and to conceal one's anger and jealousy when beaten by a rival. When I discovered this word *sprezzatura*, I liked it because it applied so well to a skill that was essential to possess in my profession, where appearance counted for everything.

You wore a white shirt, white pants, white socks, and white shoes when you played tennis. You sweated in the sun chasing after a little yellow ball. When the game was over, you shook your enemy's hand. You returned to your camp, apparently unscathed, your white shirt, your white pants, your white socks, your white shoes as clean as before. Damp with perspiration, yes, but unstained. Nothing to betray where a blow had left its mark.

The collars of my shirts remained unstained even when I played tennis into my fifties. I cannot say the same for my colleagues, friends or foes.

It has also been said of me that I am a presence when I enter a room and that people tend to gravitate toward me. Though I always hope that they do this because I have earned their respect, I have to admit once again that my height eases the way. Nevertheless I have learned that this reputation I had for attracting the attention of others, deserved or not, was no small factor in the decision of my president to appoint me one of the youngest ambassadors from any country in Africa.

I was thirty-two then. Perhaps not all that young for today's times when it is fashionable for young boys to win favor by being willing sycophants to those they neither like nor respect. Of my many faults, I do not hold that one: I have never served a man or a cause I did not believe in. I have never licked the boots of any man, even when it would have served me well and would have served my country, too.

I am not proud of the latter. Its source is the same hubris that was my undoing when I looked in the face of my good fortune and, like Adam, still reached out to pluck the fruit that was forbidden. When, though I had everything—wealth, power, the respect of my country-men, a beautiful wife, three loving and successful children—I risked my Eden for the taste of Marguerite's lips on my mouth, the scent of her hair in my nostrils, the warmth of her skin against mine.

Perhaps at thirty-two I was too young to appreciate the unique-ness of my good fortune. Even by today's standards, it is not usual that one gets to be named ambassador at such a tender age. I was certainly naïve then. I underestimated the envy my appointment engendered. In my foolish innocence I did not realize that I had made enemies of men older than me who had waited for years in patient service to my president for this honor that had been be-stowed upon me. I did not know there were serpents in my garden watching my every movement, waiting for that moment when I would slip and they could help me fall. Above all, I underestimated Bala Keye, my wife's uncle, who would be there when I wrapped my fingers around the forbidden apple. Who would save me when I did not want to be saved.

Luck was in my favor, as it would be in years to come. I was in the right place at the right time. I had the right skills. I had re-turned home to my country after graduating from university, but I did not return to my father's village. The missionaries offered me a teaching job in the elementary school that I had attended as a child. The president of my country, at fifty-one a fairly young man himself for his position, had come to the school for a meeting with officials from the ministry of education in France and I was asked to be his interpreter.

Though the official language of my country is French, it was only so because the colonizers were French, for very few of us spoke

French. I suppose the French liked to keep it that way so that we would not know how much they were stealing from our country. They had created a sort of tropical Paris in the city, with boutiques, art shops, restaurants, and bars that fed their illusion of power and security. Nearby, these *blancs*, as we called them, had built themselves a residential compound—houses of stone and our finest timber, manicured lawns they watered even in the dry season, swimming pools always brimming with blue water, and gardens full of roses, their petals withering under the sun in spite of the everlasting mist sprayed over them like fine-spun gauze.

My president, who used to live outside the city, outside this Paris before our independence came, did not speak French, nor did millions of his countrymen. When he rose to power after two world wars had reduced Europe to its knees and its control over its colonies had collapsed like a stack of dominoes, my president found himself in the painfully embarrassing position of having to rely on French interpreters to do business with the French.

I was a savior to him when he blasted the French government for its negligence, which he characterized as criminal, in leaving behind a populace of which close to 80 percent could barely read or write though their people had decimated acres of our farmland in their savage pursuit of uranium and gold. I pleased him with the accuracy with which I conveyed his anger (shortly afterwards, the French ministry sent a letter promising financial support and personnel), and he arranged with the missionaries for me to leave off teaching and work with him. Soon I became his personal interpreter and his most trusted companion. I knew his secrets and I kept them. Because I also spoke and wrote English, I was not only his interpreter with the French but also with the English. In time there was no one he relied on or trusted more than me.

He made me an assistant to his ambassador to the United States the year my country was suffering from a terrible drought and our children were dying like flies, their stomachs bloated from dysentery and starvation. He hoped that with my help as interpreter, his ambassador could stir the consciences of the world. I was twenty-eight then. Four years later, I would be ambassador myself.

For the honor of being named assistant to the ambassador, my president asked me one favor: to marry his daughter and take her with me to America. It was not a favor that was difficult for me to grant him. Nerida was a beautiful woman. She had a soft smile and shy, gentle eyes. Her skin was dark brown, at least three shades lighter than mine. It reminded me of the color of cocoa. She was wearing our traditional dress when her father introduced me to her, and though it covered her from her neck to her ankles, I could see that she was lovely.

I was not disappointed on our wedding night. She had the figure a man dreams his wife would have: small breasts, narrow waist, wide hips. It was the figure of my mother. What I remembered of my mother before I was weaned from her breasts when I was four years old. I remembered sitting on my mother's lap cushioned between her hips. When I made love to Nerida the first time, the memory was so strong, I wept. Nerida asked me why I cried. I said, "Because I am happy."

It was not a lie. I was happy, or rather I became quite happy with Nerida within a very short space of time.

Not long after our marriage, her father, my president, sent me to Geneva for six months' training in the diplomatic service before I would assume my post as assistant to his ambassador to the United States. Nerida accompanied me and, in those six months away from her family, she blossomed.

I discovered I had a wife who was not only beautiful but intelligent, not only intelligent but of such character that I grew to admire her. Never once did she complain that she was lonely or that she missed her home, though I would often leave her alone in our apartment all day and night as I honed my diplomatic skills: developing *sprezzatura*, learning to keep my thoughts to myself until they mattered, and then, presenting them, always to appear harmless, affable. I acquired this talent not only from watching others negotiate around the conference table, but from observing them trade favors at the dinner parties and lavish cocktail parties that were frequent in diplomatic circles.

Nerida came with me sometimes to these parties, but more

often than not she stayed at home. She found these occasions boring and surprised me by saying she felt useless.

"Like a piece of decoration with no function," she said.

I had thought that this was what most women lived for: to be seen, to be admired, to be complimented for their beauty, for the way they wore their hair, for their jewelry, their clothes. But this was not true for the woman I had married. It was the first of the many surprises I would discover about my wife.

I did not know, for example, that she had been to the university and that when she married me she already had a bachelor's degree in history. Her father had probably thought it unwise to tell me of this since he believed, as the men of our times believed, that a man could not be master of his home if his wife was equal to him in matters outside the home.

My male friends (and, of course, I at the time) would have approved if Nerida was an excellent cook, which she was; if she knew how to keep an attractive home, which she did; and if she could take care of the children when we had them. But more than a few of them would have thought it was a mistake to marry a woman who not only could challenge me intellectually, but had the means to earn a living if she wanted to. Such a marriage, they would claim, could not last. At the least provocation my wife would leave me.

"You can't have two man-rat in the same hole."

It was a creed they lived by.

Nerida knew our men thought this way, and so I cannot blame her for not telling me that she was a university graduate. Nor can I blame her father for making it a condition to my marriage to her that I take her to America. He saw the arrangement as a compromise with his conscience. Nerida would be a wife, a wife who understood and carried out her wifely duties, but she would be a wife in America, where there were books and libraries and places that could feed her curiosity, satisfy her hunger to know more.

I was young when I married Nerida. Today I would marry a woman even if she had a doctorate. Then, I do not know. I still had much growing up to do. As it was, it was Nerida who taught me most of what I learned, not only about women but also about history.

"I'll go to the library," she said when I asked her if she would not be bored staying at home. For three nights in a row I had had to attend official functions. Nerida had accompanied me once, reluctantly. I was trying to persuade her to do so again.

"What will you do there?"

"Read."

"Read?"

"History books. Keep up with my studies, you know."

It was then she confessed she had a bachelor's degree in history.

Later, I grew to appreciate her knowledge. She taught me better than my teachers in Geneva about the history of the United Nations. It was from her I understood the motives the European countries had for sending diplomats to sit with us at the table—the people they had once enslaved, the people they later colonized. Two world wars had so devastated Europe that it could no longer afford to maintain its armies in our countries. Without its armies it was not as easy as it had been before to lay claim to our land and the abundance of minerals that lay beneath it.

Nerida made me understand the power of the table—the new battleground where prizes were won and stolen. She taught me the importance of my job. I learned from her that it was my duty to fight for all of Africa, to stave off those who would suck us dry.

In Geneva, Nerida became my sole counselor and adviser, my friend, my lover, as she was to be for years to come. But that was before Marguerite reentered my life. That was before having schooled myself in the wisdom (and in the moral rectitude, it embarrasses me to add) of keeping my distance from her, I no longer had the will or the desire to deny myself the woman I believed I was born to love.

3

I would hear Marguerite's name for the first time in Geneva, in 1966, but I would not meet her until two years later when I was in America. Catherine, the wife of a Jamaican diplomat, told me about her, though to say told me about her is inaccurate. Catherine had merely mentioned her name and it sang in my head like the call of a lovebird: Margarete, Margarete.

"She is my best friend. She was the one who warned me when John joined the diplomatic service that it was the beginning of the end for us."

Catherine and I were at yet another of those obligatory cocktail parties that diplomats, and those of us in training to be diplomats, were required to attend. These were the laboratories where we were observed, the classrooms where we were tested to determine how well we had acquired the accoutrements of civility: the proper way to hold the wineglass, to dispose of napkin and toothpick after the hors d'oeuvres, to carry on a conversation with food in the hand tempting the mouth. The correct modulation of voice for greeting dignitaries, for arguing a point. The right pitch for pleasantries, especially for laughter. The eye contact that avoided intimacy, that maintained neutrality, particularly with the women (above all, with the women), the wives of important men from important countries.

Nerida, as had become usual, did not accompany me, but Catherine, as usual, was there with her husband, John. Catherine was the kind of woman my friends and I had been told to stay away from. She was bright and articulate. She had won a scholarship from her island in the Caribbean to study literature at Oxford. She had met John there, and when he graduated from law school and entered the diplomatic service, she deferred another scholarship to graduate school to marry him.

It was love, she said. She was too in love with him to live apart from him. I could have foretold her future when she said this to me. My mother also had been too in love with a man to live apart from him.

Catherine was beautiful, tall, slender, full-bosomed, with skin the color of tamarind shells. That evening she was wearing white— a slim silk dress that flattered her figure. Her skin glowed against it. Yet I did not think John noticed how beautiful she looked. I did not think John ever noticed how beautiful she looked.

She said to me more than once that John never made a decision that was not in his best interest politically. I often thought that when she said that she wanted me to understand that his marriage to her was one such decision. It was rumored that she had written his papers for him at the university and that without her to guide him, John would not have survived the minefields of the diplomatic world as long as he had. But I never thought she married him for convenience. She loved him. She was besotted with him. They had a two-year-old son, Eric, whom they both adored. "Everywhere John goes, Eric goes with him," she once told me. "And everywhere John and Eric go, I go with them."

We were sitting on the couch next to the wall, opposite to the bar, when she said the name of my beloved. From where we were, we could easily see John surrounded by a group of Swedish diplomats and their wives. I had noticed, from across the room, when John had walked away from Catherine. And when I saw her gazing vacantly over her glass in his direction, I excused myself from the man I was speaking to, and I went to sit with her.

I suppose it could have appeared that I did so because she seemed so alone, so abandoned. Catherine had often said to me that I was an unusual African. An unusual man, for that matter.

"You talk to me in public as if you think women have something to say," she said.

But I had not joined Catherine because I thought she had something to say. Nor had I joined her because I pitied her. I had joined her because I was drawn to her, and I believed she to me, by what, in retrospect, I know was a kind of incompleteness we recognized in each other. A yearning that neither of us understood or could name but was visible and identifiable to people like us who felt a nagging at the soul, an irrational dissatisfaction.

I say irrational because I believed then that I had everything a man would want: a wife who loved him, and the reassurance of a future of prestige and power. For I was certain that within a few years my father-in-law, the president of my country, would name me one of his ambassadors. There was no reason then for me to be dissatisfied or to have feelings of longing or yearning. What could I have longed for or yearned for? How could I know then it was for Marguerite?

And yet when Catherine said the name of her friend, my ears rang with the shrill whistle of the lovebird.

"Marguerite," she said. "That's my friend's name."

I want to say now that I do not believe in juju or in any kind of magical spiritualism. I am a Christian. But Marguerite would tell me later on, after she became my world, and life without her seemed impossible, that culturally I am African.

Once, because she worried that I had adopted the myths and beliefs of Europeans, she asked me if I remembered when the missionaries came for me. I told her they took me from my village when I was very young.

"How young?" she asked.

"Seven," I told her.

"The age of reason. You had already passed the age of myth."

Perhaps, then, it was fear that led me to say what I said next to Catherine. Perhaps I thought that in saying it I could reassure myself that my conversion was secure. That it was not juju that filled my head with the call of the lovebird, but a memory. A memory of a woman who existed only on the pages of fiction, make-believe, a woman who once upon a time had both fascinated and terrified me.

"Margarete," I said. "The woman Faust sold his soul to the devil to get."

Catherine stared at me. "You read Marlowe?"

"No, Goethe."

She tilted her head to one side. "Ah, I knew there was a reason I liked you. A man who understands passion for the flesh."

The bird shrieked in my ears at that moment. Its cry cut through bones, filled blood vessels. I doubled over in pain and clasped my hands across my ears.

Catherine touched my shoulder.

Only one word came out of my mouth.

"Headache," I said.

It took all my willpower to walk, not run, out of the room.

4

Let me explain myself. It was not the sound of Margarete's name that had terrified me, the trilling notes it made, like a love-sick bird, the penultimate vowel piercing the ear to bursting, the final consonant offering such sweet release as tortured lovers pine for. It was the memory it evoked, or, rather, the memory I had tried to stifle with a fantasy about Margarete, that pure vision Goethe had wrought and which I had perverted for my own needs, to serve my own purposes.

Let me try again.

I had buried a past that had tormented me. I had needed to heal a broken heart. A year before the president saved me by offering me his daughter's hand in marriage, I was the slave of a woman named Mulenga. I was young. I was foolish. I had not yet learned to avoid that abyss from which my mother did not return. In which her lover willingly gave his life.

Mulenga was the first woman I loved, the first woman I had allowed myself to love. I met her by accident. I was leaving the schoolyard at the end of the day when one of my students stopped me to ask a question about an exam I was going to give the next day. I became so involved in explaining to him the differences in the metric beat of poetry, tapping out lines on my hand—trochaic, iambic, dactylic—that I missed my bus. Just as I was about to cross the street, the bus going in the opposite direction from where I lived pulled up. That was when I saw Mulenga for the first time. Her beauty took my breath away.

I will be specific: the long stretch of her dazzlingly beautiful thigh took my breath away.

The buses in the village where I was teaching were old, worn-out wrecks that had already done duty in the city. Few had steps to the main platform. Passengers would grasp on to the railing at the side of the door and pull themselves up on the bus. Sometimes this was too difficult for the women and someone would lend them a hand. Mulenga did not need a hand. She was young. She was strong.

I told myself it was that strength I was admiring that day, but I knew then, and I know for certain now, that I had lied to myself. What I was looking at, what fixated me to her, was that smooth, fluid stretch of brown skin rising, it seemed interminably, when she hitched her skirt and lifted her leg to climb on the bus. Did I hope to see more? Did I think I would see her panties? I was not conscious of those thoughts, though I may have had them that day. But if I had, I was immediately put to shame by her seemingly panicked embarrassment when she realized that her skirt had been caught in the weave of the basket she was carrying on her arm, and that when she lifted the basket to her head, the skirt went with it. In what I now know was false modesty—her sudden intake of breath, her confusion, her eyes brimming with tears as she flapped her arms around trying to push down the folds of her skirt—I constructed my image of her innocence and virtue.

I ran to her aid when she dropped her basket. It was full of ground provisions—yams, edos, cassava, bananas, as well as mangoes and plantains. They rolled off the bus when the basket fell. Mulenga came down to help me pick them up. When she was ready to climb back on the bus, I put my arm around her waist to help her onto the platform. She did not object. Even today, if I shut my eyes, if I allow myself to go back to that time, I can feel the heat that rose to my neck when I cradled her in my arm.

Of course, I boarded the bus and sat down next to her. I told her I was on my way to visit a friend. I would have accompanied her to her doorway, too, had I not believed she would have found me too forward. But I could have told her another lie. I could have said, I want to help you, though the truth was that all I wanted was to be near her. I could have insisted. That basket is too heavy for you, I could have said. But she was a tall, strong woman with firm arms and wide hips. It was easy to believe her when she said she was accustomed to carrying baskets heavier than the one she had. She was distracted that day, that was all. That was why the basket had fallen. I wanted to believe her, and was all the more convinced when she told me that her parents were ill and she had to do the marketing for the family. *My saint.*

From the window of the bus, I watched her until her image receded and disappeared as the bus took me farther and farther away from her. She walked with her back stiff and erect, and her shoulders held high, but her backside swayed up and down, right and left, as if to the soundless beat of the rhythms of highlife, the music that was popular with the young those days in dance halls mushrooming all over the city. My eyes remained fastened on those hips until I could see them no more with my physical eyes, but later, lying in bed in the darkness of my room, I re-created, down to the smallest detail, the movement and roundness of her backside, and more—the curve of her breasts, the muscle stretching up her thigh, the firmness of her flesh on her arms.

I did not admit this, of course, to my conscious self when I pursued Mulenga. I always found myself conveniently visiting my "friend," conveniently at the bus stop when she came there (from where I did not ask her) with her basket full of ground provisions and fruit, and I always helped her climb up on the bus, and I always looked out of the window until her image disappeared, and I always reconstructed in my mind, in my bed at night, the lines and curves of her body, my imagination already beginning to store the building blocks.

It did not take long for Mulenga to invite me to her house. Yes, there was a mother and there was a father; yes, there were siblings—two boys and two younger girls, but only by months. Mulenga told me she was her mother's first daughter by another marriage to a man who had died long ago. But I would discover months later that that was a lie. Her mother's present husband had been her only husband. In fact, her mother did not know which of the men she had slept with was Mulenga's father. She told her husband that lie so he would marry her. It worked. He would see in her, as I so stupidly would see in her daughter—inexperienced as I was at the time with the ways of the world—virtue where there was none.

"Mango don't fall far from the tree," my father said when I left his compound the second time to accept the scholarship the missionaries had offered me to the university in London. I was ungrateful, he said. Just like my mother. He had wanted me to help him till his land.

For what should I have been grateful to him? Yet there was wisdom in his words, and had I accepted that wisdom, I could have saved myself the heartache that almost destroyed me when I discovered, within a matter of weeks, that Mulenga was no different from her mother. Time did teach me eventually, though, for in time, like my mother before me, I found myself lost in grief for someone who was not my spouse.

I never saw Mulenga's parents and siblings after that first evening when I sat with them at their table for dinner. My mother and father are well now, Mulenga told me the second time I visited her. Their fever has gone. They are strong now. Indeed, they had seemed fit that evening when I saw them for the first and last time.

And the children?

They stay with my father's mother during planting season when my parents are working in the fields.

And why not you? I wanted to ask. Why aren't you in the fields helping them?

But I did not ask her that. The answer was obvious. She was too refined to work in the fields. She had been to school. To the ninth grade, she said. She had already finished the sixth grade when her mother married. She was too good to work in the fields. But good enough to do what? Mulenga's mother had no answer to her husband's question.

To marry a rich man, my friends said to me. But they were wrong. I was not a rich man, and yet Mulenga let me court her.

It was a trap, my friends said. "If her mother cannot find a rich man for her, she will take a university man. A university man has potential," they said. "Her mother leaves you alone with her because she has a plan."

I did not care. So what? I said to myself. I was in love with her. "I may marry her," I said.

There were rumors: Mulenga is not who she seems to be. I stopped talking to those who brought me such rumors.

Yet I never asked Mulenga what she did during the day, or how it was that she was always available to me whenever I wanted to visit her at her home. If these questions arose in my mind, I always banished them with proof of her virtue: She kept her front door unlocked and allowed me to enter her house without knocking. If she had anything to hide, surely she would not have taken that risk. Then, too, she had refused my advances. She was keeping herself for her husband, she said. Why shouldn't I have believed her? And, oh, how I longed to be that husband she had saved herself for, to stroke those firm thighs, to let my fingers climb beyond those points where she stayed my hand.

I was in the habit of coming to her house on Tuesdays and Thursdays after the end of the school day. I would take the 2:30 bus and would arrive at her door at exactly 3:00, give or take fifteen minutes for the African sense of time. I would leave at 5:00 when the bus returned for the trip to my village. I would walk directly to her house and enter without knocking. She would be there waiting for me with pancakes she had just made, and a cup of tea. We would spend the afternoon talking. This was the pattern we established.

I realize now that it was I who would spend the afternoon talking. She would simply listen, holding my hand in hers. But isn't this what endears women to men? Don't we love it when they hang on our every word and look into our eyes with the kind of adulation that says, Yes, you are my hero; yes, you are my conqueror; yes, there is no one greater than you? It was vanity that brought down Lucifer, and so it was with me: the pride I took in Mulenga's seeming adoration, the praise I secretly heaped on myself for keeping my eyes on her face and not letting them stray to the places I wanted to see and touch—her satin-smooth thighs, her soft breasts, her undulating hips. We were both virtuous, she and I—she for her determination to remain a virgin for her husband, and I for not exploiting her vulnerability. There was no one home to protect her. No one would have blamed me for taking advantage of a virgin whose parents had left her at home, without a chaperon.

Yes, I planned to marry her. In spite of what the missionaries had tried to teach me, I did not believe that having sexual intercourse with a woman before I married her was sinful, but I wanted Mulenga to know that I thought she was special. I wanted to set her apart from the other women I knew. So I did not touch her, I did not make love to her, though every nerve in my body rebelled against my determination to let honor, and not carnal desire, rule my heart.

One day I missed my Tuesday bus. Mulenga did not have a telephone, so I could not get a message to her. I assumed she would be worried, that she was pining for me. I assumed that she would thank me for canceling my Wednesday plans to visit her, and so the next day I took the bus to her house.

I walked directly to her front door. There were no signs to warn me that I should have turned back, that this time, at the very least, I should have knocked on her door. Everything seemed the same as it was on any of the other days when I took that dirt road leading to her house. The children stopped what they were doing to stare at me, but they always stopped their play to wave to me. I did not notice that this time they did not wave to me. The women were at washtubs washing clothes or standing in front of those large wooden mortar pots in which they pounded the yams for the evening meal. They did not say a word to me, but they never spoke to me. I should have paid attention to the laughter at my back when I passed them, but I dismissed the chuckles and sudden outbursts as ordinary laughter among gossiping women.

Mulenga did not budge. She did not get out of the bed when I opened her bedroom door. She simply looked at me. "Oh," she said, "Oufoula. But it's not your day. It's Wednesday today." The man beneath her groaned. "Come on," he said. "Give me some more. Come on, Lenga."

Lenga.

My friends said I had to learn the hard way. They said I was so firm in my decision, so adamant, so convinced that she was the only one for me, so committed to the decision I made to marry her that nothing and no one could have persuaded me otherwise. I had to witness her deceit with my own eyes. I had made her into a saint, they said. Not even she could handle the rare air I wanted her to breathe from the mountaintop where I had placed her. She probably hoped you would catch her, they said. I did not believe that, but I could not deny that Mulenga had not shown the slightest sliver of remorse when I caught her in her bed naked, lying on top of a naked man. She was not alarmed or afraid. She did not jump out of the bed and plead with me to forgive her. *Oh, Oufoula. But it's not your day.* That was all she said before she pressed those breasts, the breasts I thought so virginal I would not touch them, on the chest of her hairy lover.

Perhaps it stretches credulity to find commonality between the names *Mulenga* and *Margarete*. Say the word *Mulenga*. It does not sound like *Margarete*; it does not sing into the air like *Margarete*; it does not bring to mind the call of a lovebird. *Mulenga.* It is a ponderous word. Say it and you feel the weight of those last two consonants which that richest of all vowels, that final *a*, cannot redeem. *Mulenga.* Say it. The breath leaves the lungs and falls heavily earthwards. But say *Margarete*. The breath flows as light as a feather upwards. To the heavens. This is perhaps why Goethe named his virgin Margarete, why Faust would dream of her. *Mar-*

garete. Faust, too, longed for redemption. He lusted for the pleasures of Hell, but it was in Heaven he hoped to spend eternity.

It was by mere coincidence that I was reading Goethe when Mulenga, that false virgin, deceived me. In my sick state of mind at that time when all virtue was vice in disguise, all goodness suspect, my tongue would linger on the lightness of the word *Margarete* only to deride it, only to mock the lie it concealed: She was no different, this pure woman Goethe created to tempt Faust with her sensuality, from that heavy-worded *Mulenga*—no, *Lenga*. So I created a fantasy to save myself, to protect myself from the abasement that more than ten times I would have inflicted upon myself when I would have gone back to Mulenga's house to beg her: *There has to be some reason. Tell me, Mulenga, was that man raping you?*

But a woman who is being raped does not press her breasts against the chest of her rapist. She does not say, when the man who loves her, when the man she claims to love, discovers someone in the act of plundering her virtue, *Oh, Oufoula. But it's not your day. It's Wednesday today.*

This is how I saved myself, how I bound my feet to keep myself from taking that bus to Mulenga's house, how I stopped my mouth from saying her name, how I washed her clean from my memory: I replaced her with a woman who bore not the slightest resemblance to her, except she had presented herself, as Mulenga had presented herself to me, as a virtuous woman, a woman who could not be moved to surrender her virginity outside the bounds of matrimony. Faust had longed to screw his Margarete, and I had longed to screw Mulenga. In the end, Faust got his wish. The virgin surrendered. But I, believing that my saint could not be corrupted, restrained myself in honor of her.

A virtuous woman is a virtuous woman. She cannot be corrupted. But a lascivious woman, even if honored by a man who respects her—by a radiant angel, it would not matter—will eventually seek her true nature. Mulenga would leave my arms to prey on garbage. I should have known she was not who she seemed to be.

For days I locked myself in my room in the missionary house. Over and over again I read the tragedy of Faust until I converted his Margarete, transformed her into the woman I was now certain she was—a woman of seeming virtue, a deceitful, lascivious woman who would open her legs for any man. Every night within the walls of this fantasy I had constructed, I made wild and passionate love to Margarete, stopping just at the point where I knew she was about to reach orgasm. I would withdraw from her then and spit out my seed on the bedsheets, turning my back to her hysterical pleadings.

I take no pleasure in recalling these times. I am ashamed of them. But the truth is that this was how I was able to erect a barrier to shield myself from a reality I could not face: I created a fantasy. It would both feed my need for revenge and satisfy those yearnings for that false virgin I once adored, yearnings that came at night no matter how hard I tried to dismiss them.

I was liberated the day I met Nerida. I was freed from Margarete's prison. From that day I dreamt of her only sporadically, and sometimes, for long stretches, never at all. For this, too, I was grateful to Nerida. When her father offered her to me, I knew that at long last I had met a genuinely virtuous woman. I cannot say I came to this conclusion based on anything Nerida said or did. I was a cautious man when I met her. I had been taught caution by a specialist of deceit. I came to this conclusion solely on the reputation of Nerida's father. It was said he was not a man to leave things to chance. He took few risks, and when he did, he calculated his risks so that almost always he got what he wanted. He got what he wanted from me. It was based on this, then, that I believed Nerida to be virtuous. I was not wrong to think this way. The bedsheets were stained on our wedding night.

After my marriage to Nerida, I no longer needed to protect myself from Mulenga. I no longer needed Margarete. Indeed, there were times I quite forgot that I had ever thought of her. I was caught off guard when Catherine said her name, perhaps because at that moment John's indifference to Catherine had caused me to think about the cruelty of men, not about the cruelty of women. Margarete's name slipped through the cracks of my consciousness, and I held up a shield to ward her off: *Margarete. The woman Faust sold his soul to the devil to get.* But Catherine would remind me: *Ah, I knew there was a reason I liked you. A man who understands passion for the flesh.* Her words shrieked through my ears, seared through barriers I had erected, and laid bare a truth so unbearable, so shameful, that the nerves in my head stood on end and glowed like live wires.

5

I would meet Catherine again at another cocktail party. It would be the last time I would see her. By the time we parted, her eyes were bloodshot red from her tears, for I had made her pay for finding me out, for guessing the reason for my sudden, panicked flight from the room that night. But she would get her revenge. Before she left, she predicted a future for me that frightened me. Frightened me all the more so because I knew that in spite of what she said, I would do nothing to prevent it. The danger she wanted to warn me about, a danger she said was endemic to the profession I had so blithely accepted, was a danger I could not avoid, would not avoid, for the lovebird had already sung to me. I already longed for Marguerite.

I waited until the party was coming to an end before I spoke to her. I had been avoiding her. I knew she wanted to talk to me, but each time she approached me, I walked away or became so engrossed in a conversation that it would have been difficult for her to interrupt me. I was afraid of her, afraid she had made a connection between my sudden headache and her last words to me, between my reaction to her friend's name and Margarete, the name of a fictive woman. That she had seen deep in my heart and discov-

ered the darkness there, the darkness that sometimes seeped out
under the cover of night, when I was in bed and safe, Nerida next
to me breathing heavily, no one to witness my shame: Mulenga, a
ghost from my past, the woman I loved before I found peace again
with Nerida. Mulenga, who had trapped my heart, who had made
me a prisoner of my passion, who had so bewitched me I forsook
my friends for her and made enemies of those who loved me, those
who tried to warn me of the suffering she would cause me. Mulenga, the scourge of days before I learned that passion could kill,
before I understood that passion had killed my mother. Mulenga,
from whom I tried to rescue myself with an illusion, an obsession
with a woman who never lived, never existed but on the pages of a
book. Mulenga, who, in spite of everything, I continued to desire.
This was the memory I had wanted to deny, I wanted to pretend I
had forgotten. The lovebird shrieked in my ears to mock me.

It was late; the cocktail party was beginning to wind down when
guilt finally overrode my fear and shame. I had treated Catherine
badly. John had abandoned her again. I could see her slumped
down in a chair, forlorn, her glass hanging limply from her hand. I
went to her.

"So, finally," she said to me when I approached her.

I believed I was in control. I thought I had the upper hand,
so I spoke to her without the slightest consideration of consequences, not the least mindful that she could find my tone of-
fensive, condescending.

"Finally what?" I asked her.

"Finally you have the courage to talk to me."

I sat down next to her. "And why should it take courage to talk to
you?"

"You tell me. It certainly seemed as though you didn't want to
talk to me."

"I didn't get a chance until now," I said.

"And have you come now because you feel sorry for me? You pity
me because I am sitting by myself all alone?"

"How does one feel sorry for a beautiful woman?" I asked her.
That night she was wearing red, a color I often thought made women

look gaudy. Nerida knew my taste and did not wear it, but it suited Catherine, more so that night when her eyes looked sadder than I had ever remembered.

"So you came to flatter me? Is that it?"

"I came to sit next to you."

She laughed. "Careful. Don't make it a habit. People will talk. You and me sitting alone again? The people who come to watch you may not like it."

I brushed off her remark. "How are you, Catherine?"

"Why didn't you return my call?"

"Nerida gave me the message. I was fine. Alka-Seltzer cleared up my head."

I had answered her thinking I did not need protection, having persuaded myself that it was a trick of my imagination that had led me to believe she could have discerned the truth that lay beneath my spontaneous outburst: *Margarete, the woman Faust sold his soul to the devil to get.* But she had been waiting to punish me, to make me pay for not returning her call, for ignoring her, rejecting her. While I walked around the room scoring points with the older diplomats with my grand gestures of deference to them, my eyes averted from any possible suggestion of intimacy with the women, she had been preparing a question for me.

"Was that all that needed clearing?" She leaned toward me. "She's not Faust's Margarete, you know." She pressed her hand on my knee and locked her eyes on mine. "She's Marguerite." She spelled out her name. "And she's more beautiful than Margarete and kinder. She won't make a man give up everything for her."

I hated her at that moment, for I was certain she knew my secret, that she had discovered me, that she knew what Mulenga had done to me, how I had needed a fantasy to save me.

My voice was flat when I answered her, when I asked her the question I knew would undo her. "Isn't she the one who told you that when John joined the diplomatic service it would be the end of the two of you?"

I should have known that evil always ricochets. That the bullet you send off always throws back sound to shatter your eardrums, to wake you up at night, if you have a conscience, if you are human. It was not long before I was withering with remorse from the tears that pooled in Catherine's eyes and the answer she gave me, knowing the words she said were true and there was nothing I could do to make them untrue, I who had forced her to face the truth again.

"Look at him," she said. "Do you see him?" Her eyes traveled in the direction I had turned my head.

He could not be missed. John was a handsome man, the kind of handsome that worked like a magnet. Wives were drawn to him. Husbands feared him. He exuded the sort of confidence and self-assurance that sparkled from men who knew they had this effect on others. He was the son of a black father and an Irish mother. He had inherited the best parts of both: a swarthy complexion (the blending of two skin tones—pale and dark), his mother's penetrating green eyes and reddish brown hair, and the fierce brow and chin I had admired on men I knew from the Caribbean. It was hard not to be mesmerized by him.

"He's having an affair with her," she said.

I knew what she was talking about. I had seen it, too. A quite ordinary grouping at the bar: a husband and wife in conversation with John, except Catherine must have noticed, as I had, the many times the woman leaned toward John, or the times he stroked her bare arm when her husband was distracted, either refreshing his drink or greeting someone who was passing by.

"Oh, Catherine," I tried feebly to dismiss her fears.

"A woman knows," she said.

Marguerite would say those same words to me years later and I would think of my wife and remember Catherine. Remember how easily she had read the secret signals that passed from the woman to John. Remember that I, too, knew when John's fingers trailed down the woman's bare arm that they were lovers.

"You and John make a perfect pair," I said, my voice faking insouciance.

"Liar. But then that is what the diplomatic service teaches you to do. Marguerite was right to warn me."

She said my beloved's name again, though then, of course, I did not know she would be my beloved, but when she said it, my heart raced in my chest and I feared the return of the lovebird.

Irritated for succumbing to a feeling that was so absolutely irrational, that could have no possible basis in fact, I shot out at her: "Your friend Marguerite doesn't know a thing about the diplomatic service. Is she married to a diplomat?"

When that question left my lips I was not aware that I wanted to ask it. So it is the subconscious plays tricks on us. But when it did, I knew it was the question of all the questions I had asked that night that I most wanted an answer to. But Catherine did not seem to have heard my question. Her mind was on her unhappiness, on John's infidelity, and what she wanted to tell me about Marguerite had nothing to do with the answers I wanted: Was Marguerite single? Was she free?

"Marguerite said it is the most corrupt institution there ever was," Catherine was saying to me now, not masking her bitterness.

So I pressed her again. "Well, is she married to a diplomat or not?"

It was by mere luck she did not hear the anxiety in my voice.

"No, she's not married. What difference does it make? She lives in New York. She knows about corruption."

She was unmarried, living in New York.

Now I wanted the evening to end. I wanted to get away from Catherine, but she was not finished with me.

"Marguerite said the diplomatic service is so corrupt, it does not know it's corrupt."

I became defensive. "Are you saying I'm corrupt?"

"No," she laughed, a dry laugh. "You are on your way to being corrupt. Very soon you'll become ambassador from your country and people will bow to you as they do to John and they will call you Your Excellency. Heady stuff. It leads to corruption."

A waiter passed. Catherine called him to her and asked him to refill her glass.

I do not drink. Sometimes, especially at social occasions, I regret this decision, for without the stupefying haze of alcohol, one sees things one may not wish to see: the private selves of people that they expose indiscriminately when alcohol invades the brain and removes inhibitions. Old wounds are laid bare—hatred, fear, lust, rage, longing. I am embarrassed by the intimacy.

"I don't think you should drink this," I said. I took her glass from her hand.

She snatched it back. "Don't do that again or you'll regret it."

I withdrew my hand.

She became chastened by my acquiescence. "I was complimenting you, not criticizing you, when I told you you'll be ambassador soon," she said. She stopped me when I began to object. "You're the most intelligent and honorable man I have met since I have been here. Your country very much needs you, and your president knows what I am saying is true. But to become a successful diplomat you will have to learn how to lie." She looked over at John. "John is a successful diplomat."

"Is that what you think diplomats do?"

"You can't make any deals for your country unless you lie."

"Diplomacy," I said, "is the art of persuasion." I believed that was what I believed.

"Diplomacy is the art of lying so it appears as the truth even to the teller of the lie." She laughed again. "That's what I think will make you able to survive, Oufoula. When you lie, you'll believe you're telling the truth. From the core of your being, you'll think you haven't lied."

She was managing to disturb me, to ruffle my calm exterior. I glanced at John. He was saying something to the woman, about the drink in his hand, I thought. She leaned over, put her lips to his glass, and grimaced when the liquid reached her tongue. They laughed. It seemed a private joke. Her husband frowned.

"I won't lie," I said.

"Then you won't be ambassador," she said. "But I predict you will be."

"I don't know what I'll do in the future. I may return home after this drought crisis is over."

"There you go. You know that is not what your father-in-law plans for you, or what you want. See, you have learned to lie already. Lying, my dear, is not always by commission. Mostly, it is by omission. That is the art you'll perfect. At all cost avoid the truth. Never commit yourself. Do not make decisions. Allow others to make your decisions for you. Always insinuate. That way no one can hold you responsible for saying anything. You will learn soon how to withhold information, how to say and not say. You'll learn the art of innuendo and nuance. You'll learn to smile when you do not want to smile. To make love when you do not want to make love. To be a husband when you no longer want your wife."

A tear rolled silently down her cheek. She swiped it away with the back of her hand, but another one followed. Her unhappiness so evident now, the tragedy of her marriage, made me realize again how fortunate I was. There was peace in my home. Harmony. Nerida was waiting for me. My lovely, beautiful, faithful, loyal Nerida. My wife. How much happier was I than Catherine, how much more contented than John. I did not need to forage, to hunt. I was lucky. All that I wanted, all I could have hoped for was there, waiting for me. I offered Catherine my handkerchief. She turned away from me, threw her head back, and drained her glass.

I went to John and told him his wife was not well. I told him he should take her home and he should do so immediately, and I pulled him away from the woman who was now looking unabashedly into his eyes.

After John left with Catherine, I ran to my car and sped home as fast as I could, Catherine's predictions weighing heavily on my heart: *A husband when you no longer want your wife.* But I wanted my wife. I wanted Nerida. I repeated those words like a prayer, as if they could protect me.

I made love to Nerida that night washed with gratitude to her for being my wife, desperate to prove Catherine wrong, to prove myself loyal, true. A man who stood by his word. Nerida was amazed by my passion and counted that moment as the time I fell in love with her. She has told me this many times since and I have never disputed her, for even then I was well on my way to mastering the art of diplomacy.

Perhaps I lied when I told Nerida that night that I loved her, but

I did not know I lied. How could I when there were no words to convey what I could not understand? No words to express the yearning, the nagging feeling of incompleteness, the feeling of wanting more, needing more—an awareness I did not want of a truth I could not avoid: that though I loved Nerida, I did not love her as I wanted and needed to love a woman. That though I did not want to betray her, I would betray her; that though I did not want to lie to her, I would lie to her. I would reach for more though I had much. For my soul had already reached out to Marguerite and I wanted her. And the folly of it all, the mystery, was that I had not even met her.

6

Shortly after Catherine predicted that my father-in-law would have plans for me, he sent me to Washington, D.C. It was a major step forward in my career, and I was excited about the opportunity to put into practice the diplomatic skills I had acquired in Geneva for the good of my country. Yet I must admit that I was keenly aware that I would be in the country where Marguerite lived. I knew, too, for my friends had told me, Washington, D.C. was less than a day's drive to New York City, where Marguerite had an apartment. I did not know her phone number or her last name and I could not ask Catherine for either without subjecting myself to her questions, to her suspicions. More than that, I did not want to risk the chance that Catherine would bare her soul to me again and force me to peer into the intimacies of her marriage.

In time, however, it ceased to matter that I did not know Marguerite's last name or her phone number. In time this intense desire I had to meet her began to subside. In time I ceased to feel the thrill that coursed through my blood when, in brief spates of what surely was nascent insanity, I believed my fantasy lived. In time I ceased to repeat in my head *Margarete, Marguerite,* merging one name into the other until only Marguerite remained. *Marguerite.*

This happened partly because I enjoyed my work, partly because I liked my life with Nerida, but mostly because I wanted to believe what my friends said of me: that I was a happy man by nature, a man who was never sad, a man who rarely seemed burdened by troubles.

I had been in Washington two years when Catherine wrote to me. During those two years I had had a son, Ayi, and Nerida was pregnant with our second child. I had all I wanted. So I made an effort to put Marguerite out of my mind. Yet when I read Catherine's letter, so filled with her unhappiness, the thought above all else that came to me was that at last I had an excuse to call Marguerite.

I would meet Marguerite two days after I received Catherine's letter. She would invite me to dinner at her apartment when I called her, but I would not go. I did not trust myself to be with her alone and after dark. I wanted the full protection of the daytime when I saw her. I wanted to be surrounded by people. I did not know if I could stop myself from saying to her words that I had spoken to her only in my dreams. I could not trust myself to remember that my dreams were not reality and that in reality I had a wife I loved, a wife who loved me. Above all I would not go to her apartment because I did not know what she looked like and what I would do if she was, as Catherine had said, more beautiful than Goethe could have imagined a Margarete for his Faust. I did not know how I would react if she did not like me. For I knew, within minutes of meeting her, it would be clear to me whether she did or not.

Catherine was right: even then in my early days in the diplomatic service, it had begun to dawn on me that the cardinal rule of my profession was never to speak the truth directly. More than once I was reminded that words can never be recanted. That truth can be conveyed in other ways, subtle ways where the message is communicated without risk of commitment, where the speaker can deny, object, claim that that was not what he meant when what he meant becomes a liability for his country.

I was learning to speak with my eyes, my tone of voice, my body.

Each movement was calculated to add, to detract, to emphasize or deny what my mouth spoke. I was beginning to know who were my enemies and who were my friends by the way their eyes focused on me or shifted away from me when they talked to me, by the expansiveness or the niggardliness of their hand movements. Soon I was able to detect a laugh that meant disapproval, a smile that warned me of the futility of attempting to negotiate an agreement.

I knew, then, that when I met Marguerite, within a short time after talking to her I would know from the way she held her fork, from the way she tilted her head, from the way she smiled or frowned, or cried (for the news from Catherine that I was bringing to her was not happy news) whether she liked me or not. And if she did not, I did not know what I would do, finding myself alone with her in her apartment with the dreams and fantasies of many restless nights crushed to smithereens with one look, one glance, one turn of her body.

I am told that people who are always surrounded by people are insecure, that they fear rejection. I do not think that this is true for me. I do not need confirmation that people like me or admire me. I know that I am liked. My wife, Nerida, loves me.

Perhaps initially I was useful to my president in the diplomatic service because of my skills in English and French. But I have long ceased to be an interpreter or a trainer of interpreters. Now I am called upon by my country and by other countries in Africa as well to negotiate agreements and to settle disputes. I am told I inspire confidence in others and put people at ease. But there are many who dislike me (Bala Keye, my wife's uncle, foremost among them), still not enough to make me so insecure that I fear rejection. Yet this talent I have for making people like me was in its incipient stage, undeveloped when I met Marguerite, and I was afraid she would reject me, that she would not like me. And I wanted her to like me.

Long after I met Marguerite, she told me that it was not insecurity but rather my natural propensity for caution that made me take such care about when and how I would meet her for the first time. I am a man, she said, who calculates the risk he would take. Catherine had told her that if I were Adam I would never have taken the apple Eve offered to me. I would have looked around Eden and calculated what I would have lost.

"Catherine said you could have been the savior of mankind," Marguerite said bitterly. "There would be no original sin in the world. No need for God to sacrifice His only son."

But Catherine had not known me well enough, though she knew me well enough to be right when she commented, after I told her how I met my wife, that I took no risk when I married Nerida. I took no chance on love. Like my mother, I married the person who was offered to me, the woman who would secure my future.

But my mother did not marry her husband willingly, and when she did marry, she paid with her life for her obedience to tradition, her loyalty to family. I, too, like my mother, was in love with someone else—Mulenga—but I married Nerida willingly. I did not die for the woman I loved. Instead, in time, I grew to love the woman who was given to me to be my wife. I grew to love Nerida.

Perhaps, though, Catherine knew me better than I knew myself in those early days in Geneva when I was beginning my career in the diplomatic service. Perhaps I am a natural-born diplomat. I have avoided making decisions. I have allowed decisions to be made for me. I had not always done so.

I had chosen Mulenga in spite of the fact that none of my friends approved of her. I declared my love for her openly and withstood the ridicule of those who disliked me. It is to her I am indebted for the invaluable lesson I learned of keeping my own counsel, of not committing myself to any act, deed, or word until I was certain of the results I wanted.

The decision I made to marry Mulenga when I was a young man and in love was the last I made without some assurance of a positive outcome. It was the last time I made a commitment to anyone or anything that had not been presented to me, the facts laid out beforehand. I had not sought out Nerida. I had not pursued a career in the diplomatic service. Both had been presented to me.

If I feared meeting Marguerite for the first time by myself, it was because I feared she could change all that, that she could awaken in me a passion I had long since suppressed when I cried like a woman, not because I had been betrayed, but because in spite of my betrayal I longed for the woman who had made a cuckold of me before my friends. Then, like Ulysses, I needed someone—something to lash me to stillness from desire.

I feared being alone with Marguerite when I met her for the first time, it was because in spite of the schooling I gave myself, I needed Margarete to live and grow in my imagination, to feed my fantasies. This fictive woman, the lascivious fantastications I had spun from her innocence and forced surrender, protected me (so I thought) from the passion that could ruin me. The passion that ruined my mother.

Margarete, or what I had made of Faust's Margarete, ruled my nights, she inhabited my dreams. She kept me from surrendering to Mulenga. Then I heard her name in the name of a woman in the flesh.

Now, faced with the reality that I could meet her, I feared I would prove myself indeed my mother's son. I would willingly seek my doom to be in the arms of my lover. Nothing anyone would say or promise, no matter what the price, would dissuade me. It would take only the first step and I would keep on walking, as my mother had done, never stopping until all breath had left my body.

It was the first step I feared. I would meet Marguerite in the daylight, protected, if not by friends, then by strangers. I would not take that risk of meeting her in the flesh, as I met her in my dreams, alone, and in the night.

7

~

This is the letter that gave me the excuse to telephone Marguerite.

Dear Oufoula,

You left Geneva before I could say good-bye to you properly. If I had not run into your wife by accident in the store, I would not have known you were leaving the next day for America, for Washington.

I cannot blame you for avoiding me. I know that was what you were doing, so don't get diplomatic with me. You didn't want to face me again. What a spectacle I must have made of myself crying all over your clean white shirt, which I bet Nerida had washed and ironed for you. She looks like a woman who would have starched it as well. She is quite beautiful, too, I must say.

I am writing to you because I need your help. I called you a liar, but I am also a liar. I pretend to be strong when I am not strong. I pretend to be brave when I am desperate. Well, I am not going to pretend with you. You would read through me, in any case. So here it is. I am desperate. John has left me and he has taken Eric with him. I need your help to get John to return Eric to me. You are good with negotiations. John told me once that nobody wants to displease you. You disarm them with your goodness and your kindness. Well, it's your goodness and kindness I am relying on.

Eric is four now—three years, eleven months, and thirty days old. Today is his birthday, as you can surmise, but I have not seen him for thirty days, so I think of him not as four but as three years, eleven months, and thirty days old.

Don't think I'm losing my mind. My mind is quite solid. I just think of things differently now. I count time in different ways. By how many times the sun dawns. By how many times night comes. There have been thirty dawns and thirty nights since John left with Eric and said he would return the next day.

I know he is in New York. I have heard he is posted to the Jamaican mission there. I know he has Eric there with him. The blonde you saw hanging on her husband's arm while she made love to the man I was married to is now playing mother to my son. One of his powerful friends called me to tell me that John wants me to know that Eric is safe. He expects me to be grateful for that information. So I gathered from his friend. He wants to warn me that if I try to reach Eric, he will take him away from me forever.

You know as well as I do that John has the power to do that. The malice also. His friend told me that John wants me to return to Jamaica and wait for him there. He said he would bring Eric to me in Jamaica. I do not believe him. I do not want to go to Jamaica. I think if I go there, John would find a way to keep me there. He owns the government of Jamaica. They will take away my passport and I will never be able to leave the island to find Eric.

I do not know what to do. I cannot stay much longer in Geneva. My money is running out. I am afraid to go to New York. I know John does not make threats lightly. I am afraid to return to Jamaica. He'll make me a prisoner there. So you see, I have no choice but to turn to you. You can negotiate this for me. I know John wants to divorce me and marry his blonde. She's rich. John's decisions are always calculated. I'll give him his divorce without an argument, but I want my son. Eric means life to me. I need him and he needs me. Every child needs a mother—his real mother, if she wants him. And I want my son.

No, I know I can't keep Eric for good. John would never give him up. I told you before that wherever John goes, he wants Eric with him. You know Jamaican men and their firstborn sons. It must be so for African men, too. Their sons belong to them.

I broke off reading. "Not so for my father. Not my father," I whispered to myself. How raw that ache remained in me! And as suddenly as it returned, it vanished and I refocused my eyes on the letter before me.

Eric belongs to John, so he believes. So, yes, I know I can't have him all the time. I am so desperate that I'll agree to have Eric go to school where John is and spend the summers with me in Jamaica. Will you tell him that for me, Oufoula, and get him to send my son to me? You are an honorable man. I know you will do it. You probably have a child now, perhaps a son. You know what your son means to you, means to your wife. Can you imagine the pain your wife would feel if your son were taken away from her? Can you imagine, Oufoula? No, don't try to imagine it. I wouldn't want even my enemies to know my hell.

Here is my phone number in Geneva: 022 555 55-55. It's a new number. Call me when you receive this letter. I am going to give you Marguerite's phone number, too. You remember I talked to you about Marguerite? Call her when you get to New York. Give her my love. Don't tell her about my troubles with John. It will only worry her, and there is nothing she can do.

Yours in love and desperation,
Catherine

Oh, P.S.: Marguerite's phone number is 212-555-5224.

I memorized the number greedily, and everything else Catherine had written to me vanished, disappeared, became unimportant, insignificant in the angles and curves of those ten blue digits. It was as if a boulder had suddenly been lifted from the memory that in recent times, content with Nerida in Washington, I had managed to suppress, and I relived at that moment the same thrill and fear I felt when Catherine told me, at that unfortunate cocktail party, that Marguerite lived in New York and in a fit of irrational desire I made that impossible leap from one world to the next.

For what man made of flesh and bones, of spirit, too, but not only, could calm the rising rivers of blood pounding through his veins if he had the chance to meet in reality the sexual fantasy of his nocturnal emissions?

Marguerite! *"And she is more beautiful than Margarete,"* Catherine said.

I could call this Marguerite. I could speak to her. I could hear with my ears the voice of the woman who spoke to me only through my dreams. I could see her. I could touch her.

I tried to steady myself, to remind myself that I did not know her, that I had no need to know her, to meet her. I had a wife. I wanted no one but my wife. Marguerite was an illusion, a figment of my imagination.

It was not enough to dissuade me. Perhaps I had gone mad, but how different was I from the rational man who goes to his therapist once a week to recapture dreams I could recapture with a telephone call, a visit?

I reasoned—I let reason beguile me—that when I saw Marguerite, when I spoke to her, I would finally put an end to the incomprehensible yearning that still persisted even when I made love to Nerida, a longing for a thing I could not see or touch or name. Perhaps, I convinced myself, calling Marguerite would strengthen my marriage, rescue me for Nerida alone.

8

I do not consider myself a callous man. I can sympathize with the pain others feel. I am moved when they weep. I am happy when things go their way. I dance at weddings, I visit the sick. I cry at funerals. I am a kind man. I put money in the tin cans beggars proffer to me. When I lived in Washington, D.C., my colleagues used to laugh at me because I did this. They told me I wasted my time, that I was a fool to succumb to beggars in a city where begging can be as much a man's job as diplomacy was mine.

It was the wrong comparison for them to make. Begging was what I did for a living and because it was, I knew too well its cost to a person's dignity. Though in the diplomatic service we tried to compensate for that loss with the airs we put on, the trappings we surrounded ourselves with, the titles we gave ourselves, the obsequiousness we required from those who served us, it was never enough to dull the humiliation when we were rebuffed, particularly when the thing we begged for was, as so often was the case, a matter of life and death for our people.

So I did not refuse beggars. I could not have a man beg me for food and deny him, or a woman beg for my help and ignore her. And yet, ultimately, that was what I did to Catherine. I tore up her letter. I never called her. I never wrote her. I never saw her again. I never heard anything more about her except through Marguerite.

I told myself I had done the wise thing by destroying Catherine's letter and not doing as she pleaded with me to do. There were many reasons I used to justify my actions. I reminded myself that first of all it would not have been manly for me to chastise a man for his treatment of his wife. Women, I believed, belonged in that arena. They were the counselors, the censors of the unfaithful, the healers of the brokenhearted. Men had to avoid that quicksand of empathy, for men knew that when they stepped on it they could be swallowed by emotions that could take them off course, make it impossible for us to make hard decisions when such decisions had to be made. Men did not have the luxury of yielding to emotions as women had. Men had households to support, women and children who relied on them for food and shelter. A man could not squander his future in the abyss of emotions. Not a manly man.

For in those days, not yet made wise and human by my love for Marguerite, I categorized everything. I put everything in a place, I gave everything a function, a role. For me, then, the private self did not belong in the world of the public self. I was convinced that not to separate the two was to court chaos, to invite disorder and confusion. A man could not know his own thoughts when the private self intruded into the public self or the public self into the private self. He could not know if he was persuaded to think the way he thought, to decide the way he decided because of his feelings for this or that person, his concerns about this or that interest.

My ancestors were warriors. I believed they were victorious because they knew their own thoughts. If they had entered wars each time one of their men had suffered a broken heart, and not when it was the right thing to do, the wise thing to do, our people would not have survived. We would not have been, as we now were, among the richest and most powerful of clans in my country. It was because of my forefathers that I had a place that one day my children could call their own.

No, I reminded myself when I discarded Catherine's letter, when I decided not to answer it, it was the Europeans who destroyed each other for the love of a woman. I thought of the ten years of war between Greece and Troy over the love Paris had for Helen; how Sampson let his people be devastated because of his obsession with Delilah. My people went to war over land, over disputes about patrimony. They traded goods when one of their own was humiliated by a woman from another tribe: thirty virgins for the one that betrayed their countryman. A hundred pounds of yam to compensate for the one who could not produce a son.

It would be war I would be entering into if I spoke to John as Catherine wanted me to do. I knew John. I had witnessed him plot revenge against a person who harmed him. There was no one I knew whose heart was more full of malice than John's. John did not try to get even with those who crossed him. He tried to destroy them, and, more often than not, he succeeded. And he would have tried to destroy me—rightly so—had I, a colleague, a friend in his public life, intruded into that space that belonged to his private self.

More than that, I knew Catherine did not have a chance against him. I knew that John would call in every favor that he had extended to anyone, he would use every iota of influence he had, to get his way. He would consort with thieves and murderers, if that became necessary. I had divined his character. I had always wondered why Catherine had not seen what I had. Why a woman otherwise so intelligent had missed what was clearly so obvious to the men I knew who knew John.

Emotions got in Catherine's way. She allowed herself to be ruled by her heart, as most women did. As my mother did. As I once did with Mulenga before I taught myself to confine such passion to the prison of my dreams.

There should be a bell that goes off in our heads when we lie to ourselves. Some noise to jar us awake when we allow ourselves to toy with reason so that it bends to our commands. I wanted Marguerite. I needed to find a way to see Marguerite. But I did not want to be disturbed by pangs of conscience. I did not want to feel guilty that I had used Catherine as I would an airline ticket, to get from one place to another. So I convinced myself this at least I could do for her: I could tell a friend of the trouble she was in. Perhaps there was something Marguerite could do. Someone she knew who had political influence. I disregarded Catherine's words that Marguerite could be of no help to her. I used a self-serving logic to suppress objective reason, reason that told me that Catherine was also my friend and I should try to help her, that perhaps there was a chance that I could penetrate John's conscience. I could move him by the very love he had for Eric and Eric for him. I could make him see that his son's happiness lay not only in having his father's love, but his mother's love, too.

Instead, I told myself that such an effort on my part would have been futile. Even if I were willing to do the unmanly thing, even if John were to admit me into his private space, I would have lost. For John was also a cunning man. He would have known how to ensnare me with his existential arguments. He would have asked me to define "mother." He would have pointed out that biology was no determinant for who was the best caretaker for a child. He would have said that he could offer his son opportunities that Catherine could not. His son would travel, go to the best schools, meet the world's most influential people. And as for love, he had enough love for Eric to make up for Catherine's absence. His new girlfriend loved Eric and was devoted to him. And, finally, he would have made a defense I could not rebut. He would have reminded me that Catherine was a closet alcoholic. Didn't I see her get drunk at one too many cocktail parties? She suffered from bouts of depression. Didn't I see her cry in public? He could not expose his child to such danger and unhappiness. So it was I concluded that it would have been useless, and perhaps not wise, for me to try to persuade John to do as Catherine wanted.

It would be this, my calculated analysis of the dangers in ceding to Catherine's pleas for my help, that would lead Catherine to say to Marguerite that if I were Adam there would be no sin in the world. Yet because I tried to be a kind man, because I did not want to be a callous man, I decided that I would speak to Marguerite. I would offer Catherine the consolation of her best friend's love.

But even as I came to this conclusion, I knew I was lying to myself again. I knew that it was for my sake I wanted to call Marguerite. That ever since that first time when Catherine mentioned her name, I longed to see my dream incarnate, my fantasies made flesh. For in spite of what Catherine had concluded, I was indeed the son of Adam. I, too, could not resist the forbidden fruit.

9

I called Marguerite the very day I received Catherine's letter, obsessed with my dark desire to see her, afraid that if I waited one more day, reason would overrule me, return me to that safe, secure place where my world was in order, where things were in place, where my life was peaceful, calm, unruffled. Where I believed I was happy. Where I lived in my cocoon with Nerida and our son.

Marguerite answered the phone on the first ring.

"Hello?"

I had to reach deep in my throat to find my voice.

"Marguerite? This is Oufoula Sindede. Catherine's friend. Catherine Simpson's friend."

"Wait," she said. "Wait a minute."

I waited, and while I waited I let myself be sucked downwards into the vortex of the forbidden. I shut my eyes and let it all come back to me—those days and nights locked in my room in the mission school when Mulenga had deceived me, made me a cuckold with her lust.

I saw Marguerite through those eyes, the eyes of my former self, myself before Nerida. I saw her naked, her body dripping wet from the shower. I saw her put down the phone, race across the room for a towel. I saw her breasts, two ripe mangoes plump and firm, their nipples brown and erect, shifting with her movements, her skin the color of butterscotch, curving around a small waist, rounded hips, parting at that triangle above her thighs, and I sucked in my breath with my desire for her, my years of longing for her.

"Hello? Hello?" She was calling to me again, but I had lost my voice winding through the dark caverns of my fantasies.

"Hello? Are you there?"

I coughed.

"God, I hope it's not the flu." Her voice was not the voice I expected, the voice I had waited to hear. It was a sweet voice, a caring voice, a sympathetic voice.

"No," I said quickly. "No, not the flu."

"It's been going around."

I coughed again.

"Take two Tylenol," she said. "Not aspirin. They could upset your stomach."

A white heat burned through me. I fought against her. The woman I created when Mulenga deceived me would not have cared, would not have said, *Not aspirin*. She would not have noticed my cough. I did not want to surface to the present where this woman was, to the real, to the mundane where she wanted me to be.

"It's not the flu," I said. "It's a dry throat."

She must have detected the irritation in my voice. "Hmm," she said, and nothing more. Then, just as I was beginning to think I should apologize (I did not want to lose her), she said my name and my world became right again.

"Oufoula."

My name never sounded so dark, so seductive, so rich with possibilities.

"Oufoula. Yes, I know who you are. Catherine Simpson's friend."

Was all well with her friend? she wanted to know.

She did not speak again of my throat, the flu, or a remedy for the flu.

"Yes," I said, "but I have a message from her to you."

"A message? It's not serious?"

"No," I said.

"What is it?" she asked.

"It would be better if I told you in person."

I was cunning. But had Catherine not wanted me to meet her?

"Then it is serious."

"Serious, not devastating."

"How soon can we meet?"

I told her I would be in New York the next day. I had not planned it. I did not know when I picked up the phone to call her that that was what I would do, but I knew it then. I knew that one more day was all I could wait to see her.

"I'll make dinner."

"No." I almost shouted the word at her.

"It won't be any trouble."

"No. Not in your apartment."

In the daylight. In a place where there are people.

She stumbled over her words. "I mean . . . I thought . . ."

I had embarrassed her. This was not how I expected Marguerite to be. When I caught Mulenga on top of her lover, she did not blink an eye. She looked directly at me. She held my eyes. "Oh, Oufoula," she said, as if she were chiding a child. "But it's not your day. It's Wednesday today." She had no remorse.

"I don't want to bother you with cooking for me." I softened my tone.

"I thought it would be more convenient," she said. "In my apartment."

"Yes. That was kind. But is there a restaurant close to you?"

A place where I would be surrounded by people.

She lived in the Village, she said. There were many restaurants close to her. I asked her to choose one, and she gave me the address. We could meet for lunch, I said.

"Twelve-thirty?"

I agreed. I did not consult my appointment book. I said twelve-thirty was a good time for me. I did not dare say more. I did not dare risk my good luck. She had said yes. I would meet her tomorrow. Tomorrow was not a long time away. Tomorrow was an afternoon, a night's sleep. Tomorrow was hours away.

There are times we wish for things we should not have: another man's wife, another man's job, another man's power. But when we wish for those things, we know that we will do nothing to actually get them. We will not steal, we will not murder. We will not betray the ones we love. We know these things we wish for are the stuff of our imaginings. Safe in the privacy of our illusionary world, we are free to make what we will of these things as if we had them. We make love to the other man's wife, we sit in the other's man castle, we drive the other man's Rolls-Royce, we use the other man's influence and power.

We do this in dreams, and we are not culpable. Behavior, we know, is what counts. We cannot control how we feel. Temptation, the devil's lethal weapon, comes to us in many forms—feelings and yearnings, the most persuasive. But we do not surrender to them, not always for fear of the loss of paradise in the next world, but for fear of the loss of the paradise we have in this world, the present world in which we live.

I had paradise in the present world, paradise that it would shatter me to lose: Nerida, my son, another child to be born in four months, a job with prestige and influence. I believed I was happy. Yet when I said good-bye to Nerida that morning before I took the shuttle from Washington to New York, it was another paradise I was thinking of—not of the next world, or of the present conscious world, but of the subconscious world, the world where I had lived in secret when the first woman I loved so devastated me, I was forced to shield what was left of my heart with a lie that consoled me.

Nerida saw the glaze in my eyes when I said to her that something had come up unexpectedly that morning and I had to go to New York.

"Why didn't they call you last night?" she asked me.

I blamed the diplomatic bureaucracy.

"They had probably given the message to someone who thought someone else had already telephoned me."

"Oh," she said. She did not take her eyes off me.

"I'll be back early," I promised. "I'll take the six o'clock flight."

"So you will have dinner at home?"

I knew she was pressing for a commitment from me.

"Yes," I said.

"I'll wait for you."

She said it as if she meant she would wait longer than the hours it would take for me to get back to Washington from a day's trip to New York. But women have this prescience. When they sense danger approaching them, they send out signals. Warnings. I'll wait for you, they say. A promissory note. They make you sign it. They throw out the rope to you that could save them. Catch it, they tell you. Reel me back into the boat with you, they say.

I wish it were so with men. We keep our fears silent, our dreams secret. We know emotions can erode our manhood. I could have said to Nerida, Reel me back in. But I did not, though I was afraid. For though I was afraid, I was not so afraid as I was desperate, desperate to see the woman of my dreams.

This is where women prove themselves more levelheaded than men. They know there is a fine line between truth and illusion. They speak their desires, their fears. They know that the unspoken world is the dangerous world. They bring the unspoken world into the open, into the daylight. They talk and talk. I see them revealing this and that to each other. I do not know exactly what they say, but I know they tell all.

We men say nothing, nothing about what touches the heart or lies in our dreams. Perhaps this is how women protect themselves from suffocating from a lifetime of fantasies. They know that if they do not give wings to the secret desires that intrude in the silent spaces of their minds, they risk pushing themselves too near that line where the vision blurs. Where they could cross over. Where they could make that fatal mistake and find themselves in a place where the unreal becomes the real.

I did not give my wife Catherine's letter to me, but I told her that

John was leaving Catherine for the blond woman he met in Geneva. My wife responded with a lecture to me, though she was far too discreet to use the tone of voice that would have revealed her intent to caution me, to have me learn from John's philandering ways.

"Men are stupid like that," she said. "They are always willing to give up the thing they have for the thing they have imagined. Nobody is perfect. Men believe in the illusion of perfection. I know this may seem odd to you, but think about it. Who are the realists, men or women? Men say they are and that we are the romantic ones, but it is they who are romantic. Women understand the necessity of compromise. They know they can never get exactly what they want. It's men who chase windmills.

"John will be no happier with that blonde than he was with Catherine. In time that blonde will prove to be imperfect to him, too. What will he do? Find another one? Pursue one of his childish dreams again? He should grow up."

My wife was an intelligent woman. I should have taken her words as a warning.

I went early to the restaurant. I wanted to be seated before Marguerite came in. I wanted to be in a place where she could not see me but I could see her when she entered the room. The restaurant she had chosen yielded to my plans. It was bright and sunny and otherwise open except for a wide column in the center of the room behind which I could hide. I calculated that if I pushed one end of the table further outside of the column, I could sit on the chair behind the column where I could not be observed from the doorway and yet could still be able to see the people as they entered the main dining room. I had just moved the table when the waiter approached me.

"Not that way, sir," he said, and stretched his arms across the table to put it back in its proper place squarely behind the column.

I had to raise my voice at him to get him to understand.

"I want the table here. Here where I had placed it."

He was a man in his sixties, someone who had spent a life waiting tables, someone who took a proprietary pride in the arrangement of the seating in a restaurant he had deluded himself into
thinking of as his own. I saw the trembling begin in the corners of
his mouth and I regretted my insensitivity. To appease him, I commented on the group of black-and-white framed drawings that
lined the wall in the back of the room. I said I was sure he had a
hand in selecting them. He didn't deny the possibility.

"It is the work of a new artist I know," he said.

"A patron of the restaurant?" I asked.

"She eats here all the time. I told the boss he should showcase
her work, but he plans to take them down soon. Put up something
more colorful. Black and white, you know." He shrugged his shoulders. "He says they don't work in a restaurant."

"But you were right to tell him to display them," I said. "They are
remarkable. You have the eye of an artist."

He beamed.

I looked at my watch. It was noon. I had called Marguerite from
the airport as soon as I had arrived. I could not bear to wait the
hour it would have taken me to reach the office of my colleagues in
the UN and telephone her from there. It was nine o'clock when I
called her.

"How will I know you?" she asked me.

"I'll probably be the darkest and tallest man in the room," I said.
She laughed.

"And me, you?"

"I'll wear something red." She paused. "A scarf. I'll tie a red scarf
around my handbag."

My heart raced. Red. The color I had seen her wear in my nocturnal wanderings. I tried to stifle my disappointment that it would
only be a scarf.

"If you want, you can go look at them." The waiter was still
standing next to my table. I did not want to offend him again. I got
up and walked to the back of the room. That was why Marguerite
saw me before I saw her. I was standing before a framed etching of
a black woman seated on a daybed, her back bent, seemingly from

years of hardship. One arm was hung limp across her lap, the other was held akimbo on her hip as if in defiance of a fate to which she would not surrender willingly. Under the etching the artist had written: "Woman Alone in her Room."

"You like that one?"

I turned around and saw a woman with a red scarf tied in a knot on her handbag.

Marguerite. She was nothing like I imagined her to be. She was short. I imagined her tall. Her hair was long, caught up in a ponytail. I imagined it in an Afro, loose and bushy around her head. Her eyes were bright, sparkling, honest, frank. I imagined them smoky, alluring—ultimately deceitful.

I could not tell if her breasts were like the mangoes I had envisioned when I spoke to her by phone the day before. She was wearing a long, white, sleeveless, loose shirt. It did not cling to her bosom and make the outlines I wanted, but I saw her arms. They were the color of butterscotch—like the color of her face—warmer than the skin of the woman in my fantasies, more alive, more radiant, more luminous. She wore a dancer's black leggings, white sneakers, and gray socks, yet in that simple outfit she was more elegant than any of those fashionable women I had seen on the streets of Georgetown, and a hundred times more beautiful.

"Oufoula, right?" She did not wait for my response to her question about the drawing. She shook my hand. I confirmed my name. "My God, I didn't think you'd be so dressed up," she said.

Suddenly I felt embarrassed by my suit—my diplomat's gray jacket and pants, white shirt, striped burgundy tie. I should have known better when she said a restaurant in the Village. I could have taken off my jacket, loosened my tie. But I was dressing for Margarete. Margarete who would have worn a low-cut dress, strappy high-heeled sandals.

"I should have picked a more fancy place," she said.

"This one is fine. Really. I like the ambiance," I said.

She smiled. I liked her smile. It was nothing like the smile of the deceitful Margarete.

"The ambiance?"

"The drawings here." I turned to them.

"So you like art?"

"When it's good."

"Are these good?"

"Sad," I said.

The other drawings next to the etching in front of which I was standing were all similar—black-and-white images of black women, heroically stoic in the face of misfortune. I was struck by one other: a woman with a baby in her arms, two toddlers tugging at either side of her skirt, three older children standing behind her, a boy, not more than ten, with the disturbing eyes of a man.

"Don't you think that's reality?" she asked.

I was startled by the irony of the word she had chosen.

"Reality?" I had not anticipated it. Not from the Marguerite I had come to meet.

"Yes, reality. There are women who live these lives, you know. We want to pretend this world does not exist, but it is real for some women."

It was as if she had read my soul, known that I was a man who lived in two worlds.

"Don't you think the drawings portray the reality of women's lives?"

"Sad," I said again. It was all I could think to say.

"Ah, but you are missing their strength. These women are not submitting to hardships in their lives."

I examined the first etching again.

"Yes," I said. "I thought that's what that arm on the hip meant."

She was pleased with my answer. "I like you. A man with perception. An instinct for art and a knowledge of women. Okay, I'll confess. I had a reason for having you meet me here." I turned toward her expectantly. Her eyes were shining. "This is my work," she said.

On my way to the restaurant I had rehearsed much different words for her to say to me, but now it did not matter that she had not said them. Now the simplicity of her admission, those four words shimmering with the pride of girlhood dreams now fulfilled, stirred in me emotions I had never before felt: a tenderness toward her that made the muscles on the sides of my neck quiver, a sudden overwhelming desire to protect her, from whom I did not know. People who could harm her? She was not much younger than my wife, twenty-three perhaps. In my country, a woman of her age would have been married. She would have had children, a husband to care for her, a wide arc of aunts, uncles, brothers, sisters, cousins, a mother, a father, grandparents added to the ones she already had. Women who had not achieved this status by Marguerite's age were to be pitied. They were among the undesired. Yet Marguerite seemed unaware she could be perceived this way. She said, *This is my work,* as if her art meant everything to her, as if it conferred pride and confidence in her worth as a human being, as a woman for whom gender was no limitation.

I would not call the emotions I felt at that moment love, though it would not be long before I would say with certainty that I loved her. Tenderness toward her, yes; admiration for the courage it must have taken for her to rise above doubt and disapproval, yes; but gratitude also. For when her face became transformed with her joy and pride expressed in those few words, she transformed me. The Margarete of my fantasies vanished. A heaviness was released from my soul: the liberation of a lovebird. It broke out of the prison of its cage. It stretched its wings and soared. I would not need it to sing to me again, I would not need it to console me.

This was no mirage before me, no dark fantasy I had contained in my dreams when Mulenga deceived me. This was not Margarete, a character I had taken from a book and distorted to serve my sexual fantasies. This was Marguerite, a real person, a flesh-and-blood person. She was real. I was real. I was in a real place, in a real time, with a real Marguerite, a beautiful, real Marguerite. Not a seductive Marguerite. An honest Marguerite with honest black hair, honest dark brown eyes, honest butterscotch skin. A kind Marguerite with a heart and a soul. No one who made those drawings could not have a heart and a soul.

The thought flashed through my mind that this was a woman with whom I could be alone in the sunlight or in the dark. A woman I did not have to fear. She would not arouse in me dreams that could lead to my destruction. She would not take me to the brink of the abyss.

I regretted I had not accepted her first invitation. I could have had dinner with this woman alone in her apartment.

"So you must tell me, is my work any good?"

She was looking directly into my eyes. There was no subterfuge there, no trickery. No plot to bait me so I would fall into a trap she had laid for me.

"I don't mean to put you on the spot," she said when I had not answered her. "I meant to ask you when you could be honest. When you didn't know it was my work."

"No," I said. "It would not have mattered when you asked. Your work is good. I like it."

She left it like that. She did not press me for more. I liked that she did not press me for more.

At the table she refused wine and asked the beaming waiter for sparkling water. I observed this. My Margarete would have asked for wine.

"So what did Catherine want you to tell me?"

"Catherine?" I had almost forgotten.

"That's why you're here, isn't it? What does she want me to know?"

"John has left her."

"The bastard. I knew he would."

Exactly. Exactly the word I would have used for him. But I would not have said it aloud. Not to someone I had met just twenty minutes ago. The diplomatic service teaches you the wisdom of such caution. Discretion is our badge of courage.

"And what's to become of Eric?"

"John wants to keep Eric."

"He's that kind of bastard," she said. "Where is Catherine now? Still in Geneva?"

"Yes," I said.

"And Eric?"

"With John."

"Where?"

I thought it prudent to not tell her that John was in New York. Did I fear she would take action? A woman who could portray such strength in the face of defeat in her drawings, who did not hold back her tongue to name a bastard when she recognized him, could do such a thing. She could prove an embarrassment for me if she approached John and told him the source of her information. I lied, and as I lied, I acknowledged to myself that she was a better person than me.

"That's the problem. Catherine doesn't know where he is," I said.

It was not a total lie. Catherine did not know where exactly John lived. New York City was a big place.

"I'll call Catherine in Geneva."

Ashamed of my earlier lie, I told her Catherine had a new number. I gave it to her.

She seemed surprised. "I told Catherine diplomats were corrupt. You are an exception."

I looked away from her.

"No, I mean it. You didn't have to give me Catherine's new number. Diplomats don't like to get involved in such intimate matters, the domestic squabbles between a husband and wife. You're different."

It is sometimes to the advantage of people with skin like mine, especially in my profession, that we do not change color, not always perceptibly that is, when we are embarrassed, when we are guilty of allowing an innocent person to make an assumption which we know to be false, but which presents us in a favorable light. The blood gets hot, but the skin guards its secret. It was to my advantage that day, for the truth was I did not want to get involved.

"Like what you said about my drawings," she said. "You did not carry on. You did not praise me more than was necessary."

Grateful that she had not pursued the subject of diplomats and their inclination to corruption that reminded me so vividly of Catherine's warnings to me, I responded quickly, "But I like them."

"Yes. It was just refreshing to hear unadorned honesty from a member of your profession. Knowing how to give praise must be a qualification for the diplomatic service, no?"

I did not answer her, and she sensed my discomfort immediately.

"I don't mean it in a bad way." She reached for my hand. My skin tingled where she touched me.

"Diplomats have to lie or they won't get anything done. No agreements or treaties. I know that."

She was speaking in general terms but it felt as if her words were meant for me alone. As if she was saying to me she understood me.

"You're being kind."

"No. I can see you're not like the rest. You're not corrupt."

Our eyes met. "So you forgive me?"

For a second, and that was all it took, something passed between us. A recognition? A meeting of our souls? I did not have to answer her question. She knew: there would be no need for forgiveness between us.

And then the eternity of that second passed and she flinched as if she felt for the first time the heat of my hand under hers. She pulled away, but it was already too late. She had told me all I needed to know. The feelings I had when we stood before her drawings would not be in vain.

She ordered a salad and ate it quickly. Ten minutes later she announced that she had to leave. I tried to persuade her to stay a little longer. "I can't," she said. She was already out of her chair. "I have to go." She fumbled with her handbag. "How can I reach you?" She looked up at me. "So I can tell you what Catherine says," she added quickly, as if she had to explain why she had asked. But we both knew that Catherine had nothing to do with her question or with her sudden need to leave.

I wrote the phone number of my office in Washington on a piece of paper and gave it to her.

Nerida was waiting to have dinner with me as she had promised. Since we arrived in Washington, she had stopped wearing the traditional African dress except for official social functions. Now she had on a light blue jumper over a white silk blouse. The fabric of the jumper curved softly over her rounded belly. It was my child she was carrying. Ours. Perhaps another son, or a daughter. Nerida was beautiful when she was pregnant. She was beautiful that night. I kissed her on her mouth.

"Long day?" she asked.

I nodded.

"I made your favorite. Oxtails with gravy and rice. Ayi is asleep."

My son. I sat down and she massaged the space between my shoulder blades.

"I should have told you to stay in New York," she said. "It has to be tiring making two trips by plane in one day."

"Short trips," I said. "Less than an hour and a half one way."

"But you are exhausted. You should have spent the night in New York."

Innocent Nerida. If only she could have read my heart then, the hands that caressed my neck would have grown stiff with her anger. She had echoed a desire that had come over me. A desire to be where I was in a dining room, to have a woman's hands on the back of my neck, to have a woman breathe in my ear, except I wanted that dining room to be in New York; those hands to be Marguerite's; that sweet breath, Marguerite's; those lips that kissed me in bed that night, Marguerite's; the breasts I cupped in my hands, Marguerite's.

The next morning Marguerite called. Catherine had left Geneva. She had telephoned her and got a message with a forwarding phone number in Jamaica. She spoke to her in Jamaica. Catherine said she had decided to follow John's instructions and wait for him in Jamaica. He said he would be bringing Eric to her and they could discuss the details about Eric's custody there.

"Did she say if she knew where John was?" I needed to know if I had been caught in a lie. I needed to prepare an answer.

"If she knew, she didn't mention it. Do you think John will bring Eric to her?"

"No." I was relieved. I answered her honestly. "No, I don't think he'll bring Eric to her."

"I don't think so either." Her voice was sad. The sadness penetrated my heart.

"Catherine will be okay." I said. "She's a fighter."

"I don't know . . ." She paused, a pause that grew into a palpable silence.

"Hello? Hello?" I called to her.

"I'm here," she said.

"You were so quiet."

"Poor Catherine. She told me she only wanted you to give me her love. She didn't want to worry me. She didn't want to burden me with her troubles."

"Was she angry that I did?"

"No, she seemed pleased. I think she felt better knowing that I knew what had happened to her. She was relieved to talk about it. But I also think that secretly she wanted you to meet me. Something about your reaction to my name."

I held my breath.

"What was it about my name? She said you'd tell me."

"I liked it," I said.

"I got the impression from Catherine that it bothered you."

My diplomatic training rescued me. "I wouldn't say bothered me. Intrigued me, perhaps. I mentioned to Catherine that Marguerite was the name of a woman in a story I read at the university. Catherine said you were much more beautiful than that woman. I couldn't wait to see you."

She laughed. "You couldn't wait to be disappointed, huh?" It was a nervous laugh.

"I wasn't disappointed. You are more beautiful than I could ever have imagined."

She did not speak at once, but I could feel her holding my answer in her heart. I was not wrong. Something had passed between us when she looked into my eyes in the restaurant. The emotion that had filled my heart to bursting could not have been merely exhilaration—the overwhelming relief I experienced when at last I was freed from the bondage of a dark fantasy that had consumed me, which, in spite of the respite marriage often gave me, returned to haunt me with that slip of the tongue that caused Catherine to remind me: *Ah, a man who understands passion for the flesh.* It was more than that. It had to be more than that. I had fallen in love with her and I was beginning to believe it was possible that she had fallen in love with me, too.

"Can I see you again?" I asked her.

"Yes," she said. Her answer was simple. Direct.

"When?"

"When will you be in New York?"

"Monday," I said.

"Yes, I can see you Monday."

"We could meet for lunch. In the same restaurant if you like. I'd like to see your drawings again."

"They took them down," she said.

"I thought they were going to be there for one more week."

"Me too," she said.

"So where are they?"

"In my apartment."

The line was quiet between us.

At last she said softly, "You can see them there if you like."

My heart beat wildly in my chest. I could not respond without revealing my excitement. *In her apartment.*

"I'll make lunch," she said.

I sometimes think we live too much in the future. We waste our lives preparing for it, thinking we can give it shape, that we can control it. But often when we reach that future, it is not what we want, and we find ourselves squandering days and nights plotting another future while the present slips from us.

Sometimes it is the past that consumes us. I had lived with the past too long. I had allowed a broken heart to lead me to my future. I married Nerida to heal that heart. I sought out Marguerite to avenge that heart, to find the incarnation of a fantasy that would satisfy my dark desires. Instead, I found a good person, a kind person, a compassionate person. Instead, I fell in love with Marguerite. I did not know how that happened, or why. It simply did, and my acceptance of that fact was the beginning of a lesson life would teach me: it is the present that matters—the people and things we love in the present that we need.

Though later I would come to a deeper understanding of the present, I believed then that if we stood still and listened to the present, we would hear all we needed to hear, have all we needed to have. Marguerite had stood still in the present with me. She said yes. I said yes. We did not consider yesterday. We did not consider the consequences of tomorrow. Today was what we had. It would take us to another today. We would have lunch. In her apartment. Monday would be the present for us. It would show us the way to the other present. I did not fear that other present.

10

I have seen two swans make love on a lake in the heat of the noonday sun in my country in Africa. I was in my second year teaching at the mission school. A man I knew, an Irishman, called me to his house to see them. His name was Patrick O'Malley. He was a farmer with a missionary's calling and a patriot's love for literature and hatred for the English. The only English poet he would concede he admired was Dylan Thomas, and he would remind me that he was Welsh. He compared him with his favorite Irish poet, William Butler Yeats. One spoke of death, the other of conception. Both sides of the same coin, he would say. They both understood the fight man has to wage against the forces that would destroy him. "Do not go gentle into that good night," he would shout at me, quoting Dylan Thomas. "Rage, rage against the dying of the light."

It was rage that kept us alive, he would say. Passion. "The Englishman is too cerebral to know passion. Passion terrifies him."

I had meant the same thing when I said to Catherine that it was not the Englishman with his obsession with the intellect I was thinking of when she said her friend's name was Marguerite.

O'Malley wanted me to see rage, he said. To witness with my own eyes what Yeats had in mind when he wrote his famous poem

"Leda and the Swan." He wanted me to see that it is rage that engenders life. That without rage we would be like lambs to the slaughter. It is rage that allows us to keep our dignity in the face of inevitable defeat, he said. Each act of sexual intercourse is an act of rage.

"Do you think we would happily create a generation whose purpose it is to make us obsolete?" he asked me. "No, we have sex because it feels good to us. Yet we resent the trick God played on us. So we 'Rage, rage against the dying of the light.'"

He had dug a lake in the back of his house that he fed with underground pipes that channeled water to it from the river. No one had objected when he stole water from the river to make a lake on which he bred white swans he had imported from Europe. But it was not only a lake he had intended to build. He wanted to crisscross the country with pipes and bring water to the interior. He wanted to show us that it was possible to grow food in the drought.

His plan failed. My people believed he would drain the river dry and incur the wrath of the river gods. Those of us who should have known better, the educated ones of us, did not contest them. Who were we to know where the gods lived? Christianity was still a generation new for us. It had yet to penetrate our myths.

Today we are laying his pipes across my country, but he did not live to see his plan become a reality. He died not long after that day he called me to his lake to witness rage, to see righteous resentment of a God who forced us into conspiracy with Him to fashion our own destruction.

Fool's gold, he called children. We console ourselves with the lie that they make us immortal. That after we die, our seed will live on in them. He would buy no fool's gold, he said. So he never married, he never had children. He never raised animals, as some of the Europeans did. He found no comfort in pets, no solace from dogs. Only swans comforted him. They are honest birds, he said. "One day I'll show you."

That day came when two of his swans were mating. He called me to his house, his voice quivering with urgency.

I remember the distance the other swans kept from the mating pair, except for one, a female swan that circled them, her long neck curved stiff with indignation. Three times the male swan tried to drive her off. Three times she returned and circled them, and when finally he had defeated her, she did not go far. She turned, stayed still, and watched them.

We watched them, too. We watched the water churn angrily with the flapping of their wings. We watched the struggle: the rage of the male swan, the passionate resistance and eventual capitulation of the female swan.

The male swan sunk his rigid beak into the nape of the female's neck and she beat him off. He straddled her, dug his webbed feet into the feathers on her back, and she fought him. For half an hour they turned those placid waters into their battleground, arching their powerful wings like weapons above each other. White feathers flew into the still air, the water fretted. Again and again the male pounced, and again and again the female beat him back, and then he pushed her so deep below the surface of the water, I thought he would drown her. But he did not drown her. He pulled her head up again, her skin clamped in the vise of his powerful beak.

The female seemed to know now he had conquered her. She did not resist him again. She allowed him the ritual. She seemed to know each time he plunged her head beneath the water, he would not drown her. He would pull her out again. She waited for the end, and when it came, she stayed beneath the water and let him swim away above her. She knew, his work finished, he would not look back at her again.

The swan that had seen it all seemed to pity her. She floated to her and took her to the edge of the lake. On the bank, the female stretched out her wings. Powerful shudders erupted through her body. Back and forth she twisted her long neck, the tremors through her body increasing as if she could expel the thing that had been planted in her.

"Rage and shame," said O'Malley. "Look at the male swan. He can't bear to face her. He knows he's been duped into using her to destroy them both."

I would think of these swans after Marguerite and I made love for the first time.

I had come to her apartment for lunch as we had arranged, but we did not have lunch, not then, not later. Later, I was sated. Later, I did not need food. Later, Marguerite was all I wanted, all I needed.

I had followed Marguerite to her bedroom with no conscious thought on my mind other than that I wanted to see more of the drawings that had intrigued me in the restaurant. I will confess that when she opened the front door and I saw her—her hair brushing against her neck where it fell from a ponytail, the sweet simplicity of the faded blue jeans and white T-shirt she was wearing, her bare feet (it was the bare feet that undid me)—desire cascaded over me and I ached to fold her in my arms. But she held out her hand to me in a gesture that, though friendly, was decisively formal, and I forced my mind to refocus, to remember that it was to see her drawings that she had invited me here.

I know now with the wisdom of years of plans thwarted in spite of my best efforts, realized beyond my best hopes, that life flows on its own accord. The universe, the elders tell us, is unfolding as it should. Marguerite was pointing something out to me on one of her drawings and stepped back so I could take a closer look at it. She tripped on something on the floor, perhaps her shoes, and fell backwards on her bed. I reached to help her up—that was my intent—but she was already coming forward and our bodies touched.

She did not resist me when I lowered her back onto the bed. She seemed to have sensed the inevitability of what was to happen between us. She stayed still. She did not say a word. Sound and movement came only in the end: in the low moan that escaped her lips, in the shudder that rippled through her body, coinciding with mine.

Then the battle began.

She tore at the buttons on my shirt and when they resisted her, she ripped them from the threads that bound them. With the force of her heels she shoved off my pants that were tangled at my ankles. She sank her fingers deep in the thick of my matted hair. I found arms to pull through the holes of her T-shirt, a head to tear it off of. I ripped apart a bra, sunk my mouth into nipples, clamped skin between my teeth.

And yet I say there was no rage when we made love that first time. Greed. Desperate greed. The ravenous greed of the hungry, the starving. We had both crossed deserts, our throats parched with thirst, our bellies shriveled from want of food, and we had found sustenance in each other.

I have seen men lost for days crawl out of the desert on their hands and knees. They choked on the water we gave to them.

"Calm down. Calm down," we told them. "There's more. You have time to take more."

That was what Marguerite and I had to tell each other.

"Calm down. Calm down. We have eternity to love each other."

For I did not feel the threat of the end of my mortality then, as O'Malley had predicted I would. I felt no rage. I was complete with Marguerite. I was immortal. We had not entered a subversive pact to breed a generation to replace us. We made love for the sake of it, for the happiness of it. I felt no shame looking at the body that glistened with the pleasure I had given to it. She felt no shame looking at mine, knowing it was she who had caused my body to tremble as if with ague.

"What if I got pregnant?" Marguerite asked when we were spent, lying in each other's arms.

We had not paused to consider that possibility. Not even for a fleeting second had I considered the future, had my mind been willing to leave the present, to go beyond it to wonder whether she was on the pill, whether she needed to use a diaphragm. But, now suddenly, I thought of the future, and I remembered the past. I remembered Nerida. I remembered I had a wife, a wife who was pregnant. I remembered I had a child, a son I adored.

But Marguerite did not want an answer to her question. It was as if it had slipped to her tongue without her being conscious of it. She would not make that mistake again. She would take a firm hold on what was in her heart, in her mind. She would prevent it from leaking into words that could come between us, that could spoil our happiness. She would exercise this control until I pushed her, until I forced her into admitting what she knew, what she feared. But for now I let her drift into unconsciousness. I said nothing to stop her from turning on her side, throwing her arm across my chest, closing her eyes, and slipping happily into oblivion.

11

The apartment where I lived with my wife had style. Everything in it had been carefully planned, had been deliberately designed. Nothing in it was the result of spontaneity or impulse. Yet when I entered it, I could not be sure that what I saw there was a reflection of my wife's taste, for my wife decorated our apartment for me, to please me.

Marguerite's apartment did not have style, at least not the kind of style likely to get photographed in magazines about home decorating, but it made a statement. You knew when you were there that you were in a place where an artist lived. My wife was not interested in making statements about her personal tastes. She was interested in my welfare, in the welfare of our son, the welfare of our family.

We did not have much money, though we had things that people would have needed money to obtain. We had a beautiful apartment overlooking the Potomac River. It did not belong to us. It belonged to the government of my country. Ordinarily it would not have been assigned to us. I was not yet an ambassador. I was merely part of the retinue of an ambassador, but I was the husband of the daughter of a president, so my apartment was larger than most and located in the stylish part of Washington where, if he wanted to, the president of my country could visit his daughter without embarrassment.

Nerida seemed surprised that others could have been jealous of our good fortune, and, indeed, she did nothing to cause them to be so. Though we had an allowance for furniture, she never bought more than she thought we needed: a bed, a dresser, a full-length mirror for our bedroom, the same for my son's room, a mahogany dining room set for the dining room, a couch and two armchairs for the living room. She kept all the walls in the apartment white. She said it helped to simplify things, to keep our apartment from feeling too small or too cluttered. To keep me from feeling hemmed in.

My wife knew that though I slept and worked within concrete walls in my country in Africa, only a door separated me from the vast openness of the grasslands. She wanted to give me this feeling of space in Washington. She gave similar reasons for the potted plants in the living room and the earth tones of the fabric that covered our furniture. She said they were closer to the colors I had left behind in Africa. Sometimes I wondered what colors she would have chosen if she were not choosing colors for me. I did not know what colors she would have preferred. I did not feel the need to ask her. I liked the way our apartment looked. It made me feel at peace. Calm. It was the way my wife had planned it. She was making a home for a husband who provided the food on her table and the financial support for her child. In this view of the role of a wife, Nerida was traditional. The hunter deserved rest when he returned home from the kill. How surprised her old suitors would have been to know that there was no need for them to have been intimidated by her just because she had been to university!

Marguerite had not created rooms with me in mind. She decorated them for herself. Color was splashed everywhere. Her bedroom was pink, her bathroom orange, her kitchen yellow. Only the walls of the outer room that served as her living room, dining room, and studio remained neutral. And yet they were not white like the walls my wife had painted for me. Dove gray, Marguerite called the color of her outer room, and she kept it from being somber with huge canvases of her art, most of them paintings in bright colors.

She said the ones I saw in the restaurant, the black-and-white etchings, were part of a new phase for her. She had just started experimenting with shadings of black and white. Chiaroscuro, she said the technique was called. One could use color to achieve a similar effect of light and dark, but she preferred to work with black and white. "For a change," she said, smiling at me and indicating the bold colored paintings on her wall. But she was not ready to hang those black-and-white etchings in her apartment just yet. They were still evolving, she said. "Anyhow they can be painful to look at. Maybe," she added, "that was why nobody wanted them."

I knew she said that as a concession to me. When she had first asked me what I thought of the paintings I saw in the restaurant, I said they were sad.

Marguerite had put wicker baskets everywhere in her apartment— on top of shelves, at the sides of kitchen chairs, in corners of the room, under the bathroom sink. She filled them with bunches of dried wildflowers and roses, most of them pink and red. She used a futon for her couch, huge pillows for armchairs. Some were covered in orange, yellow, and red batik prints, some were in solid colors, some were striped.

She worked in the front of the room, her back to the only window in the apartment. Cans of paintbrushes, soaked in water, were lined neatly on the floor next to her easel, which held her latest painting, but it was always covered when I was there. The rest of her work that was not on her walls was stacked against her bedroom wall. This was the only order in Marguerite's apartment: the order in which she catalogued her work, in which she defined her space to work, in which she organized the tools of her work. Yet I did not feel closed in there. I did not suffer from the claustrophobia and confusion Nerida feared would come from the juxtaposition of different patterns, the placement of one color against another, the disorder of pillows piled on the floors.

Less than a week after Marguerite and I made love for the first time, I was back in her apartment again. I gave Nerida some explanation about needing to be at the UN for two days, so that I could spend a night with Marguerite. If Nerida had any doubts about the legitimacy of my trip to New York, she did not voice them then, nor in the weeks that followed when more and more I found excuses to stay overnight in New York. It was not long before Marguerite's apartment felt like home, my second home, and Marguerite my wife, my second wife. I was as much at ease with the explosion of color, the jumble of baskets, flowers, and furniture there as I was with the quiet order of the rooms Nerida had prepared for me, the subtle arrangement of shapes and shades meant to soothe me. But soon I began to grow less at ease, less comfortable, less certain of my place with Marguerite, less secure of her than I was of Nerida, and I found myself wondering if she knew the secret that was not voiced between us. If she had guessed, suspected, that I had a wife. If the comfort I felt was a false comfort, the ease I assumed, a false ease—make-believe woven by desire, by love, by longing gratified. Made real because I had wished myself into believing it real, into thinking Marguerite was my second wife, her apartment my second home.

Marguerite never asked me where I was or what I did when I was not with her, but now I wondered if it was because she did not want to know. If it was because she was afraid of the answers I would give her.

I came to New York and I left New York and it seemed in that space in between, before I returned to her again, she would bury me deep in some place in her heart where I lay dormant, frozen, never being quite real for her until she saw me again. Often the first thing she did when we met was to press her ear against my heart and listen to my heartbeat. It was as if she needed to reassure herself that I was alive.

She never telephoned me, though, of course, the only phone number I had given her was my office number in Washington. But she never used it, except for that one time she called to give me news of Catherine, and then, of course, that was before I went to her apartment. That was before we made love.

Often I did not know until the very last minute when I was required to be at the UN in New York. Often my longing for her would become so intense that my head would ache and a hollow pit would open in my stomach. I would call her then, perhaps giving her notice of just a few hours, but even at those times she would be waiting for me without questions. Waiting if I came directly to her in the morning from the airport or late at night after work at the UN. It was as if time stood still for her and there was no time between the time I left her and the time I returned to her. Yet I knew she had not spent her days and nights in a vacuum waiting for me. There was always a new drawing she had to show me, or a painting she had begun or was finishing.

I told myself that because she was an artist, she liked the arrangement we had—the long periods of two and three weeks of absence between the brief days we spent together. She told me that she had been offered a position teaching art full-time at a small college but she had turned it down. She needed unobstructed time for her art, she said. She could not do as some of her friends did—draw or paint for a few hours in the morning and then go to work. That was not how her ideas developed. She needed a full day. The reassurance of no obligations, the freedom from commitments. It was only then her imagination was freed to construct images she could not conceive with her conscious mind. The mere idea that she had something to do or someone to see that day stymied her ability to dream. Her body was the instrument of her talent, she said. She had to release it from the world so it could serve her art.

I envied her. I had no such consuming preoccupation to distract me from her. My wife and my son were important to me, but they could not build a wall strong enough, or solid enough, to prevent Marguerite from filtering through my everyday thoughts, my everynight dreams. I woke up thinking of Marguerite, I went to sleep thinking of Marguerite.

I liked my job, but I could not say it was the reason for my existence, the purpose of my life. If I had asked Marguerite who she was, she would have said an artist. If someone had asked me the same question I would have floundered through the many identities

I have, the many things I do. I would have said I am a man, an African. I am a delegate in the diplomatic service of my country. I am a husband, a father. I am the lover of a woman I adore. I am Marguerite's.

And yet when Marguerite was with me, I seemed to be her consuming preoccupation. If I did not ask her about her work, she would not mention it to me. If I did not say I wanted to see what she was working on, she would not show it to me. But when she did, I knew from every movement of her body, from every inflection in her tone, from the way she bent her head from one side to another to point out this or that line to me, this or that color I had barely observed, that her art was the center of her universe and I, a fortunate occupant.

That was not my place in her world, but the center was her place in my universe. Since that first day when I clung to her, a man found his way through the desert ravenous for drink and food, since that afternoon when a yearning I used to feel, for what, I did not know, was suddenly recognizable, understood, fulfilled, everything in my life took its reference and meaning from her. She had become the star by which I measured my place in the world. My compass. I would say this and wonder if she would have approved my saying so. I would hear that and wonder if she would have agreed. I would smell this perfume, sometimes perfume on my wife, and I would say to myself, I must get this for Marguerite. I would see a dress on a mannequin in a store, a dress on a passing woman, and would compare how it fit her with how it would fit my Marguerite. Always, it fitted my Marguerite better. Always, it curved around her breasts more softly, dipped more deeply into her waist, fell more demurely above her knees.

I was not dissuaded that Marguerite never used perfume, that she rarely wore dresses. I would imagine her even in ways I had not seen her. Ways perhaps I wanted to see her.

Perhaps I imagined my Marguerite this way—with perfume, wearing a dress—because I saw her in the future with me, at a cocktail party at the United Nations, at a dinner party at the ambassador's house. And yet I had not imagined that I would leave my wife, though when I kissed her, I thought of Marguerite's lips on mine. When I made love to her, I felt Marguerite's heartbeat next to mine. When I put my son to bed, I saw the contours of Marguerite's face on his—her deep-set eyes, her high cheekbones, her determined chin.

When people made appointments with me, I thought like this: Yes, Wednesday. We could meet on Wednesday. It was six days before I would see Marguerite. Or, No, not the seventh of the month. It was the day when I would be with Marguerite. Yes, in New York. Any day in New York. I could be with Marguerite. My life ebbed and flowed around her, the days I could be with her, the nights I could spend with her. But it was not so with her.

She may have gained time for her art when she turned down that full-time job she was offered, but not without a price, one she willingly paid, though it was painful for her. It had denied her the one luxury she had yearned for: a trip to Jamaica to revisit her homeland. She would have liked, she said, to see coconut trees again, beaches where sea-almond trees grew, cashew nuts that hung from fleshly red fruit like nipples on the udders of cows. Grass as green as emeralds, sky blinding with the color of turquoise. She would have loved to see donkeys straddled by old men in straw hats, stray dogs sniffing the heels of women balancing yam and cassava on their heads. She would have loved to hear cane fields whispering in the wind, waterfalls making music over granite boulders, the timpani of rain on galvanized rooftops. She wanted to meet cousins who had probably forgotten her, uncles and aunts who were grateful for her sake when she was given the opportunity to go to America. But she would forgo all that for her art. She had forgone the money a job could have given her for all that. She did it for her art.

My heart sunk when she told this to me, for I glimpsed then the strength of my competitor. I understood my ranking in relation to it.

Marguerite's story was similar to mine. She, too, was rescued by missionaries. She, too, was an only child. She, too, had lost her mother, but she was not abandoned, she was not rejected. Her

father was also dead. When the missionaries came, she had no father to say without feeling: *Take him. He'll return.*

The Catholic missionaries in Jamaica recognized that Marguerite had talent and recommended her to nuns in Chicago who
gave her scholarships to do her bachelor's degree and master's degree in art at Loyola University. By the time she was twenty-three,
one year before I met her, she had graduated from Loyola, had already sold one painting, and the etchings I had seen in the restaurant had been on exhibit in a small gallery in New York.

She lived on grants, she told me, that were awarded to her by
the government and private endowments for her art, and on the income she earned teaching two classes, two nights a week, at the
New School, on Tuesdays and Thursdays. I arranged my work so
that I was never in New York on Tuesdays and Thursdays. I did not
think I could be in the same place where Marguerite was and not
be able to see her.

There were days when I was relieved that she had her art to distract her. Those were the days I was driven either by guilt or by
jealousy. I had a wife I loved, whom I knew I would not divorce. I
thought Marguerite too young, too full of promise, to deny her
what I had—a spouse and a child. On those days, guilt forced me
to find contentment with the times we spent apart, but those days.
were few. For most of the time I was tortured by thoughts of the
opportunities my absences could make possible. Marguerite was a
beautiful woman. I knew other men would desire her. I was tormented by images of her in the arms of another man, kissing another man, making love to another man. I would find relief only by
remembering that she spent her time shut up in a studio with her
drawing pencils and her paints and her brushes. I was grateful for
those times, then, grateful that her work demanded so much of her
attention, required so much from her.

There were other days, days when I doubted Marguerite loved
me, when I could not understand why she was not plagued by
thoughts of me in my absence, as I was of her. When I could not
understand how she could erase me from her mind like chalk from

a blackboard each time we said good-bye. How she could empty her head so completely of me and fill it with her art alone.

I bought books to help me understand, to assuage the doubts when they arose. I wanted to know how talent was nurtured, where inspiration came from. When did it come? How did the artist court it? But the most I understood from my reading was that the creative force was nebulous. Fickle and elusive. Those who worshipped at its feet would have to be its willing slaves. They would have to be ready, brush in hand, canvas on the easel, waiting for it to come. That when it came, they would have to relinquish their all to it. It brooked no distraction, no movement from it to the conscious, this muse. It was a jealous master, and I was jealous of it.

"Don't you miss me when I'm not with you?" I asked Marguerite one fateful day when jealousy so consumed me, I could not contain it, when it made me a slave and I had to serve it.

"You are always with me," she said.

"But don't you mind when I'm gone?"

"You are always in my heart."

"Aren't you curious? Jealous?"

"Jealous? Jealous about what?"

"What I do when I'm away from you," I said.

I knew I was nearing the edge of the cliff when I asked her these questions, but I couldn't stop myself. My insecurities were deepening. My doubts and fears about her affection for me reaching the low point where I was willing to throw caution to the wind and face the precipice. If she had asked me to jump to the rocks below, I would have. If she had asked me if I was married, I would have admitted it all. I would have said I have a wife. I have a son. I have a baby on the way. But she never asked. She never pushed me over that edge.

"It's men who worry about what women do when they are apart," she said. "It's in your genes. It's all biological." She laughed.

"Biological?" My emotions looped like a yo-yo. I was giddy with relief—she had put me firmly back on safe ground again—but my fears intensified. She seemed so indifferent. Mulenga, too, had been indifferent when I'd uncovered her lies. There had been no trace of remorse in her eyes.

"Yes. Women always know for sure that their children are theirs. Men can never be certain."

"Ah, there are blood tests now," I said.

"That's my point. That's the only way to know for sure, but long before blood tests, men had that insecurity planted in them genetically."

"And there's resemblance." She was making me uncomfortable.

"Haven't you seen siblings who bear little resemblance to each other? I have. I have cousins, children of the same parents, some are light skinned, some are dark. You'd barely know they were related."

I became desperate for her reassurance. "But I trust you," I said.

"Why shouldn't you? I've given you no reason not to trust me."

"And you? Do you trust me?" I was skirting on the edges of danger again, but I had to know. She had greeted me with such open affection when I came to her apartment, though I had been away more than two weeks. She asked no questions. She accepted my presence as if I had been there the day before and no significant time had elapsed between then and the time I saw her last. While I was tortured with suspicions, she seemed unconcerned, unaffected by my absence.

Men say this is what they want: a woman who does not nag them, who does not keep track of everything they do. A woman who gives them space to breathe. But we lie when we say this. Either we are certain of the every movement of our wives or girlfriends— where they are at this or that time, who they are with at this or that time—or we have ceased to care, and it no longer matters to us what they do or with whom. We do not love them. But I loved Marguerite and I was tormented by thoughts of what was possible when I was not with her. I asked her if she trusted me, risking discovery of the secrets I concealed for the uncertainty in her voice— hesitation in her answer that would let me know she cared, that she loved me, that she, too, found sleep difficult when we were not together. But her answer came swiftly, without the slightest pause.

"Of course I trust you. Why not?"

I was enflamed with jealousy.

. . .

I would return to this topic again—of whether or not she was disturbed by my frequent absences—and when I did, I would set in motion the beginning of my end.

We were in the park at Washington Square near her apartment. Marguerite loved to walk. She would stop and observe things I barely noticed: a streetlamp with a broken pane, a park bench with a missing slat, a tuft of grass struggling to grow between the stones. The crowds that pressed around singers with their guitars, mimes with their clown faces, dancers, their bodies twisting to the latest craze, had no appeal to her. She preferred solitary faces or the faces of lovers lost in each other's gaze.

I was becoming accustomed to the sudden turn of her head when we passed by someone she found interesting—someone peeling an orange on a park bench, two men huddled over a chessboard, two lovers embracing. I knew when her voice trailed she had shifted her attention to a particular slant of a body, expression on a face, or unusual coloring—skin, hair, eyes. I was learning to be patient. I was trying to understand that it was the demands of her art, not her disaffection for me, that caused her distraction.

At first when she used to ask me to go walking with her, I was wary. I worried I would meet someone who knew me or knew my wife. Someone who could put an end to the happiness I had with Nerida and my son. But my fears soon gave way to my desire to please Marguerite. She would say to me, after we made love, that she wanted to celebrate her happiness with life. She wanted to breathe in air without walls, she wanted to see trees, even the ravaged ones there were in Manhattan. She wanted to look into faces. She would so move me with her innocence and freshness, I would feel old, though I was only thirty, just six years older than she. I would take risks then to regain my youth with her. I would take risks because the risks I took made her happy.

Yet she did not know I took risks. That she, too, took risks. That each time I stepped out of her apartment with her, came out of a restaurant, a cinema, an art gallery, we could have been discovered.

That she, too, risked the end of the happiness she wanted us to celebrate.

The conversation I had with Marguerite that day in the park seemed harmless enough. Yet it would plant the seeds for my unraveling to my end, our end, Marguerite's and mine. It was unusually hot and still. Marguerite's apartment had no air conditioner, and the air in the room hung heavy around us. I could barely breathe. Even if it were one of the days I feared discovery, I would have gone to the park with her.

"Have you ever read Wole Soyinka?" she asked me suddenly, pulling me down on a bench next to her.

"Soyinka?"

"Yes, Soyinka. Have you read *Death and the King's Horseman?*"

I shook my head.

"My god, you've become so Europeanized. You've filled your head with European literature. Art, you know, enters the soul. I hope you have not allowed the Europeans to replace your myths with theirs."

I frowned. That was when she asked me how old was I when the missionaries took me from my village to their school in the city. I said I was seven.

"Good," she said. "Seven is the age of reason. You had already passed the age of myth."

"And do I get a prize for that?" I asked her.

She kissed me. "I love you," she said.

Her answer was not enough for me. I had to ask my question again. "And are you jealous of me? Of the time I spend away from you?"

She knew the real question I was asking. "Oh, Oufoula!" She put her hand on my forehead and smoothed away my furrowed brow. "You have no need to be jealous. You know I am always with you."

That was not what I wanted. I wanted her to say that she could not live without me, that nothing in her life mattered to her more than me. That when I was not with her, she spent her time dreaming of me.

"What I know," I said, nursing my hurt like a spoilt, overindulged child, "is there are many days when we are apart."

She became serious. "Those separations do not matter. We are never apart. You should understand that. You were born in Africa. You know our spirits can travel. You know that we can put ourselves wherever we want at any time. Nothing can prevent us, not people, not things, not distance."

I had heard that sort of romanticized view of African beliefs before. Mostly from black people outside of Africa who were desperate for an identity, a past that took them beyond the brutality of slavery. But I had heard it, too, from white people who needed to reassure themselves of their superiority. They made us their barometers and measured their success by our failure: our failure to reject the mystical, our failure to base *all* our truths on the tangible, the seen, the scientific. For both these people, black and white, Africa had to remain in the bush. Their sense of self, their identities, depended on that fantasy.

I smiled to hide my irritation. Marguerite found my smile condescending and lashed out at me.

"Maybe you should have read Soyinka. Maybe you need to read *Death and the King's Horseman*. Even though the son of the Horseman was educated in England, he wasn't so brainwashed that he denied that his people had the power to move their spirits."

She was chastising me, and I became contrite. I decided to put aside my cynicism and listen to her.

"Tell me," I said. "Tell me about *Death and the King's Horseman*."

"I saw the play, here, in the city," she began. "White people began walking out even before it began. The drumming made them uncomfortable. I think they were scared when those masked men came up the aisles. The ones covered in straw. You know who I mean?"

"The Egwugwu," I said.

"Yes."

She was pleased I was listening to her, that I could give her the African word she needed. She forgave me now. I had proven I had not forgotten my past. "Well, in the story, the king's Horseman must will his spirit to leave his body so that he can prepare the way for the king, who has died and now must live in the world of the dead. It takes a while for the king's Horseman to do this not because he cannot, but because he will not. Everybody knows that if he wills it, he can make his spirit go to where the king is. Everybody expects him to do that—the people in his kingdom, his wives, his children. Even his English-educated son."

She looked sternly at me. I had the presence of mind to look properly chastened.

"The son packs up his bags to return home when he hears that the king is dead. He knows that his father is dead, too. That he had willed his spirit to be with the king."

I understood what she wanted to say to me through this story. I did not need her to speak the words.

"That is what I do when I am not with you," she said. "I will my spirit to be with you. I am never not with you."

My guilt deepened. She loved me. I had practically badgered her for this admission. But could I say the same? Could I say she was always with me, every time I was in bed with Nerida? I had not known how much she loved me until then. I had not loved her as much as I loved her then.

Marguerite would teach me other lessons, lessons about integrity that I could not allow myself to take to heart without jeopardizing the relationship I had with her. She never stopped trying to find ways to remind me that my profession was a profession of compromise. Some event would make the news involving a diplomat, and she would say to me: "I wonder what lie he had to tell to get what he got for his country."

I would try to convince her that compromise was not a bad thing in itself. "If what we want is good for the majority," I would say, "then it is worth it if a minority suffers."

"Only if that minority is not made of flesh and blood," she would respond. "No compromise is good if people suffer, even a single person."

She had definite views on capital punishment. "It dehumanizes us all," she said. "Human life is too sacred, even the life of our worst enemy. We lose our dignity when we fail to acknowledge that. We bring ourselves down to the level of the murderer when we take his life. No, lower than that, for we take his life without passion, in a cold, calculated way, with injections or electric wires. It's even more disgusting when we have the priest and the doctor there—one to save his soul and the other his life when our intention is to have neither occur."

She was adamant about the importance of truth. Lies, she said, always hurt the person they are intended to deceive, if not at the beginning, then at the end of the relationship.

I was beginning to be more and more afraid that she would discover the lie I had not articulated. I did not know which terrified me the most: that she would leave me because I had not told her the truth, or that she would leave me if I told her the truth, or that I would have to leave my wife if I told her the truth. That last I knew I could not do because though I loved Marguerite with every fiber of my being, I loved Nerida, too. She was my wife, my friend, the mother of my son. Sister from my homeland.

It was Nerida I was thinking of and the life we had in Geneva and now in Washington, a life I loved, when I said one day to Marguerite that I used to think I was a happy man. I said it not because I was unhappy with Nerida but because every day I spent with Marguerite I was discovering how much happier it was possible for me to be.

"And weren't you always a happy man?" Marguerite asked me.

"I thought happiness was wanting what I had. I know better now."

We were in bed. We had just made love. Perhaps it was the ecstasy of our lovemaking that had made me reckless, forgetful of my customary caution.

"And what was that?" She sat up in the bed and looked at me.

"What was what?"

"What you had? What used to make you happy?"

She was jealous. Hadn't I longed for this evidence that she loved me? But that longing was a double-edged sword: I could destroy myself with the answer I gave her. "You," I said. "You make me happy now."

I tried to pull her down to the bed with me, but she wriggled out of my arms.

"I mean before me." She turned and faced me.

I kissed her.

"What made you happy before me?" She pushed me away.

"My life before you seems dull now," I said.

"And yet you said you were happy."

"I did not know what happiness was." I ran my hand through her hair. She stopped me.

"I want to know what made you happy before me. Tell me." She was speaking softly now, but I could hear fear quivering beneath her words. She knew. She had not been indifferent to those times I was away from her.

"The same things that make me happy now," I said. "Only they make me happier because of you."

She shut her eyes, but before I could bring her back to where we had been, locked in each other's arms until ecstasy had led me to make my foolish statement, threatened to ruin me, she opened them again. "Besides me?" She probed me for more.

"Besides you?"

"What makes you happy besides me?" She was looking steadily at me. Lie, her eyes seemed to say. Lie.

"My job," I said. "I get to travel. Meet people like you."

I think she saw the stop sign then, the one held in front of her. I think she sensed the danger in going any further. She opened her eyes wide and flung back her hands in mock surprise. "Meet people like me?" she asked.

"Meet you." I lifted her hair and nuzzled the back of her neck.

She brushed me away. "Just like a man."

But it was a halfhearted rebuke. The crisis had passed. She was rebuffing me in jest, playing with me.

"Just like a man to find happiness in your job." She buried her face in the pit of my belly.

I joined her, laughing, pretending machismo. "And don't you forget I am a man." I turned her on her back and climbed on top of her. "Don't you forget it!"

Our lovemaking was no different than it had been before. We kissed the same way, held each other the same way, reached orgasm the same way. But something had changed. Something had intruded. Someone. Nerida. I felt her unspoken presence between us, my lie suspended heavily between Marguerite and me. Marguerite's lie, too. For I knew that she knew that I was hiding something from her. That it could not have been my job that had made me happy. My job did not mean to me what art meant to her. I had told her how I got it. How it was a series of circumstances that had led me into the diplomatic service. I had not sought my position. It was given to me. I was simply a man who was in a certain place at a certain time, an African man who spoke two European languages. I had thought to do no more with those skills than to teach.

But Marguerite asked no more questions, and now I knew the answers to mine. Though she would say she did not mind the long periods of time when we were apart, because she had her art, though she would insist that she did not need to call me, because her spirit was with me, she was afraid. She had lost her nerve. She who claimed she could handle the truth, she who found no room for compromise, for half-truths. She did not want to know what I did when I was not with her. She did not want to know with whom. She wanted to shield herself, to shield us from the answer she sensed could hurt us.

Marguerite and I entered a silent conspiracy on that day. It would eat away at our happiness one nibble at a time. It would erode the confidence we had in each other. It would force me finally to reveal the truth to her to save us both.

12

I had never seen Marguerite draw or paint. When I arrived at her apartment, her easel would always be covered with a cloth or stacked against the wall. But the next time I came there, she had left a drawing uncovered on the easel. It was different from the others I had seen in the restaurant. She had drawn only the head of the woman, not the entire body, and the style she used was not realistic. I barely recognized nose, lips, and chin from among the angular lines that shaped the woman's face, but the eyes struck me. I felt pulled to them. They were large and mysterious and seemed to contain a wisdom that had been garnered over centuries. Yet I knew they were not the eyes of an old woman but of a woman not long past her teenage years.

"Who?" I asked Marguerite.

"Why should there be a 'who'?"

"She reminds me of someone."

"She should," she said.

I came closer to the drawing. "You?"

"Yes, me. It's a self-portrait."

I studied it. "Yes, yes. I can see that."

"Do you like it?"

Like? I would not have used such a term to describe its effect on me. I could not say whether I liked it or I did not like it. I found it at once familiar and disturbing. A likeness of Marguerite, yes, but of someone else I had known.

"Does it look sad, like you thought the others were?" she asked when I did not answer her.

"No, I wouldn't say sad." Then I remembered. The year before my mother walked to her death, she had taken me to the shed behind my father's hut. I had seen faces like this one there, mysterious and all knowing, laced with cobwebs. I had returned to the shed twice when I was a teenager, before my father traded the wood carvings for some brass pots that he had taken a liking to. Many years have passed, but I have not since witnessed any thought or feeling that had worked itself on a man's or woman's face that was not there in that shed, sculpted out of wood. "It reminds me of the masks of faces we make in Africa," I said to Marguerite.

She seemed pleased with my answer. She smiled and kissed me. "I would have thought you would have said, like the copycats Picasso drew."

I did not know what she was talking about. Then she told me that Picasso and the Cubists had copied their style from the African masks. "Now everybody has forgotten their source," she said. "They believe Cubism began with Picasso." She removed the drawing from the wall.

"Here," she said. "It's for you. So you will remember me when I'm not with you."

It was another step in our conspiracy of silence, our agreement not to give voice to the thing that could cause our unhappiness. But it was a more fragile step. More dangerous. She was giving me a likeness of herself, a likeness not so easily identifiable, but a likeness of a woman nonetheless—a portrait of herself. She wanted me to take it with me, to hang it in the place where I lived. She didn't say that. She said only, *Here. It's for you,* but I knew what she meant. We had not spoken about where I lived. She had never asked me to take her there, but she wanted her portrait there. She was daring me to hang it there. To put it where I slept.

I took the portrait from her hands, her silent challenge thickening the air between us. But I did not take it to my home in Washington. I did not hang it in the place where I lived with my wife, the place that was our sanctuary. I wrapped it in brown paper and I went to my office at the UN. I put it in a closet and I left it there. The impulse to do that did not come out of weakness or cowardice. Quite the opposite. Discretion, I reminded myself, I reassured myself, is the better part of valor.

13

I think sometimes that in those days I was as in love with the life Marguerite unknowingly dared me to live as I was in love with her. She filled a need in my soul Nerida never guessed existed. She gave me glimpses of a life I lacked the courage to live. She had taken control of the reins of her life and turned them to the direction she had chosen. Since she was a child she had known she was an artist. She had pursued her conviction without compromise. I had merely followed the times and the opportunity. When the wind blew, I let myself be carried with it. I never resisted. I never sought another direction. I never asked if there was something different I could do. If there was something else I wanted to do.

With Marguerite I had begun to take chances. I had begun to seek my dream, not in my fantasies, but in reality. In real life. I had pursued Marguerite of my own volition. I had sought her out. I had deceived my wife for her. I had taken the risk of losing my wife for her.

Still, if someone had asked me why I did not want to leave Nerida, I would have said because I need her, too. If they had asked me why, I would have said because she gives me security. Because she gives me stability. Because she creates spaces where things remain the same, where I can delude myself with the possibility of permanence.

The walls of my apartment, I would say, will always be white, my furniture will always be mahogany, the colors of the upholstery will always be earth tones, my bed will always be made, my son will always be fed and dressed and in bed if I am home too late. Dinner will always be ready. Nerida will be waiting for me. Always.

This, above all, is what marriage does, why in spite of other passions that tempt us, dissatisfactions that may cause us to stray, we return to it, we hold on to it. Marriage offers us this: the illusion of forever. It is part of that great denial of our mortality that is so much at the heart of our modern age: technology, the new god, stretching limits beyond reasonable hope and belief. We talk of advances in medicine as if the cures they offer could be permanent. We promote health clubs, health food, cosmetic surgery as if they could break that free-fall to old age. We marry, we divorce, we remarry. Why? Because marriage eases the fear of our mortality. In middle age and old age we could pretend to start again. We could make the same promises of forever. Nothing will end. We could swear an oath that the law would validate, that the church in the name of God would sanction.

Many years later, when I had seen much, experienced much, I would wonder that so many could blind themselves to this irony: We have invented an industry marketed by psychologists and analysts to cure the very ill we have used to sustain us. Marguerite would admit to falling victim of that sickness. Denial, she would confess to me, was what allowed her to love me without question.

And the illusion marriage promised is what bound me to Nerida. That and more. For Nerida offered me an anchor to Africa, to home, to history, to tradition. To the past, to the future. When I sensed a threat to this permanence I had with her, as I sensed it the day Marguerite gave me permission to lie, to break her golden rule about integrity and truth, I retreated. I ran.

I had made love to Marguerite that day, enlisted her in my conspiracy of lies of omissions, encouraged her fears of loss (which I suspected had to be the consequences of her loss of Jamaica), all to squelch the answer to her question: "What used to make you happy?" For I did not want Marguerite to leave me. For I did not want to leave Nerida.

Marguerite said I had read too many books by the Europeans. We had made our peace over Wole Soyinka and I had read *Death and the King's Horseman*, at first, admittedly, only to satisfy her, but afterwards because I found it as rich as any play I had read. She began to buy novels, plays, and books of poetry by African and Caribbean writers for me. I read most of them but not all, and the ones I read, I read because Nerida read them to me.

Nerida was pleased when I brought home the books Marguerite bought for me. She thought I had started taking an interest in literature again. When I said I did not think I would find the time to read because the ambassador was keeping me too busy, Nerida sympathized with me and said she would read to me in bed. So comfortable had I made myself with my world then, that I saw no contradiction, no conflict, in my wife reading to me books that the woman I also made love to had bought for me. I had not faced the details, the questions of legality, the prohibitions of my Christian religion, for my spirit was at ease with loving them both, needing them both.

I think back now and I realize that in those days when I thought wife, I thought of them both, for each of them was an aspect of wife that was essential to me. I could not think of one as my wife without thinking of the other. I could not imagine living with one without being able to be with the other.

Nerida read only the parts of novels she thought I would find interesting—excerpts of plays, and short poems—but it was enough for me to sound knowledgeable and convincing to Marguerite when I discussed them with her. The only novel that I read on my own was Chinua Achebe's *Things Fall Apart* and that was because when Nerida pointed out I would be fascinated by what Achebe made of "The Second Coming," a poem by Yeats, I remembered O'Malley and his swans and his interpretation of another poem by Yeats. I remembered the first time I made love to Marguerite.

We fought for hours, Marguerite and I, over what it seemed to me was Achebe's premise: that the Igbo clan in Nigeria fell apart because they had no unity among themselves. She, however, insisted it was because of English colonialism. The English, she said, brought their values, their philosophy, their system of law, education, and government, and, of course, their guns, and threw the Igbos into confusion. I agreed with the first part of what she said, but argued that it would not have been possible for the English to weaken the culture of the Igbos if the Igbos had remained loyal to each other and to their traditions. She was glad to hear me say this but only because it gave her a chance to repeat to me once more that I had filled my head with too many books by European writers.

I knew she was intimating that I, too, had not been loyal to my traditions. Marguerite was romantic about Africa. She wanted to see Africa through the rose-colored glasses of the young people I saw in the streets of New York and Washington who wore dashikis and African beads and insisted on a purity of tradition that was no longer possible, who wanted Africa to freeze in time for them, who could not understand that irreconcilable opposites could coexist, do coexist. Africa had a past, but was also entitled to a future. I could be African and yet a man of the modern world. I could remain loyal to my traditions and yet admire and desire the accomplishments of the European world.

"Africa is in my heart," I said, "but my heart beats in the present. If I took Africa out of my heart, my heart would stop beating. I would die."

But in her youthful enthusiasm, Marguerite did not believe it was possible for an African to love Africa and still love the literature of the European. She had left Jamaica at too early an age to understand that. She had forgotten that when we were young we lived in colonial countries and that in colonial countries we lived two lives: the life at home and the life among the Europeans. She had forgotten that in school we read only their literature. The Europeans were training workers to serve them: hands and feet to do their labor; minds of young people like me to perform clerical tasks for them in their civil service. They did not take risks with what they would have called subversive literature, literature by the people. By the time I understood their intent, it was too late for me to revolt against them. I had already fallen in love with their literature. I had found universal truths there that spoke even to me, a black boy born in the bush in Africa. I made their literature mine. I claimed it. It belonged to the world and I was in the world. I was human.

It was one such book, a novel, that led me, subconsciously, so I thought once, to push Marguerite into the discovery of my lies, the admission of hers. It was from Dostoyevsky I learned that the guilty returns to the scene of his crime. Like Raskolnikov in *Crime and Punishment*, I too found confession seductive, the danger of being found out irresistible and cathartic.

I had spent two nights with Marguerite and was packing my bags to return to Nerida. It felt good leaving Marguerite, returning to Nerida, knowing I would be back again with Marguerite. It was perhaps this feeling of anticipation without guilt of being with Nerida and our son again, and the absence of sadness in saying good-bye to Marguerite because of the certainty I had of seeing her again, that led me to ask Marguerite foolishly if she also agreed with the tradition still existing in some parts of Africa that a man was permitted to have more than one wife.

Marguerite was in the kitchen when I asked her that question. I was in the bedroom. She did not answer me. I repeated the question and gave it context, shouting though I knew it was not necessary. The wall that separated us was too thin and the door was open.

"You said the European literature I read has made me forget my traditions. I wanted to know if one of them you thought I should not forget is that a man usually had more than one wife."

It was after I personalized the question that I realized the danger I had placed myself in. But Marguerite seemed oblivious to the possibility of danger to herself. Or perhaps by then she had perfected the art of denial. She may have heard me the first time, and her initial hesitation to respond was probably a reflexive action, the human instinct we share with animals to brace ourselves when trouble approaches us. But reason prevailed when I asked her again, the control she used to squelch the questions that would have made it difficult, if not impossible, for her to continue her relationship with me.

"I don't think it's such a bad tradition," she said.

I came out of the bedroom. "You don't?"

"No, I don't."

I sat down on the stool in front of the counter that separated the kitchen from the living room and stared at her, my mind paralyzed by the impossibility of a thought that had come so recklessly to me—the sudden awareness of a possibility that must have been always with me.

"Don't look at me like that," she said. "Why should you be surprised that I would think that way? Jamaicans haven't lost their connection to Africa, you know."

"I would think from your drawings I saw in the restaurant—"

"What about my drawings?" she cut me off.

"Well, you seem so concerned about women."

"I *am* concerned about women."

"Women's pain," I said.

"That precisely."

"And still you would think that it's not a bad tradition for a man to have more than one wife?"

"I think so precisely because I feel women's pain. I've seen too many women grieve for their children when their live-in boyfriends or their husbands find a new love interest. It's one thing for a woman to throw a man out if there are no children, but if there are children, I think the man should not leave and the woman should not put him out."

I looked away from her. I did not want her to read my eyes. "And what about the new woman, his love interest, as you call it?"

"That's a separate thing. I'm not talking about that. I'm talking about the relationship between a man and his wife if there are children. The man leaves his wife, divorces his wife, and what then? What happens to the children? They are left without a father. He may start off seeing them a lot in the beginning but eventually when his new wife has children, he begins to see less and less of them, he begins to give less and less to them. It becomes easy for him to think of his new wife and new children as his only family.

"His new wife encourages that view, society endorses that view, and it becomes convenient for him to have that view. When people ask him about his wife and his children, they mean his new wife and his new children. As his financial situation improves, the new children benefit. They live in a bigger house than the other children, they go to better schools, they have more opportunities, they travel, they meet important people who put in a good word for them to the colleges they want to go to or the jobs they eventually get. Divorce too often means deprivation to a set of children who did nothing to deserve it. To me there is no greater pain for a woman than to see her children denied their birthright, especially if there was something she could have done to stop it."

"So," I began carefully, "you wouldn't divorce your husband if he were having an affair?"

"Not if I had children."

"And you don't think a husband should divorce his wife if he's in love with another woman?"

"What would the husband do in Africa?" she asked me.

"He'd marry the other woman," I said.

"But he wouldn't divorce his wife?"

"No," I said. "He wouldn't divorce the woman he married first."

"And he'd have two families and all his children would be treated the same, right?"

"In fact, his first wife would be treated with more respect," I said. "And her children, too."

She put her arms around my neck. "See, I'm more African than you think. I agree with that tradition."

"Are you sure?"

"Yes, I'm sure."

"You think it's a tradition we should keep?"

She kissed me. "Yes, it's a tradition you should keep."

Slowly I removed her arms from around my neck. "Do you think I should keep it?"

She began to answer me: "Yes, you should . . ." But her voice faltered. She cleared her throat. "Africa, I mean." She gained confidence. "Africa should keep that tradition."

"What about me?"

She lost her footing again with my question. I think this time she sensed it was not academic. She tried to laugh, but the laugh stuck in her throat.

"You ask me that as if you were married," she said. I saw her eyes travel to my left hand, a hand that by now she knew as well as her own. I did not wear a wedding band. I never did. "You are not married, are you?"

I did not answer her.

"Well, are you?" There was still hope in her voice.

I cast my eyes anywhere but in her direction.

"You're scaring me. Are you married?" She tried to force my eyes to meet hers. "Tell me, Oufoula."

I remained silent.

"Are you? Are you?" Her voice was tense now. "Look at me."

Again I did not answer her. I did not look at her.

"Oufoula, stop it. You're really frightening me now. Tell me you're not married."

But she knew my answer. She heard the truth in my silence.

"Say it, dammit. Say it. Don't just stand there. Say it."

"What do you want me to say?"

"Say it!"

"I'm married."

"Liar. Say it's not true." But she was looking at me with glazed eyes, the eyes of dead fish laid out on trays in the market.

"It's true, Marguerite."

"Liar." There was no conviction in her voice.

"No, Marguerite. It's true."

My words must have finally penetrated the defenses she had mounted in her brain. She opened her mouth to speak again, but no sound came. It was as if she suddenly understood what I had said to her and, understanding, could not trust herself to use words again. For words had trapped her, deceived her. When they rose on her tongue she swallowed them, pushed them deep into her throat and buried them. The moan that eventually came through her lips was not unlike the mournful lowing I had heard from animals caught in a hunter's snare.

I stood still next to her, wishing I could absorb her pain, take it away from her. I did not touch her. I did not speak to her. I wanted her to hurl curses upon me, shout, scream at me. I wanted to be punished. But when finally she spoke, her voice was almost a whisper: "Children?"

"A son. A baby on the way."

"Leave," she said. She did not raise her voice. "Leave and don't come back. *Ever.*"

I knew she meant it and there was nothing I could do to persuade her to change her mind. I went back to the bedroom, threw the rest of my clothes in my bag, zipped it closed, put on my jacket. She did not look at me when I came back into the living room. She did not move. She did not stop me when I opened the front door. She did not say good-bye.

I asked the cab that took me to the airport to stop first at the UN. I went directly to my office. I walked to the closet where I had hidden Marguerite's portrait. I took it out and brought it home with me to Washington.

14

$\mathcal{H}$ow can I describe the days that followed, the weeks afterwards? Self-recrimination was not enough to ease my pain. It did not bring relief. How could it when what I had said to Marguerite was the truth? When finally I had been honest with her? How could I expect guilt to assuage my pain when I was guilty only of ending the lies, the lies I told to Marguerite, the lies I allowed Nerida to believe when I gave her the impression that my visits to New York were for business only?

The truth, I was told by the missionaries, sets you free. I was anything but free. I came to Nerida that night a prisoner, locked out from the woman I loved, locked in to the woman I loved. An iron gate stood between the life I had with Nerida and the one I wanted with Marguerite. On one side of that gate I was free to love Nerida, our son, the child we would soon have, but it was a freedom I could not enjoy. It barred me from the freedom I also wanted, the freedom to be with the other woman I loved.

I know now that there is no such thing as freedom. I know now that whatever freedom we experience comes when we voluntarily submit ourselves to the opposite of what we think is freedom. When we impose limits on ourselves. When we deny ourselves choice. I remind myself of that when I do mundane things, things of little import or consequence, like choosing the shaving cream I use. I know that there is much available to me: the kind that has moisturizer in it, the kind that has perfumes, the kind that will not burn me if I cut my face. I have the money. I can buy whatever I want, but I limit myself to one kind. I disregard the others. I buy only one brand. I do not think of the attributes of the others. I am not plagued by indecision. I am not tormented by doubts that there are others better than the one I bought. It is I who voluntarily excluded the others. That fact alone gives me contentment with what I have.

I know that now as a man of fifty-five, though every day I must remind myself. Every day I must tell myself that freedom comes from voluntary exclusion. I did not understand that then, so I grieved without restraint for the loss of Marguerite. I did not choose to give her up. I had not voluntarily imposed that limitation on myself. I wanted her, I longed for her. So I took my grief and my longing to Nerida. It brought me discontent and unhappiness. It made me a prisoner of myself in my home.

Nerida saw the change in me when I returned to Washington with Marguerite's portrait in my hand. She attributed it to the exhaustion.

"You really have to tell the ambassador that you cannot be expected to make so many trips to New York," she said.

My kind Nerida, my sweet Nerida. I walked past her to the cabinet where I stored my tools. I did not wait to take off my jacket. I took out my hammer and a nail from the drawer and went to our bedroom and hammered the nail on the wall above our bed and hung the portrait of my Marguerite there.

"It looks like a mask from back home," Nerida said.

But I knew she wanted to ask me other questions: Where I did I get it? Did I know who drew it? Did I know the artist personally? Why did I want it hung on our bedroom wall? Why not in the dining room or the living room? Why couldn't I wait until the next morning to hang it up? Why did it have to be done as soon as I arrived? Why now, when I was so exhausted?

But Nerida did not ask me these questions though they were probably fermenting in her brain. Instead, she comforted me, worried that I had overworked myself. That it was the accumulation of my many trips to New York that had made me so listless, so distant. But I was certain when she said this it was merely a subterfuge, a cover-up for the true fears that gnawed at her.

She had cooked salmon for dinner. It was a fish I liked. That night I barely touched it.

"You're not eating." She slid my plate gently toward me.

"I'm not hungry." I pushed it away.

She said again that she thought I was overworked. "You look tired. You can hardly hold up your head."

"I just need to sleep," I said.

"I'll tell my father to speak to the ambassador. Either you work here where we live or we move to New York."

"No!" I saw her flinch when I hit the table with my fist. "We will *not* move to New York."

I could not live with Nerida and our son in the same city where Marguerite lived and not make love to Marguerite. The thought alone set my head on fire.

Nerida picked up our son from his chair. "I'll put Ayi to sleep." She brought him to me. "Kiss Baba."

I did not take my son from her arms.

"Kiss Baba. He had a hard day."

My son sensed the rigidity in my body. He pulled his head away from me.

"Kiss Baba," Nerida told my son again. She leaned him toward me. "Kiss Baba." She pushed his head against my face.

My son began to cry. His tears wet my cheeks.

"Kiss Baba."

He refused.

Nerida was almost shouting now, my calm Nerida who always spoke so gently to her son. "Kiss Baba." She was crying, holding him tightly to her breasts. Tears ran down both their eyes.

"See, see," she said to my son. "See how you made Baba unhappy and he is so tired. Look how we made him unhappy."

Only my son spoke the truth that night. Only my son who could not yet talk in sentences that would have made his feelings clear, only he said I was the guilty one. He and his mother were the innocent ones. They had not made me unhappy. I was the one who had made them unhappy. They were the ones who were crying. I was the one sitting like a stone, unmoved by their tears. I did not deserve his kisses. He would not kiss me. His mother could not make him say he loved me. I did not deserve his love.

We lied to each other that night, Nerida and I. When she touched me in bed hoping I would put my arms around her and comfort her, I turned my back on her.

"Sleep," she said. "I know you're tired."

I allowed myself to accept her lie as the truth. I kissed her and said I would be better the next night after I had some sleep, after I had the rest I needed. She allowed herself to accept my lie as the truth.

I made love to Nerida the next night with the portrait of Marguerite looking down on us above my head. I could not see the eyes, but I knew the eyes saw me. I told Nerida I loved her. It was not a lie. I did not tell her that I also loved Marguerite, the woman in the room with us. That was a lie of omission. It was the same kind of lie I had used with Marguerite.

I was a man divided into two selves, each self a different self, desiring and needing a different love. But I could not exist if my two selves remained divided. I could not survive if they were separated. I needed Nerida, but I needed Marguerite, too. I loved Nerida, but I loved Marguerite, too.

Mornings were the worst for me. I would wake up and see Nerida lying on the bed next to me and I would be happy that she was my wife, the mother of my son and my unborn child. I would be grateful for the family I had. But soon the serpent of discontent would slither into my Eden and I would yearn for Marguerite. She would enter my mind and it would be she I would see on my bed lying next to me, not Nerida.

I would see her as I had seen her many mornings, her hair loose from the ponytail she wore during the day. She would have pushed it off her neck. It would have splayed across her pillow. Her large eyes would still be closed, her full lips slightly parted, her brown face smooth and silky soft when I touched it, her legs entangled in the bedsheets. How many times had she pulled the sheets off me during the night? She laughed at me when I complained.

"You're too tall for my sheets," she said.

I would pull her on top of me. If our heads met, there would be a full twelve inches of my legs left bare from where her feet touched my calves.

When memories of my mornings with Marguerite tormented me, I would rush to the office to call her. Always there would be no answer. Sometimes Nerida would still be in bed when I left the apartment. Those were the days when my desperation turned to fear, the mornings when I tried to convince myself that I needed to call her earlier, that if I called her earlier, she would not yet have started to paint or draw, that she would answer the phone when it rang.

Nerida never questioned me. She apologized instead that she had not woken up in time to make breakfast for me. But how was Nerida to know that I would leave our apartment at five in the morning? I myself did not know. I did not know until four that morning when I would be plagued with doubts that I would calm with excuses that gave rise to other doubts. Marguerite was waking up earlier to do her art, I said to myself, and then I would remember she needed the light from the sun. But no matter what time I called during the day, she never answered the phone.

I began leaving my house at all hours in the night to call her from the phone booth in the street. Still, she did not answer. Soon the excuses I had used to calm my anxiety ceased to work. It was foolish to believe Marguerite would never answer the phone. She had friends who called her, her students, people she hoped would purchase her work or exhibit it. She would answer the phone for them, and if it was me she did not want to hear from, she could put down the phone when she heard my voice or she could change her number.

I concluded now that Marguerite was not in her apartment. I became obsessed with this thought, finding relief only when I imagined that she had gone to Jamaica for a holiday. But that thought also did not bring me relief. I would remember that she had no money to go to Jamaica and that she had to stay in New York because she taught two nights a week at the New School. Finally, I was left to confront the only other probability. She was with someone else. She had moved in with him. There was someone to whom she was giving her love.

I was determined to find out if this was true, but it had become impossible for me to go to New York. Nerida had made good on her promises and had telephoned her father. He gave the ambassador strict orders to restrict all my responsibilities to Washington. I was not to be required to travel except in an emergency when my services were absolutely needed.

I did not know what Nerida said to her father to warrant this extreme injunction, though I could surmise what she could have said. She could have said to her father that I was becoming distant from her, irritable sometimes without reason. That I had been going to New York every two weeks, that often I stayed overnight. That the last time when I came back home after spending two nights in New York, I slammed my fist on the dining room table and made her and our son cry.

She could have said that when I started going to New York regularly, I began to bring back books I did not read. That more than twice I had asked her to come with me to an art gallery. That before that, she never knew I had any interest in art.

That I had brought back a drawing of a head of a woman and hung it on our bedroom wall.

She could have said that lately I was going to work before dawn and that late at night I would remember I had forgotten something in the office or that I needed to speak to someone in person. That I was overworked and tired most of the time. That I rarely slept.

Her father would have decoded her message. He would have known the truth. He was a man. He understood what men could do.

But I knew Nerida. I knew how much she loved me, how much she cared for me, how much she worried about my welfare. She was a wife who thought it her duty to calm her husband's nerves when he returned home from the hunt, who thought she must have patience when her husband needed to play.

That was what I told her when I decided I would go to New York on a Saturday to assuage my fears that Marguerite was living with another man. I said I needed the distraction. I needed to be with friends. I needed to relax. I needed to play. But I went to New York because I needed to reassure myself, to prove to myself that Marguerite still lived alone in her apartment, that no one else—a man—lived with her.

I told Nerida that one of my old friends from the University of London was coming through Washington on his way to California. He would have only a day in Washington, and I wanted to see him. Nerida was happy to let me go. Before I could say it, she said that she didn't think she and our son should go with me. She said my friend and I would have things to talk about that she wouldn't know. She had not been with me in London. She could only be in the way.

"Go, Oufoula," she said. "You need to do something else besides work. Give your friend my regards."

I had mastered the lie of omission. I was learning to master the lie of commission. How much more complicated that lie turned out to be. It left a trail behind it that required more lies to cover the lies I had already told. Before, there were no questions for Nerida to ask me. I was going to New York on business for the diplomatic service. What questions were there to ask? Why should she have guessed that my main reason for going there was to see Marguerite?

Now I had to invent reasons for my absence, and with each invention I pulled myself deeper into a web of deception. I learned better how to tailor my lies, how to make my inventions plausible. It was not by accident I made up the story of a friend passing through the airport in Washington. I had assessed the risks, anticipated the possibility of discovery. If I was seen at the airport by someone who knew Nerida and told her she had seen me, Nerida would not be surprised. She would say she expected me to be at the airport. She knew I was there to meet a friend from England, whom she could not identify since I had taken care to give her neither a name nor a photograph, and, so, therefore, she was not in a position to know that I was there to take the early morning shuttle to New York. I was there to go to Marguerite.

I was in front of Marguerite's apartment building by nine o'clock that Saturday morning. I knew she slept late on Saturdays and that she had breakfast in the coffee shop that faced her building. I decided I would wait for her there. I could see her when she came out of her apartment. I could be waiting for her in the booth where she ate. By eleven o'clock I was beginning to despair. There were women who came out of the building who looked like Marguerite: tiny women with bodies like Marguerite's, the same small breasts, narrow waists, and rounded hips. But none of these women had Marguerite's fluid movements—the graceful stride of a woman who had balanced heavy baskets on her head and knew how to keep her shoulders straight, her back erect while her hips glided like sailboats across a silken sea.

By eleven-thirty I had convinced myself that I had been right. Marguerite was no longer living in her apartment. She had moved in with a man. This thought was not as irrational as it seemed. Marguerite had told me that she knew that when her grant ended she would have to move to a less expensive place. She had told me she had an artist friend who had offered to share an apartment with her. She had not told me whether that friend was a man or a woman. Then, in my arrogance, when I felt the intensity of her love for me, I had assumed it was a woman. Then, there was no question in my mind that she would not live with another man, whether her relationship with him would be platonic or not. Now it seemed that there was never a doubt. That she had told me many times before that her friend was a man.

Frantic, I searched my brain for a name. And then I saw her. She was coming out of her building holding the hand of the very man I had imagined. She was laughing, turning her face up to him. She had taken her hair out of her ponytail band. It swung free on her shoulders. She was wearing the pink shirt that I liked. She wore it over a white short skirt that exposed her legs, the legs I had kissed, the legs she usually concealed from the public under leggings or covered under pants.

The young man was African. He had the confident eyes of an African, the air of insouciance I rarely saw in African Americans, vigilant as they were to the nuances of American racism that we black foreigners often understood too late. I knew he was not Caribbean, either. He was lighter in complexion than me, but he was not mixed with other bloods as were the men from the Caribbean.

They crossed the street and came toward the coffee shop. I panicked. I did not know what I would say or do if they came inside. Would I snatch her hand from out of his? Would I push him down? Would I say to him she is mine? She is the woman I love, the woman who loves me. But I did not get the chance to do such things, to say such things. When they reached the front of the coffee shop, she tugged his sleeve and forced him to bend his head down toward her. What she said made the insouciant man laugh. He nibbled on her ear. Nibbled on my Marguerite's ear. He fondled her neck. The back of my Marguerite's neck.

I knew she had seen me. Now she looked straight in my direction. The eyes were my Marguerite's brown eyes, but they were hard. Unyielding.

The man hugged her by her waist. She put her head on his shoulder, held my eyes for a second longer, and then turned and whispered in his ear again. He tightened his grip and led her across the street toward her apartment. I knew what they would do. I knew she had whispered to him about love. She had whispered like that to me.

Three days later I received a letter from her. She had mailed it to my office.

Dear Oufoula,

Do not follow me again. Do not call me again. It is over between us. Go home and love your wife. I should have known better. Lying is the

necessary qualification for the diplomat. How well you will succeed in
your chosen career! I congratulate you in anticipation of that happy day.
Marguerite

I would remember these words when I was named an ambassador for my country. I would remember when I had power and prestige bestowed on me that Catherine had said those very words to me in Geneva.

15

⁓

I viewed the next days with the impassioned detachment with which the contrite sinner accepts his punishment. When I received mine, I knew that God's justice had been meted out. I speak not only of the loss of Marguerite. That was to be temporary, though more than twenty-five years would pass by before I could say that with certainty. I speak of a greater penalty, the kind that lets us know that God's laws must not be transgressed. The kind that made Adam understand that he had not lost Eden because of an apple. He had lost it because he had looked in the face of God and challenged Him. Because he was ungrateful.

God had given me everything. He had sent Christian missionaries to educate me, to give me a scholarship to a university in England. He had paved the way for the president of my country to take me under his wing, to open doors for me to a career that would bring me more successes than I could have dreamed of. He had given me Nerida, my devoted wife, and Ayi, my loving son. And yet I had risked them all. All for Marguerite, who in spite of my punishment, I would continue to love.

Perhaps my punishment was severe because I was not the Christian I thought I was. Perhaps Marguerite was right. I had learned to be a Christian but I was not a Christian in my soul. Perhaps I had only memorized Bible stories, commandments, laws, but they had not become articles of faith for me. They had not penetrated my spirit, resided in my subconscious the way myths always do, the way the myths of my people had done—the beliefs I acquired as a child in my mother's lap without consciousness or effort.

Perhaps the Margarete that first disturbed my dreams, the Margarete of my fantasies, was not spawned there by a European play I had read at the university in London about a tormented man who made a bargain with the devil in the hope that satiety with the pleasures of the flesh would finally bring him respite from his ceaseless yearnings. Perhaps the Margarete of my fantasies was not put there by a woman who had deceived me when I was too young to know that all that was said with sincerity was not necessarily sincere. Perhaps I had dreamed of Margarete because I had dreamed of what my father had, what his father before him had. Perhaps as a boy I had wanted, as they were allowed to have, two, even more wives.

Boys learn at the feet of their fathers to be men, and though my own did not care for me, perhaps I had still learned from him. Perhaps I harbored in my soul a secret longing for the life my father had, his happiness and his pleasure, too: the love of two wives, the pleasure of two wives. And when I learned to be Christian, when I was taught to trust my brain and not my heart, and reason informed me that the world of my ancestors was chaotic and the laws of the Christian God would bring order to my life, I became ashamed of my boyhood desires. I determined I would love one woman in the flesh as the Christian God had commanded. I would marry one woman.

Yet my desires persisted, and when I was deceived by the first woman I loved, when Mulenga betrayed me, I unconsciously blamed my misfortunes on my pigheaded insistence on the Christian way. Now I would have two wives, but since the one I wanted did not want me, I would create another, but she would burn with desire for me and I would reject her. So I invented a fantasy, a destroyer of men who would not destroy me, and I confined her to my dreams, to that erotic cesspool of my nocturnal scavenging. Until I met Marguerite. Until I met Marguerite who was good and honest and beautiful. Marguerite with whom I fell in love. And I wanted her, too, as I wanted my wife.

This may have been the reason why I had asked Marguerite that question that led to her rejection of me. The impulse to ask her may have had nothing at all to do with the influence of Dostoyevsky's Raskolnikov on my psyche. It may have had nothing at all to do with guilt or my desire for catharsis. For I did not feel the need for catharsis. For I had not felt guilty for loving Marguerite. I did not feel guilty when I made love to her. For the truth was that when I asked her if she thought I should follow in the tradition of my forefathers and marry two wives, I had hoped she would say yes. As difficult as it is for me to imagine that possibility now, I had imagined it then. And it is for this reason I believed I was punished. Not because I had had an affair, not because I had broken the sixth commandment of the Christian God, but because for one long moment, for one immeasurable pause in time, I had considered the unthinkable: the reversion to a system of belief the missionaries had devoted their lives to eradicating from my soul and from the souls of Africans like me—the abandonment of all I had come to espouse, the submission to all I had believed no longer had merit.

I was punished for my ingratitude. And for my hubris. It was a punishment so severe that had I not considered it in the light of this justice, I would not have been able to go forward with my life. I would not have been able to commit myself to the service of my country. I would not have been granted the privileges I now have that give me power and bring me wealth.

Five days after I saw Marguerite, my wife went shopping with my son. They were crossing the street. My son's hand was in my wife's hand. The crosswalk sign in front of them was green. It gave them permission to walk. They had just stepped off the curb when a car careened toward them. It was a drunken driver, the police told me. A young man of nineteen full of beer and cheap wine from a fraternity party that had begun at noon.

It was five o'clock when his car struck my wife and my son. My son died on the spot. My wife remained in the intensive care unit of the hospital for a week. Our daughter was born dead.

16

My president recalled us to Africa. He thought I would not be able to breathe air in the country where my son had lost his life, where my daughter never had a chance to begin hers. I left without saying good-bye to Marguerite. I did not answer her letter, I did not call her, I did not try to see her again. I left directly from Washington when my wife regained consciousness. She went with me on a stretcher to Africa, needles feeding liquids into her veins to keep her alive. She wanted to be in Africa when I buried our son, when we said good-bye to a daughter we had never heard cry or ever seen in her eyes the faintest flicker of life.

There are no words that come close to conveying the grief a parent feels at the loss of a child, much less the loss of two children. Nerida and I bore our grief in different ways. She wanted no reminders of their physical existence. She left all our son's clothes, all his toys, in the apartment in Washington, the baby things, too, she had bought for the child we were expecting. Her babies had gone to the ancestors, she said. They were spirits now. She would keep them in her spirit. She did not return to their graves after the funeral. That was not where they were, she said. They were everywhere. They were in her heart.

Nerida is a Christian as I am, but she became a Christian for me. When I insisted on marrying in the Church. To please her, I had allowed the priest from her clan to bless us and the drums to beat nine days for us. I presented her with a dowry of wood carvings and gold, and I had ten cows slaughtered and a feast prepared for the people in her village. But I did those things so her father would allow her to marry me in a church and so that the missionaries from Canada, who had paid for my education, would officiate at the ceremony.

Nerida indulged me because she loved me, but she did not believe as I said I believed. She did not believe in a Resurrection of the flesh. She did not believe that one day our spirits would return to our dead bodies and we would rise again inside our physical selves, the selves we had on earth, to await God's judgment. She believed that when we died, we joined our ancestors. That the body that carried our spirit no longer had value. It returned to the earth from whence it came.

My wife recovered fully from the accident that took our children's lives. Today she bears no physical scars, but still she rarely speaks about our dead son and our stillborn daughter. In the early days she refused to talk to me about them at all, so profound and lasting was her grief. She did not intend to cause me pain, though talking to her would have relieved my pain. Only two people really know the intensity of the suffering the death of children bring— the child's father and the child's mother. I could have talked to others, but no one but Nerida could have begun to comprehend my anguish. But Nerida did not want to talk to me. She said I was a mirror in which she saw the reflection of her pain. Talking to me about our dead children only caused her suffering to be twice as excruciating.

I went alone to the gravesites of my children and there were days, I confess, when I longed to weep like a child. When I wanted to bury my head in the bosom of a woman who loved me, a woman who would comfort me with her affection for me. But my mother was dead, and Nerida did not want to weep with me. Those were the times I ached for Marguerite—for the softness of her skin against mine, for the solace of her courage that had forced me to tell her the truth. To tell her about Nerida.

Marguerite would not have wanted me to pretend. She would not have wanted me to act strong when I felt weak, to smile when I wanted to cry. She would have let me soak her hair with my tears. She would have known that though my Christian beliefs had assured me that my children were in Heaven, I was not consoled. I wanted my son in the flesh. I wanted to touch him, to hear his voice, to see his face. I wanted to kiss the cheeks of my stillborn child. I wanted to open her eyes. I wanted to loosen her tongue. I wanted to hear her call my name, Baba, Baba. I wanted to see her take her first step. No religious belief could take away those longings from my heart, diminish those feelings. I wanted my children back. I wanted them alive.

On those days when I was desperate for Marguerite's understanding, I told myself that a good God would not have been so cruel as to punish me this way for loving her. Then, I refused to make any connection between her and the death of my children. Then, I did not think my pain was due to retribution for my ingratitude to the missionaries for saving me from the darkness of the spirit world of my ancestors. From illiteracy. I did not think it was hubris that caused me to look into the fires of the Christian Hell and still reach back, grasp on to the beliefs of my ancestors for affirmation, for validation that would let me keep Nerida, and Marguerite, too.

I would have called Marguerite again. I wanted to call her. Only the memory of seeing her from the window of the coffee shop stopped me, only the image indelibly imprinted on my mind of her unyielding eyes, of her laughter in the arms of her lover, arrested me. I knew which words she whispered in his ear. I knew why she had crossed the street to return to her apartment. I knew she had lain naked with him on the bed where she had lain naked with me. I could not bear those images. I could not bear the possibility that even now she was making love to another man.

I had brought her portrait and the books she had given me to Africa. I did not unpack them. I left them in the boxes that had been shipped to my home. I did not want reminders of her. I wanted to forget her.

It was shortly after I returned to Africa that my president named me his ambassador to Ghana. I was thirty-two. Those who envied me when the president made me his trusted confidant, gave me his daughter's hand in marriage and sent me to Geneva and then to Washington, hated me now and wished me misfortune. But I did not have misfortune in Ghana. God smiled on me in Ghana. A month after I arrived there, my wife was pregnant again. We had a son and, after him, two daughters, twins born the following year. In the four years I spent in Ghana, my life was restored. My three children eased the pain of the two I had lost. I believed I had wiped Marguerite out of my memory. I embraced Nerida and my love for her grew stronger. I believed she was all I needed, that Marguerite no longer mattered, that Nerida could fill the spaces Marguerite had left yawning in me. I believed I was happy, that my wife and my children were all I desired.

My work was absorbing. It brought me happiness and satisfaction. I became involved not only in the concerns of my country but in the concerns of other nations in Africa. Often I was asked to resolve disputes between nations or to be the voice of African countries in their negotiations with the Europeans. As more and more gold, oil, and uranium were discovered in Africa, particularly in countries around the equator, I was the one most entrusted by governments to represent their interests. I was considered fair and honest. An impartial judge who did not take sides in quarrels between Africans but who fought steadfastly for Africa when African countries, not only mine, were involved. I was considered a man of principle and integrity. A man who could be relied on to say the truth, even to those who did not want the truth.

I would often think that Marguerite would have found it ironic that I should have gained this reputation. Indeed, if it was true that I was a man who told the truth, it was because Marguerite had taught me the painful consequences of not telling the truth. And yet there were many occasions when I found it prudent not to reveal all I knew. There were times when I knew the truth could hurt my country, could harm Africa. In these instances, I did not tell the truth. Was I a liar? I do not call these untruths lies when I withheld such knowledge from the Europeans or even from another African, but I sometimes wondered about the position Marguerite would have taken. Would she make a distinction between discretion and lies? Would she say, as the missionaries had taught me, that a lie of commission and a lie of omission were both sins against God? Would she repeat to me that lies always hurt the one they are intended to deceive, if not at the time they are told, then later?

What if the person who was deceived deserved to be harmed? What if it was my intention to cause retribution to the one who devastated my people? Would she still say no and tell me that the truth sets you free? What if the truth caused the imprisonment or death of a good man?

I have been in situations where I lied for my brothers in South Africa, where I used my contacts within the diplomatic world to raise money for the outlawed MK—Umkhonto we Sizwe, The Spear of the Nation—the military force that was once headed by Nelson Mandela and was intensely feared and hated by White South Africa. MK was held responsible for the sporadic uprisings in Johannesburg. It was said that it was MK that supplied the guns and the explosives for these uprisings. That it was MK that trained young children and women in the tactics of guerilla warfare. The founders and leaders of MK were in jail, but there were thousands willing to risk their lives and their livelihood, willing to die for their freedom.

Publicly I decried their acts of violence. I told my sponsors I was raising money for support of a peaceful resolution to the crime of apartheid. Privately I had long since ceased to believe that such a solution was possible. I had learned my lesson from America. It was Malcolm X's threat of "by any means necessary" that stemmed the bloodtide of America's vicious racist policies. Not Martin Luther King's dream. But no one knew I thought this way. Not even Nerida. If these kinds of lies made me a good diplomat, then I was proud to be a diplomat. I was proud to be a man of discretion.

But Marguerite had meant another kind of lie, the lie I told her. And try as I did, I could not convince myself that I had withheld the truth from her to protect her from the hurt of a broken heart, or that I had deceived Nerida to save her from the pain of betrayal. No, I knew too well I had lied to them both because of my selfish desires: I loved them both. I wanted them both.

Still, there were many who did not think me a selfish man. Those I served found me altruistic, my motives untainted by greed for personal gain, and though this was true, I also profited. When I was posted to Nigeria, I lived in a house as large as the president's, his gift to me for negotiating an oil deal from which he became rich and our country's citizens not as poor as they once were. When I went to Ethiopia, money was deposited in Swiss banks for me for persuading the Americans to dig water wells in areas suffering from drought. In Mali I was given gold bars for uncovering hidden clauses in a contract between a European mining company and the government that would have robbed the country of millions of dollars. More money was deposited in my name by other African countries, including my own, for trade agreements I had obtained for them with the larger developed countries. I never requested the vast sums I received in excess of my fees, but I never refused payment either. Most of the time the money was given to me without my knowledge.

Before I was forty I was a rich man. I was able to provide my family with more opportunities than I had imagined would have been possible. My children traveled all over the world, they went to the best schools, and met the most important people. Before they left home to go to university, they spoke not only two African languages but also three European languages—French, German, and English—two more that I did.

Nerida, too, enjoyed our wealth but she was never extravagant. She never bought more clothes or jewelry than were necessary for the social functions we attended. Though she no longer had the need to create reminders of Africa for me in our home since we now lived in Africa, our furnishings remained conservative. The colors in our home were muted; wood carvings were placed everywhere, as were woven baskets and potted plants. It did not take me long to realize that this style was actually a reflection of Nerida's own taste, not merely her attempt to please me, as I once believed. When we entertained heads of state from other countries, I was always proud of the way she had decorated our home and the elegance with which she had meals prepared and served.

She did not become involved in the diplomatic social circles, however. She went back to university and completed a master's and then a Ph.D. in history. Both the children and I profited from her knowledge. She continued to teach me about the history of Europe and about the European exploitation of Africa and Asia. There are more times than I can count that I have been grateful to her for that education.

In those years, I saw Marguerite twice—the first time, ten years after I looked into her eyes and the Margarete of my youthful fantasies died, burned to ashes in the intensity of my passion, the suddenness of the love that I felt for the woman in front of me, the real Marguerite, the true Marguerite. I saw her briefly then, that first time, ten years later. I was forty and the ambassador for my country in Chad. My president had asked me to go to the UN to persuade the West African countries to put pressure on Nigeria to unload shipments of food waiting in the harbor. Nigeria was undergoing another period of unrest, and most of its harbors were closed. My country, like Chad was landlocked, and though we had rivers that led to the interior, nothing could get to the rivers unless it passed through Nigeria's harbor.

My president was apologetic. He assumed that I did not want to set foot on the earth of the country where my son and my daughter had been violently killed. This was true, but it was also true that the moment he asked me, the moment I realized that there was a possibility that I would go to New York, Marguerite returned to my heart, Marguerite whom I had fooled myself into believing I had forgotten. Now she consumed me, took control of my waking hours and my dreams until more than anything else I desired, I wanted to go to New York. I wanted a chance to see her again.

17

I telephoned Marguerite at her apartment the afternoon I arrived in New York. A man answered. I would have put down the receiver had I not realized that his accent was American. He was not the African I had seen nibbling on her ear, fondling her neck in front of the coffee shop. He told me that Marguerite no longer lived in the apartment. He did not know where she lived, but he knew she was still teaching at the New School.

I told myself, when I called her, that I no longer desired her, that she was a friend from the past. That was all. In the ten years I was away from her in Africa, I had made love only to my wife. I had desired no one else but my wife. Nerida had become my confidant, my companion in life, my world. Had I not thought this, I would not have had the courage to call Marguerite. I would have feared I would have fallen to my knees at her feet. I would have begged her forgiveness. I would have pleaded with her to take me back. I would have cried with rage and jealousy over the man who had replaced me. But these are the tricks the mind plays to give us what we want when conscience or fear stands in our way. So when I dialed the number to Marguerite's office I did so with a lightness of spirit, believing myself safe, my heart repaired.

"Oufoula!" She seemed happy to hear from me. "When did you come to New York?"

The sudden racing of my heart should have warned me, the joy I felt on hearing her voice. But I did not want to be warned. I wanted to remember. I wanted to hear her speak again. I wanted to see her.

"Yesterday," I said.

"How long are you staying?"

"Three days."

Three days. It was not a long time, even if I weakened.

"Three days! Will I get to see you?"

"I called because I wanted to see you," I said.

"It's been a long time."

"Yes," I said. "Can we meet?"

"Of course, of course," she answered quickly, her voice almost officious.

"Today?"

She hesitated. Consulting her appointment book? I had not consulted mine when I let her choose the time and place for our first meeting. "Tomorrow," she said finally.

"When tomorrow?"

"In the early evening. Say about seven?"

I tried and failed to control my anxiety. "For dinner?"

"Yes," she said. "Dinner would be fine."

"In the same restaurant?" Memory propelled me to imprudence, to take the risk of immersing myself in the entanglement of emotions I should have known I could not resist. My hope was that she would refuse me. It was a hope I did not want fulfilled.

"In the same restaurant," she said. But there was no acknowledgment in her voice that that was a special place for her.

I came to the restaurant fearing for myself, but when I saw her, the muscles that had constricted my chest loosened and I was able to breathe again. She had changed. She seemed more mature, more womanly, less of the carefree girl that I had fallen in love with ten years ago, a shadow of the image I had struggled to smother. I did not think she seemed that way to me because she was older, or because she had cut her hair and no longer wore it in the ponytail I remembered. I did not think it was because she no longer had the body of a girl and that her breasts were fuller, her hips slightly wider. Or that the clothes she wore—a fitted navy jacket that buttoned over a white blouse and a narrow dark brown skirt that ended mid-calf—were completely unlike the casual attire I had known her to wear. I barely noticed these differences. She was as beautiful, as much the same as before, and yet there was a darkness that clouded her eyes that made her so different from the woman I had loved that I could approach her now without the flutterings in my heart that had surfaced when I heard her voice for the first time on the telephone.

She came immediately toward me. "Oufoula." She did not embrace me. "It's nice to see you again." She held out her hand.

I noticed at once the ring on the second finger of her left hand. I made myself find comfort in it. We would be friends. Nothing else was possible.

"You look beautiful," I said.

"You haven't changed."

"I tried calling you at your apartment. I see you've moved."

"Yes. When I got married," she said.

The waiter came to seat us. He was not the same waiter who had pointed me to Marguerite's etchings in the back of the room. This was a young man, a boy barely in his twenties who wore an earring in his left ear. But nothing in the restaurant was the same. The etchings on the walls had been replaced by signed photographs of famous people. Track lighting crossed the ceilings where old fixtures once hung. Small round tables were crammed into the dining room, and the space between the wall and the column, where I had tried to hide from Marguerite, had been sealed to the height of a table counter. Behind it was a bar from which loud voices and laughter filtered into the dining room.

"It's gone the way of most of the Village restaurants," Marguerite said when I made these observations to her. "I hardly come here anymore."

But I was glad, relieved that there was little to remind me of the place where I had fallen in love with her. Glad of the new decor, the ring on Marguerite's left hand. Both would keep me from losing my balance. Both would remind me of the stability of my life with Nerida.

"When did you get married?" I asked Marguerite. We were at the table. I was feeling secure now, confident. There were no traces of resentment in my voice when I asked her that question. I asked it as I would have of a friend I had not seen for years, a friend whose joy I was happy to share.

"Nine years ago," she answered me.

And suddenly the jealousy returned. Suddenly my mind registered this single fact: Nine years ago was exactly one year after the year she put me out of her apartment.

"The African?" My blood rushed to my head.

"The who?" She looked surprised.

"The man I saw you with."

"You saw me?"

"Ten years ago, outside your apartment building. I was in the coffee shop."

She looked away from me. "Oh," she said.

"Was it he you married?"

"I saw you, too." Her voice was quiet.

"I thought you did. Then I got your letter and I was certain you had."

"I turned away deliberately."

She was talking about whispering in his ear, leaning against his chest when he put his arm around her waist. Running across the street with him to her apartment. My jealousy engulfed me, left me no space to breathe, to be kind, to be gracious.

"I used to think you were in love with me," I said bitterly.

"He meant nothing to me." I had to strain my ears to hear her.

"It doesn't seem so. And so soon after we had broken up."

"I had to get over you," she said.

"Well, that took you no time at all, did it?"

She had been avoiding my eyes, but now she looked directly at me. "It was the quickest way," she said.

The pain naked on her face pierced my heart. I crumbled. "Marguerite." I said her name and reached for her hand, hating myself. Loving her.

"Don't." She pulled away from me.

"Marguerite." I said her name again, wanting to fold her in my arms, to press her to my heart.

"I had to cut you out of my system. There was no other way."

"I'm sorry. I'm sorry, Marguerite. I didn't mean to hurt you."

"I know you didn't, but you did." The tone she used now was flat, without emotion. She opened her napkin and placed it on her lap.

"I loved you."

"We loved each other." She was stating a fact, about something that had happened in the past, but there was no room for a present in that past.

"I still love you."

"No. Don't talk about love now. We're friends. Let's be friends." The waiter came toward us. "Let's order," she said.

"I never forgot you."

"Stop. Don't."

The waiter stood in front of us. "I'll have the chicken cutlets. And you?" She turned back to me. "What will you have?" Her voice was controlled, steady.

"I'll have the same," I barely responded.

When the waiter left she spoke to me as if nothing had passed between us, as if I had inquired about her marriage the way I thought I had—as a friend, believing that that was all she meant to me.

"My husband's name is Harold. Harold Gifford. He's American," she said.

"American?"

"African American."

"An artist like you?"

"A politician."

"A politician? I'm surprised."

She heard the cynicism in my voice, my jealousy lingering though I fought hard to banish it. "Why?" she lashed out at me. "I thought you knew I liked men who ride that fine line between honesty and dishonesty."

I cringed at the reference to the lie that had separated us. This was a new Marguerite, a Marguerite who would not soften the sting of the truth for my sake, who would not be a willing conspirator in my lies of omission.

"I deserve that," I said.

But she was remorseful. "No, I shouldn't have said it."

The waiter had brought our salads. She stuck her fork in hers and I felt her release her anger. "It's all in the past now."

Guilt swept over me. "It was my fault," I said, desperate to find a way to cover up my cynicism, to make my comment appear benign. "I only meant that as a politician's wife your life would be busy and you would not have time for your art."

"I don't," she said.

"You don't what?"

"Have time for my art."

She said what I thought she would say, but it was not what I wanted her to say. For the truth was there was malice indeed in my intent when I said I was surprised she had married a politician, the kind of malice men revert to when they want to disguise their fear of a loss they sense is irreparable. I wanted to hurt her, to imply that she had chosen to marry a politician for the same reason she had chosen to be with me. Both of us gave her time for her only true love: her art. But even as I said so, I was also afraid of the other possibility: that in that contest where I had never dared to enter, he had won. That while I was afraid to challenge her, he had not been.

Though I had been consumed with jealousy for her devotion to her art, in time I had learned to be grateful. In time I understood that Marguerite was attentive and loving to me because of the time we were apart. Because of the time my absence gave her to devote herself to her art.

So it was with creative people, I had concluded. The longer the hours they spent with the imagination, the greater their desire for the tangible. They wanted to touch, see, smell, taste then. Love with their senses. Feel with their bodies what their spirits had experienced. I had discovered that there would be benefits to be reaped if I left her alone, if I was not demanding of her time, if I had patience. And truly, after each absence, I found her more passionate, more responsive to me when we made love. So I never asked her to see me more than the day or two we were together twice every month, more than the infrequent weekends, though there were times I could have arranged to be in New York and Nerida would not have suspected me.

"We needed the money," Marguerite was saying to me now. "I teach full time at the New School."

But I did not believe her. I knew the truth. It was not money that had driven her to give up the hours she needed for her art. It was her husband's jealousy. Like me he feared the thing that could erase him from her mind, that could make him cease to exist for her. He would have known, as I did, that in those hours when she was at her easel, her paintbrush in her hand, she thought of no one, she loved no one, she wanted no one but her art. He would have seen that as I had. Except she had chosen him. Except when he demanded she have no gods but him, she picked him.

"So you don't paint anymore?" I was wracked with jealousy.

"Not as much."

"But you were so good. It meant so much to you."

"It didn't mean more to me than my son," she said.

A son! She had a son! I had braced myself for the worst, but I didn't get the worst. This was better. It was a son, not a husband, she had chosen.

"You have a son?"

Air moved freely through my lungs; the muscles in my jaw slackened. Then, without warning, they tightened again and a familiar pain squeezed my heart. It was the image of my son. Ayi. He flashed before my eyes, rebuking me. Ayi, my son who turned his lips away from me, who would not be moved when his mother pressed his face against mine. *Kiss Baba.* But he could tell, even though a child, that I was not worthy. That I had deceived his mother.

"Yes, I have a son. Paul. He's eight," Marguerite was saying. "I can take poverty, but I can't deprive him. I can't have Paul suffer for my sake. My husband, you see, is a politician without a job. He's running for a seat in Congress, but that takes time and money. There are bills to be paid, so I work. Anyhow, my art wasn't selling. It was gathering dust against my bedroom wall. Now I know how Catherine felt."

"Catherine?" I was still struggling to force the image of my dead son from my mind.

"What she would have given up to have had her son!"

"Eric?"

"John never took him to her in Jamaica. She waited for him and he never came. Eventually John called her and said she could have her son in the summer months if she gave up her rights to all the assets they shared and to any alimony payments she may be entitled to. She told me that she didn't hesitate one second to sign the papers he sent her. She gave up the beachfront land they had in Montego Bay, a wedding present from his father to both of them, all the money they had together in the bank. I think it was over fifty thousand U.S. She did all that to have her son for just three months out of the year. John insisted that Eric stay with him in New York to go to school. Going to work full-time so I could have money to give my son a chance for a decent childhood, and giving up my art temporarily so I could have time for my son, are nothing compared with what Catherine sacrificed."

I could not look at her. I could not let her see my eyes, see the remorse and sorrow in them. Remorse for my selfishness, for my lack of generosity to my son and to Catherine. To my son who only wanted my love, the sincerity of my love that day for him and for his mother; to Catherine who only asked for me to intercede with John on her behalf. But I did not stop to think of my son's feelings when I sat like a stone before him. I did not stop to think of

Catherine's feelings when I mounted my case against acceding to her request.

How easy it had been for me to find excuses not to help Catherine. How easy it had been for me to convince myself that it was wrong to interfere in her relationship with her husband, to say that John was a brutal man, that it was useless to enter a war with him that I would surely lose. Would I say the same things today? Would I, now that I knew the pain of losing a son, losing a daughter?

"What?" Marguerite leaned toward me. "What? Is something wrong?"

I had remained with my head bent, not saying a word to her, tortured with regret and the pain of my memories.

"Is something wrong?"

I looked up at her and saw the Marguerite I had known, the Marguerite whose eyes were always full of tenderness for me.

"I should have done something to help Catherine," I said.

She reached for my hand. "You did. You called me. Remember?"

I allowed her to believe that lie, for when her hand touched mine I felt such hope, slim though it was, that I did not want to take the risk of shattering it. I let her believe what she believed. That I had called her that first time because I wanted to help Catherine, because I wanted to connect Catherine to a friend who could console her. I did not tell her the truth: that I called her because I wanted to meet in the flesh the woman who had tormented me in my dreams. I slipped my hand above hers and held it. It was seconds before she withdrew it.

After dinner I asked her if I could see her the next day.

"It would be difficult," she said, but I thought not with conviction.

"I am leaving tomorrow night," I pressed her.

"I don't know."

"Even for lunch? I will be gone after that," I said. "There will be three thousand miles between you and me."

"Three thousand miles?" She fingered her napkin.

"You'll be safe."

"I don't feel unsafe now."

"I'll be gone tomorrow."

"I don't know."

"Please. For old times' sake."

She rested her fingers on her napkin. "For old times' sake."

"For lunch then?"

"Yes."

"Here at one?"

"Here at one."

18

That night I lay on my bed in a state suspended between sleep and wakefulness, trying to hold on to a dream I did not want to end and yet so fearing its meaning I willed myself to wake, to prove to myself that the world in which I had entered was a dreamworld and everything in it was false.

I had dreamed of Marguerite but not of Marguerite alone. I had dreamed she was with my dead son and my stillborn daughter. I had dreamed of my son and my daughter many times before. Though I did not love the three children I now had any less than I had loved those two, it was they who often invaded my sleeping hours, who, when I put my head on my pillow, returned to me in the flesh as they were in life. On those nights I dreamed of them, I did not want to wake, and when I did, my grief returned so much more acutely than it had been before that Nerida was forced to part that curtain she kept closed between us, the curtain that protected her from remembering, from looking into the mirror of her pain.

She would tell me, then, I should go to their gravesites—Nerida who did not believe that the body stayed there, under the earth, to be redeemed on Judgment Day, Nerida who only had to look inside herself and around herself to find comfort and consolation. For that was where she said her children resided: in her heart, in her soul, in the spaces around her, protected always by the ancestors. But she would be so pained by my grief that even when we were in Ghana, so many hundreds of miles from my country, she would book a flight for me back home, make excuses to the children for me, and urge me on: "Go. Go cry for them until your tears have dried up."

But that night, the second that I spent in America, in the country where my two children lost their lives, the first after I had seen Marguerite and knew without doubt I would never cease to love her, the dream I had of my dead children did not bring me to tears on awakening. It brought me fear. Fear that I had lost Marguerite, fear that I had lost the woman I loved.

In that dream, I had returned with my children to the place where my mother had taken her life for love, where my father did not look back when missionaries from Canada took his eldest son, the first and only child he had from the woman he had made his second wife. Things had changed since. My father and his wives no longer lived in huts built with red clay and sand and encircled by the low wall that separated them from the rest of the village. My father had torn down the wall and the huts and replaced them with two large concrete structures, one for himself and one for his two wives. They stood there in the middle of the vast lands that he had inherited from his warrior ancestors, grotesque evidence of a modernity that was rapidly taking over parts of Africa and destroying the natural symmetry of land, sky, trees, birds, animals.

My father's lands once stretched to the edge of the Sahara Desert. They were dry and barren. Before he married three more times, before he found a way to have others do his labor for him, I do not doubt that he had cursed his misfortune for being doomed to make his living on land that grudgingly yielded the sorghum, dates, and millet he farmed on it only by his sweat, by the long hours he was forced to spend tilling the ground, sifting out sand and stone, watering it with the heavy buckets of water he carried on his shoulders back and forth all day on that long trek from the water wells. And yet my father's lands were beautiful. Trees fanned out like giant umbrellas spaced at graceful distances from each other across brown grasslands. Giraffes moved in packs, their long necks arched against a perennially blue sunlit sky.

The birds that flew over my father's land were enormous: vultures, birds of prey, the kind that fed on carrion and could fly great distances without water. Yet they, too, added grace to my father's land and when my father sold most of this land to the Europeans, I was saddened that such beauty had passed so carelessly from the descendants of warriors, who had fought valiantly to attain it, to a people who saw its worth no more, no less than the value of the minerals that lay buried beneath it.

I say carelessly, because my father sold the land without inquiring of its worth. He wanted houses like the others he had seen in the villages around him. He did not want to farm any longer, to break his back in the burning sun. He took the European offer and did not regret it when they mined uranium from the earth and became richer than he could ever have imagined. My father reacted then the way he always did, the way he always dealt with adversity. The way he dealt with the news that my mother had left him, with the news that I was leaving with the missionaries to go to their school in the city. He shrugged his shoulders when people told him he could have been a wealthy man if he had not sold his father's land to the albinos. He opened up the palms of hands and, with the same indifference, the same detachment with which he responded to my mother's death and to my departure, he said: "What will be, will be."

My father built his concrete houses on the lands that remained from his inheritance. Years later I would bring in bulldozers to mow them down. I would build my country retreat of wood and clay there in that place where a griot still sings of my father's father and his father's father, but not of my father. Not of the man who shamed them when he surrendered to the albinos land his ancestors had conquered in wars. Not of the man who gave the albinos his firstborn son. The griot sings of me—of my power and wealth.

Of the two rhinoceros with the speed of the harmattan that sit in
my driveway. Of the justice come at last to my warrior ancestors
through the things I have accomplished.

But in the dream I had that night after I saw Marguerite for the
first time since she had forced me to reveal my lie, I had not yet
built my house of wood and clay, and my father's concrete houses
were the way they were before he died, the yard that surrounded
them as barren and as dry. For when my father got the money from
the Europeans for the land he sold to them, he no longer farmed,
he no longer watered his land. The water he needed for his domestic use he got from pipes he had laid underground, which stretched
from his water wells to his houses, so that he did not have to carry
the buckets of water he once lifted on his shoulders. Still, one
great tree survived my father's prosperity and the burning sun. My
father had built a wooden bench that encircled it. On hot after-
noons he would sit under its shade, watching his grandchildren
play in the dirt. It was also in this open space, in front of that tree,
that the people from my father's village celebrated their feast days.
It was about such a day I dreamed, when my father's dirt yard pul-
sated with the beat of drums and the stomping of feet of the men,
women, and children who danced in the dirt.

But in my dream, my father was not the one who sat on the
bench beneath the tree presiding over the festivities. It was Marguerite. It was she who sat there, dressed in a long white gown, like
a bride. She wore nothing on her head. Her hair had not been cut
as it was when I saw her in the restaurant. It was the length it had
been when I first met her, but it was not tied in a ponytail off her
neck. It was plaited. Long braids fell to her shoulders knotted at
the ends with ivory cowrie shells. She held a baby in her arms. A
little girl. I knew immediately that the little girl was my stillborn
daughter. At her side was a little boy. I knew, too, that the little boy
was my son who had been crushed to death under the wheels of a
car in the streets of Washington, D.C.

I did not remember that they were dead. In my dream they
seemed alive to me. Both were dressed in the elaborate finery of
our traditional garb. My baby daughter wore a long, white cotton

dress embroidered in gold threads; my son, a stiff, light-colored caftan and close-fitting cotton leggings.

I had been taking a shower in my father's indoor bathroom when I saw them. From between the latticed white bricks that decorated the top of his unpainted concrete shower wall, I watched them, happy that they were together. I did not find it strange that no one else was dressed as they. That no one else's skin was as cool and dry, their clothes as spotless. That everyone else was sweating profusely in the hot sun and their clothes were dusted with the dry dirt that swirled everywhere. I was basking in my contentment with the idyllic scene in front of me: my children gazing lovingly up to Marguerite, she beaming down on them.

I was washing out the suds from my hair that I had just shampooed when I saw Marguerite bend her head down toward my son when he tugged her sleeves. She seemed pleased by what he said to her. She smiled, stood up, held his hand and, with the baby in her arms, she walked with him to the other side of the tree. My son pointed to the sky and I saw a shaft of light descend toward them. They were still smiling when the light encircled them, when it pulled them up to the sky and they disappeared with it into the clouds.

I woke with a start, knowing then I had dreamed of the dead. Realizing then, for the first time, that I had dreamed not only of the dead but also of the living. I woke up terrified for Marguerite, afraid I had lost her, desperate to see her again.

"I dreamed of you," I said to Marguerite when we met for lunch.

She saw the fear in my eyes. "A bad dream?" she asked.

"You were with my son and my daughter."

"A good dream," she said.

She wanted to know if it was the daughter I had when my wife was pregnant. When I confessed that I had lied to her. When I admitted I had a son and another child on the way. I told her that they were both dead—the son I had and the daughter I had been expecting.

"Dead?"

Her eyes were already brimming with tears for me before I could tell her how they had died, tears Nerida had hidden from me, tears Nerida wanted me to conceal from her. I told Marguerite everything: about the senseless killing of my children, of my grief. I did not tell her of my guilt, but she must have guessed my guilt.

"You were not responsible," she said. "It was their fate."

Tears rolled down her cheeks and mine. She let me weep. She leaned toward me and handed me her handkerchief. "It's good to cry," she said. "Cry."

The people in the restaurant seemed to pity us. They lowered their voices and turned their heads away from us. The waiter brought us water. He did not say a word to us. He did not return until we had dried our eyes and Marguerite was smiling at the photographs I was showing her of my other three children.

"They must make life easier for you and your wife. They must help you forget."

But I was not listening to her. I was still thinking of my dream. "I don't want anything to happen to you," I said.

"It was only a dream. I am here. I am fine," she said. "I am healthy."

"You were with them," I said.

"You had not seen me for ten years, remember? It must have seemed as though I had died with your son and your daughter."

But I knew she had not died with my son and my daughter. Even in those years I fooled myself into believing I had forgotten her, she was always alive in my heart, able to set it aflame again with the merest reminder I had of the time we had spent together. I had wrapped her portrait in brown paper, stored it with the books she had given me and with the mementos of my son that had escaped Nerida's eyes, but it was not enough. When my president asked me to go to New York, the years peeled back. I did not hesitate. I wanted to be with her again.

"I never forgot you," I said.

She averted her eyes. "And your wife? How is she? How is your marriage?"

I did not lie. "Good," I said. "Very good."

She brought her glass to her lips and sipped the water slowly. "I sometimes wondered," she said, "if I had caused a problem in your marriage. If I . . ." Her voice broke. She bit her lower lip.

"Nerida never knew," I said.

"But I knew." She put down her glass. "I never asked you about your life. What you did in the weeks in between when I did not see you."

"You were preoccupied," I said.

"I occupied myself so I would not have the need to ask. I was afraid of your answer, but I knew. I guessed something was wrong. You never invited me to visit you in Washington. I knew there was someone else. I didn't want to believe it was a wife. Then when you told me there were children. . . ."

"It was my fault, Marguerite."

"It was mine. I have been riddled with guilt ever since, wondering."

"I loved you apart from Nerida. I still love you. I loved two women. I can't explain it. I say it to you as a fact I accept. I was not in love with Nerida when I married her, but I grew to love her. I did not think I would love anyone else, and then I met you. I did not love you because I stopped loving Nerida. I loved you in spite of loving Nerida."

"How foolish I must have seemed to you. I fell in your trap."

I knew what trap she meant. "I was the first in my family to have only one wife," I said, trying to explain myself to her.

"Did you really think you could have two?"

"I don't know. I still don't know."

"You still don't know?" Her eyes stretched open wide.

"You thought the same thing at one time," I said.

"I was a romantic young woman. I was talking about nameless, faceless women. I know a different reality now." She spoke softly, and I felt ashamed for reminding her of ideas she once had, ideas she now obviously found embarrassing.

"We were both untested," I said.

"We should have known better. I should have known better."

"I thought I believed in one man, one wife. I am a Christian, you remember."

"All those silly things I said about a man marrying two women. About admiring the old traditions in Africa."

"When I fell in love with you, I wanted to get back that way of life. You know, the old traditions. I refused to believe loving you was sinful, the way the missionaries taught me to believe. You wanted to believe that everything in Africa was good and right, and then you fell in love with me and discovered you wanted a way of life the Europeans had taught you to admire."

"I am not so sure their way of life is all that admirable." She was looking at me now. The eyes that had filled with tears for my dead children were now unabashedly facing mine. I did not dare to hope, and yet I did. Yet at that moment I believed she wanted to tell me that she, too, had not stopped loving me. That though she was married, she still wanted me, too. But she did not say that, though I wanted to believe that that was what she had intended.

"Sometimes people stay together when they shouldn't," she said.

I asked her if she was speaking personally. She turned away from me. "Marriages would last," she said, "if people stopped sleeping with other people's mates."

Her voice vibrated with a restrained anger, the source of which I was uncertain. I did not know if she was speaking of herself or of me. Whether she was blaming me for making love to her when I was married, or blaming herself for interfering in my marriage, for not admitting to herself that I was married. I said to her again that my marriage was strong; it was good and that nothing we had done had weakened it. But she repeated her statement, this time with emphasis, her anger specifically targeted to women.

"Women want power," she said, "but they will never get power until they stop sleeping with other women's men."

I did not know then that she was thinking of her own marriage. I did not know then that she was battling her husband's infidelity. I took her comment as an accusation against herself and the affair she had had with me. I saw it as her resolve not to repeat what she now viewed as reprehensible in the light of a morality that had more to do with politics—the protest rallies in support of equality for women that were an everyday occurrence these days—than with cultural beliefs or religious ethics, and I felt the hope that had sprung in my heart only moments before drain out of me.

We said good-bye as friends. She reminded me to find comfort in the children I now had and to put my dead son and daughter to rest in the past. She congratulated me when I told her I had been ambassador to Ghana and Ethiopia from my country and that I was now going to take up a similar post in Chad. She was proud of me, she said, and happy for me. I asked her again about her art. She said she still painted on weekends.

"When my husband has gone campaigning and my son's busy playing or is asleep."

"Do you miss it?" I asked.

"I'll get back to it as soon as my husband gets elected or finds a job and my son is older."

"Do you miss me?" I asked.

"Always," she said. "I have put you in a vault in my heart, locked the door, and thrown away the key."

For years I prayed she would find that key again, but that day did not come until fifteen years later, and when it did, we both knew that the love we felt for each other that first time in New York, when we were young, was a lasting love. That it would burn for a lifetime and stay with us even to eternity.

19

$\sim$

When I returned home to Africa, to Nerida, I knew that I could no longer do as I had pretended to do in the past. I could no longer say to myself that I could forget Marguerite, bury her in my memory, live as though she ceased to matter to me, as if I no longer loved her. Now I had to live with the truth of knowing I loved her, that I would always love her. I had to face the possibility—the fact it now seemed to me—that I might never again hold her in my arms, make love to her, feel her skin warm against mine, her heart beat fast against mine.

Some would say it is a gift, this ability to see all, to understand, to perceive the truth even when the truth has been covered up, concealed, when all traces have been removed from the eye. But those who say that do not know the inconsolable loneliness, the pain this awareness brings of seeing into the secret passages of the human heart. Your own heart. Of carrying inside of you the terrible burden of knowledge—your knowledge of your own truth. For it is only you who see this truth. Only you who know that nothing, not even what you know, what you may tell others you know, can change the irrefutable, immutable facts that lie before you: I loved Marguerite. I could not have Marguerite.

Every day brought me to a newer and newer understanding of my mother, closer and closer to forgiving her. My mother could have lived with my father if all that it took to live was food; if all that she needed was shelter. She could have been content in his village if all that it took for contentment was work, work that was meaningful, work that contributed to the community where she lived. If all that it took for happiness was the approval of friends, of her society—a good reputation, a place in her community. I do not think my mother disliked my father. I think she could have learned to make love to him and not feel disgust. And yet I know that none of these mattered to her. That no one, not her mother, not her father, not her friends, not her work, not her love for me could have concealed from her the truth that she knew: she loved another man. She wanted another man. In the end she could not bear that truth and live. In the end she could not make love to my father and breathe.

I loved another woman, but I also loved my wife. I longed for Marguerite but I also desired my wife. I did not want one or the other. I wanted them both. I did not have my mother's tragic good fortune. I could not choose not to live with one because I wanted the other. But now I had to accept the painful truth that I must live without Marguerite, that I must bear the heartache of knowing I loved her, of knowing I wanted her. Of knowing I could not have her. It was a reality I did not know how I could change.

I gave up all pretense when I said good-bye to Marguerite in New York. Now, in Africa, I unwrapped her portrait. I removed the brown paper that I once thought would protect me from seeing her, from remembering her. I unpacked the books she had given me. I brought them all into my bedroom. I hung her portrait on the wall above my bed. I put her books among Nerida's in the bookcase next to the side of the bed where I slept.

Nerida did not oppose me. She found reasons to hope. She took my actions as evidence of my restoration, my return to a system of beliefs she had not abandoned, my acknowledgment of the fluidity of time, the unity of past, present, and future. She did not know that the portrait of the head of a woman that had reminded her of an African mask was the portrait of a woman I loved, the portrait of my Marguerite. She did not know that the books I put in her book-case were the books my Marguerite had given me, the books I had deceived her into believing I bought, and which, in that happy ignorance, she had read to me in our bed in Washington. She thought that the portrait and the books were symbols of a past, a past I was wrong to bury when I buried my son, when I buried my daughter. She said to me that it was our children who had died, not the life we had before them or with them. It was only *their* things she had left behind her in Washington ten years ago, not *our* things.

Nerida dealt with her anguish in ways I could not. The past, present, and future fused for her in ways they had not for me. She could bring our children in the present with her, let them live in her heart and her soul. She could strip the past of the things that confined it, that imprisoned it, and free it to merge with the now. She could discard this thing, she could keep that thing from the past, and each thing she discarded, each thing she kept seemed to allow her the wholeness of time. She would leave the clothes of our dead children in Washington but she would bring their spirits with her to the present, to Africa. She would pack our furniture from our apartment in Washington and take it with her to our house in Africa, carrying the past with her to her present as she had carried it once before when she put baskets and plants in our apartment and decorated it in colors that reminded her of Africa.

There was no past, no present, no future for Nerida. Only the now that contained them all. She had not learned, like I had, to segment time, to struggle with it as if it could be conquered. She had not been allowed to leave her home, when she was a child, to go to schools taught by Europeans. She kept the traditional beliefs. The dead, the ancestors, were as present for her in her life as were the living. The future moved her toward a past when she would become part of the living, an ancestor who existed in the present.

I was not as fortunate as she. To live in the present I had to bury the past. To exist in the now I had to conceive a future. I had buried my children, visited their graves, acknowledged they had died, confronted the reality that they belonged to a past I could never resurrect. Then I had planned the children of my future. I had told myself they would ease the pain of the past. I had covered Marguerite's portrait, put away her books. In time I convinced myself that I loved only Nerida. I convinced myself of this because I could not bear the torment of the loss, the knowledge that never again would my lips press against Marguerite's, my hands cup her breasts. I could not withstand the pain of that truth, so I invented another truth, a truth I could bear.

My mother's courage to accept the fact that she loved another man caused her to take her life. I had not been so brave. I had been afraid. I did not know if I could face the truth and live. But all that had changed, now that I had seen Marguerite and knew I loved her, I had always loved her, I would always love her. Now I could admit to myself that the children I had could not replace the ones I lost. That Nerida could not fill the spaces in my heart that ached for Marguerite. How that knowledge would affect me I did not know.

There were times during those years when my job required me to return to New York. I stayed no more than two or three days. I dared not test myself beyond those brief periods. I did not call Marguerite. I did not try to see her. She was married. I was married.

Marguerite's portrait remained hung above my bed. Nerida thought it was good I had put it where it had been when we lived in Washington. I now lived with the past in anguish, Nerida with acceptance, even contentment. At times I envied her—the ease with which she found peace in the knowledge that the present contained her past; her future written in the moment in which she lived.

There was a time when I thought people spent too much time planning the future. That was when I was a young man and I carried a fantasy in my heart: a past I spent my present hoping to meet again. Then I met Marguerite and severed myself from that past. I believed then in the present, only in the present when I said yes to Marguerite, when I pretended my future with Nerida did not exist. When all that I wanted was the now, the present. Now I knew that now was the present, the future, and the past. I tried to have the courage to live with that knowledge, that insight.

20

My future continued as my life had been for the past ten years—redolent of good fortune. Even I was beginning to find it hard to contest the contention of my friends that I had been born with a silver spoon in my mouth, or the conviction of my enemies that a juju man was working his magic on me.

I was respected and in demand in diplomatic circles. More and more countries in Africa depended on my diplomatic skills and my understanding of the European mind. But I was trusted less for this skill in unmasking the European motives than for my loyalty to Africa. Time and time again when I was offered posts out of Africa, I declined. I could have been ambassador to France, Germany, Sweden—any European country I wanted. My president would have sent me there, or to South America, the Caribbean, Australia, India, China, Russia—wherever I wanted. But I did not want to leave Africa. I wanted to live on African soil. I wanted my children to grow up on African soil. I was praised for my patriotism. I was trusted because of it. It was believed that I could not be bought. That always I would put Africa first.

People, I think, say unkind things about Africa because they are afraid of Africa, afraid of the commitment Africa demands of them.

Everywhere you turn in Africa there is someone in need, someone who wants your help. Someone who has a hundred, if not a thousand times less than you. Someone wanting what you have. Not to give is to live with guilt. To give is to require sacrifice of yourself more than seems reasonable. Or fair.

Africa drains you. Africa demands of you. Africa asks you to be human. You leave her when you fear the high price of the toll she would exact from you.

I stayed in Africa because I wanted to help build a better Africa for my children. For the children of Africa. Many laugh at me. They say you can only be human out of Africa, for out of Africa you can acquire the things that make you human: the house with the convenient gadgetry; electronic equipment that defies space and time—the fax machine, the computer, E-mail, the Internet. Out of Africa you can buy cars that can be discarded when they break down; you can accumulate things you will never use. Things you dream about. But people who say such things have turned their backs on the routes to the heart, to the spirit. Why deny yourself? they ask. There is no need for sacrifice when you can have all that you want. You can be more human in the developed countries, they say. I have never said or believed that.

After Chad, I was sent to Zimbabwe. There, I became involved with the underground in South Africa, men and women fighting for the overthrow of apartheid and the release of Nelson Mandela. Nothing I had done so far in my life had given me such fulfillment. No work I had done, no assignment I had carried out, had made me feel so close to fulfilling my potential as a human being. I took risks with my life, meeting in places where I knew I could be assassinated, or worse, tortured, as I knew had happened to too many who were part of my group. But though I loved my life, though I loved my family, though I did not want to lose my life, and though I often thought of the pain the loss of my life would cause Nerida and my children, I never hesitated when I was asked to do something that would contribute to the destruction of the racist policies in South Africa, that would bring justice to a people so long denied it.

Many time I was offered money from governments in countries

neighboring South Africa that relied on my skills in diplomacy, on my tact and discretion to conceal their hands in incidents that were illegal, sometimes bloody, but always necessary for the liberation of South Africa. I never accepted it. Often I was called to temper the anger of those who could not wait, of those who wanted a free South Africa now. Of those who thought a bloody revolution was the only way out. I never accepted money for doing this either.

It was said that I was successful because I had the ability to make people feel at ease in my presence. I could make them laugh. I could take the edge off the most tense of negotiations. I seemed a man with no hidden agendas, a man with no troubles burdening his shoulders. A carefree man. A happy man.

More than once I had occasion to wonder if this personality, this talent I had, was not inherited. There were times I seethed with anger under my skin over injustices and cruelties painfully evident before my eyes. Yet few detected my anger, my outrage. I could shrug my shoulders even in such situations and adopt an air of insouciance. Those were the times I thought I was indeed my father's child. My father who could throw open the palms of his hands and say without emotion: *What will be, will be.* My father who could appear indifferent when he was told of my mother's betrayal, of her death near the village where her lover took his life because of her. My father who never stopped me once or protested once when I left his compound with the missionaries from Canada.

This control I had over my passions when I faced the white man who had persecuted or killed my brothers in South Africa was not a skill I had learned. It came to me without effort. I could appear calm no matter the situation. I could seem harmless to the enemy even while I laid the groundwork for his destruction. It was a talent that had fooled Nerida as well, though I never planned to hurt her. She did not see my longing for Marguerite until much, much later (so I thought). She never guessed that those times when I immersed myself in the books on the shelves near the portrait of the head of a woman I had hung on our bedroom wall, over our bed, that I was overcome by desires so acute, so unbearable, that I dared not speak to her. I dared not let her see my eyes.

Perhaps my father who had given me very little else when I was a child had bequeathed me this: his genes, his talent. It enabled me to deceive my wife, to conceal from her the pain of my need for Marguerite. It enabled me to become valuable to governments.

I was beginning to believe that my career in diplomacy was not accidental. It was not, as I once thought, the result of a series of unrelated events that culminated with my being in a certain place at a particular time when the president of my country needed an interpreter. I was beginning to think that it was possible that my future was determined at my birth. My father had those same skills that had made me useful as a diplomat. It was to his compound the people of the village came on the feast days. He was the one who made them feel at ease, who gave them the illusion of a life without problems. That they could eat and drink today and nothing would change tomorrow. He had turned his back on the problems that threatened to dull his joy. He had refused to burden his shoulders. My father's friends liked him for this. For the respite he gave them from the harshness of reality. They let down their guard in his presence. They told him everything, even their secrets. They believed him a harmless man, a man too much in love with a life of ease to plot their destruction.

When I made this observation to Nerida she reminded me that nothing we do can break our connection to our ancestors. I was my father's son as my father was his father's son. My people were warriors. They knew the strategies of war. They knew how to make others yield to them. The people in my father's village yielded to him. Heads of state yielded to me. The conference table was my battleground, she said, where I waged my wars. The stony grasslands of the African plains were the battlegrounds where my ancestors waged their wars. They won their wars. I won mine. The present, Nerida said to me, was the past, was the future.

But I was not a harmless man like my father's friends thought my father. I did not allow the enemies of my country to use me, to make a fool of me. To use Africa, to make a fool of Africa. Even when I laughed with heads of state, I thought of Africa. Even when I plied them with drink, Africa stayed on my mind. I may have inherited my diplomatic skills from my father, but I had made better use of them. I had not eschewed responsibility. I had not turned my back on my son.

And yet I could not say that my father had abandoned me. His skill for giving people the illusion that they had nothing to worry about, nothing to fear, had come naturally to me, had allowed me to earn my living. Because of this talent I inherited from him, I made more money than he and his entire village ever saw. But isn't this the hope of fathers? Isn't this what fathers want for their sons? Perhaps this was what my father wanted for me.

21

In September 1989, I was asked to go to the United Nations to join a team of representatives from African nations that had been trying to persuade the world to keep the pressure on the newly sworn South African president, F. W. de Klerk, for the release of Nelson Mandela. It was fifteen years since I had been to New York, fifteen years since I had seen Marguerite.

Three years since Nerida and I had stopped sleeping in the same bedroom.

I was the first one to leave our marriage bed. I did not leave because I no longer wanted to make love to Nerida. I had not then, nor have I since, ceased to love Nerida, though there were times when the memory of Marguerite returned with such intensity that being in the same room with Nerida became unbearable. But such times had long become infrequent.

Il faut savior gérer le malheur. One has to know how to manage one's unhappiness. A countryman had said this to me. He was a man I admired for his stoicism that never wavered even when the death of his favorite wife dealt him a blow from which few men recover. I, too, was learning how to manage my unhappiness—*gérer mon malheur*—how to live with the anguish of losing Marguerite, with the knowledge of never seeing her again. But though this acceptance gave me reprieve during my waking hours, deliverance from the futility of longing for Marguerite, I had developed no such ability to control my dreams during my sleeping hours. Indeed, it seemed that the more I was able to accept the loss of Marguerite when I was awake, the less I seemed able to suppress my yearning for her when I was asleep.

More and more frequently I disturbed Nerida's nights with dreams that woke me in a panic, sweat pouring down my face, my heart beating wildly, my breath coming short and fast through my mouth. They were dreams like the one I had the day before I saw Marguerite the last time. Always Marguerite was happy. Always she was with my dead children. Always I feared she, too, had died. Except now, in the past year, I would remember she was alive and in New York. That she had a husband.

It was at that part of the dream, the part when memory took me to her bedroom where she was making love to her husband, that I would bound up from my bed in panic.

Nerida would wake up, too. She would wipe my brow, press my head back against my pillow, and comfort me. It was a dream, she would say. A silly dream. It will pass. Everything will be fine. She was here. She was next to me here.

But I did not want Nerida next to me. I did not want her lying on the bed with me when I woke up with dreams of Marguerite. I wanted Marguerite. I wanted to make love to Marguerite.

It was guilt that finally drove me out of the bedroom. I told Nerida it was my work—the troubles I was having with some agreement I was trying to finalize. I will be back soon, I promised. But when I came back, six months later, after I had learned to sleep with the new dreams I was having of Marguerite, Nerida did not want me back.

At first I did not think she knew I was dreaming of another woman. I did not think she felt I had left her bed because I loved her less. She said to me that she slept better when she slept alone. That I could come to her whenever I wanted. Whenever I felt the need.

I wanted to believe her. I, too, slept better with my dreams of

Marguerite when Nerida was not next to me. Yet there were nights I wanted Nerida in the bed with me again, when I wanted to hold her in my arms and make love to her, but she made excuses and turned me away. She was too tired, she said. She was not in the mood. She was not feeling well. Eventually the times we made love dwindled from once a week to twice a month. In the past three years we made love fewer than once in six months.

Ultimately I grew to accept Nerida's lack of interest in sex. My good friend Ibrahim Musima explained it to me, though I never quite believed that the reason he gave me was the only one there was. But to him the explanation was simple.

It comes with menopause, he said. Nerida's disinterest in sex was not particular to me.

Ibrahim Musima was a Moslem. He had four wives, the fourth younger than his eldest daughter, the first my wife's age—fifty-four. It was said it was his gap tooth that made him irresistible to women. But Ibrahim Musima thought otherwise. He said to me that he understood women, he knew what made them happy. And what would make my wife happy, he told me, would be for me to get a mistress.

Women desire us when we can be of use to them, he said. When we can fertilize their eggs and give them babies. When they have no more eggs, they lose interest in having sex with us. They want us to leave them alone. Nerida no longer desires you. Give her the peace she deserves. Get a mistress.

When I protested, when I told Ibrahim that I suspected I was the one to be blamed, that Nerida had not lost her desire for sex, rather, it was more probable that she had lost her desire for sex with me, he called me a foolish man, a vain and arrogant man. A man who did not have enough sense to know he could not change the laws of Nature.

The survival of the human race depends on men, Ibrahim said to me. (These were not his exact words, but they were the exact words he meant to say to me.) We are the ones who ensure that human life will not cease to exist on earth. Nature gave us men the ability to impregnate a woman even when we are a hundred. God didn't do that for a man to waste his seed on an infertile woman.

I continued to insist that it was not I who no longer wished to sleep with Nerida, but she who no longer wished to sleep with me. Ibrahim was not unsympathetic. He was a sensitive man.

I am not saying you should leave Nerida. I did not divorce my infertile wife. But Nerida has dried out. I don't doubt she loves you, but she has lost her desire. Give her a rest. Get a mistress. You have a duty to get a mistress, a responsibility to impregnate a fertile woman, a young woman.

Ibrahim argued his case with me in front of his friends. Darwinians all, though I doubted they could identify a letter in the alphabet, they nodded their heads in agreement. They were his evidence that what he said was true. They all had more than two wives. They believed that the young women who agreed to marry them did so because they knew that not only could older men give them babies, but they could feed them, clothe them, give them shelter.

When you were a pup, could you take care of a woman as well as you can today? Ibrahim asked me. No, Oufoula. He slapped me on the back. With your money, God will punish you for not marrying another wife. Okay, you are a Christian, but God will punish you all the same for not having a mistress. Fathers will hate you for not taking their daughters off their hands. Daughters will despise you for leaving them barren.

And what about the young men? I asked him. What will be left for them if the old men take the prettiest women?

He shrugged. "Their turn will come," he said.

I did not tell him about the new research I had heard about: The seed of old men is spoilt. It sometimes produces fruit with tragic defects.

Had I said this to Ibrahim Musima, he would have shrugged again. What I had heard was Western propaganda circulated by Western women who want to rule the world, he would have said. Ibrahim Musima had fifteen children. All his children were healthy.

But I was not persuaded by what Ibrahim Musima said to me. I did not get a mistress. I did not turn to younger women when Nerida no longer wanted to sleep with me. There were only two women I wanted, two women I loved, one with the calm and serenity that come with a good marriage, the other with a passion that in spite of my best efforts remained alive, burning in me.

I threw myself more intensely into my work. It was her work, her art, that had distracted Marguerite in my absence, that had made it possible for her to suppress troubling questions, to prevent them from surfacing. Soon I found the intrinsic virtues in work that had quite eluded my father. For work occupies the mind, consumes it. Work tires the body, dampens the carnal passions, suppresses the libido. I discovered that it was not as difficult as I once thought for Mahatma Gandhi to deny himself sex. Work ennobles the spirit. It satisfies the soul, especially when one's work transcends personal needs, when it aspires to the service of others.

Work is the Sisyphian climb up the mountain when we defy the pull of gravity, when we triumph over our lot, our fated mortality. When we breathe the air of the gods.

By the sweat of thy brow. Work is the paradox in the original curse: in our condemnation is our salvation.

My work for the liberation of South Africa transcended my desire for personal reward. Its goal was the freedom of my black brothers and sisters, the end of their torture and suffering. I found my work ennobling. I found it fulfilling. It gave meaning to my life. Purpose.

Nerida compensated me in other ways—by her loyalty to me, by her friendship, by her commitment to our children. Now I relied almost completely on her opinion about the work I did. If she did not approve of an idea I had, I discarded it. If she did not review my plans before a negotiation, I postponed it. If she did not critique a speech before I was to deliver it, I did not present it. If she suspected that an invitation I received could incur negative political consequences, I rejected it.

I had already deferred to her in the upbringing and education of our children, less by intent than by the circumstances of my work

life that required me to be away from home for long hours, sometimes for days and weeks. She did not disappoint me. Our children
were loving and kind to each other, considerate of others, generous
and well mannered. They excelled in their studies. My son and one
of my twin daughters were at the top of their classes in the premed
program at the university. My other daughter brought home prizes
for her photography. I never tired of boasting of them—of Nerida's
part in their success, of her dedication and commitment to them.
Indeed, except for the dreams I had of Marguerite, I was a contented man.

And then I was asked to go to New York for six weeks to join the
team at the UN.

Nerida was overjoyed. She, like me, believed that Mandela's release was imminent. She, like me, was convinced that not only
would he be free but he would become the leader of Black South
Africa. Neither of us had dared to dream he would become president of a country that had once declared white supremacy legal,
that had robbed him of his youth in his fight for the rights of his
black brothers, that had denied his wife a husband, his children a
father, he both wife and children. That had almost blinded him in
the stone mines of Robben Island. That had tried but had never
succeeded in breaking him.

But while Nerida was happy to see me go to New York for the
sake of Mandela, I battled and lost against the temptation to antici-
pate other joys besides: the joy of seeing Marguerite again, the joy
of being with her.

My male friends, too, believed that other pleasures awaited me
in New York. How lucky I was, they said, to be free of my wife for
six weeks, to have any woman I wanted in my bed all night. Women
half my wife's age, women who had bodies like the bodies they saw
in magazines from America. They envied me.

But I did not tell them that these were not the women I wanted.
That the woman I wanted was almost my wife's age.

Marguerite, I estimated, was fifty years old now, a menopausal
woman, a woman, my friends believed, long past the stage of being

sexually desirable. Yet it was she who occupied my mind when I packed my bags for New York. She I wanted. She I hoped still remembered passionate days when we made love like the swans on O'Malley's lake, ripping off clothes like feathers, though not with the rage O'Malley pressed me to see through his jaundiced eyes. She I hoped had never forgotten nights when, like lost travelers rescued from the desert, we sated ourselves on love, devoured each other until gorged, until either she or I, exhausted, spent, broke loose only to try again. "Calm down. Calm down," we told each other. Such was our thirst, such was our hunger, as I remembered.

22

I arrived in New York at night. I called Marguerite at the New School the next morning. No one answered, but Marguerite had left a recorded message on her answering machine. I memorized it. I called her over and over that day just to hear the sound of her voice in my ear, to remember and to hope: "This is Marguerite Hollingsworth. I will be out of the country until September twentieth. You may call back then or leave a message after the beep."

Marguerite Hollingsworth. She had not said Marguerite Gifford. She had not used her married name. She was no longer married. She was no longer the wife of the man I had never met and yet hated. The man who entered my dreams at night, who had taken my place in her bed.

September 20 was five days away. Five days to be in the city where Marguerite lived. Five days to be in the place she called home and not be with her. Five days after fifteen years of smothering memories that broke free like embers from the ashes of a dying fire only to flare up again. Fifteen years of dreams I could not repress. I paced the floor of the tiny apartment my country had rented for me for the six weeks I was to be in New York, trying to block out the deadening drone of cars, buses, and trucks, broken only by the ghoulish wail of a police siren or ambulance—life in New York. From the window of the twenty-fourth floor where I was, gray buildings rose from the streets like giant tombstones. At night, when the light from office buildings lit up windowpanes, I would think of them as prisons—stone walls through which slivers of light escaped from the windows of tiny cells crammed with inmates in business suits. Even the bright multicolored lights on the Empire State Building, meant to be festive, seemed cold and impersonal to me—manufactured.

I would not have come to New York if not for Mandela. I would not have come if not for the hope of seeing Marguerite. Cities depressed me. Since I had returned to Africa from my first appointment in America, I rarely stayed in one longer than my work required of me. I knew the insides of hotels, boardrooms, and restaurants like the markings on my hand, rarely anything about the life that passed before me on sidewalks. I had only stopped to ponder the miracle that life could exist at all in places where concrete and stone seemed to grow out of the earth—macabre vegetation strangling trees.

In cities I immersed myself in work so that the hours and days I spent away from Africa passed quickly before I had the chance to miss the wide, open, uncluttered spaces I loved. Now I immersed myself again as much to blind myself to the lights, the buildings, the people who talked and walked as if they could stop time, as to keep myself from thinking of Marguerite, from riding that seesaw that one minute had me up with hope that she was free to love me again, and down again with despair that nothing had changed. I was married. She had left me because I was married. She would not want me because I was married.

For the five days I waited for Marguerite to return, I became a man possessed with my mission to liberate Mandela. I was up before dawn and in bed well after midnight. When my colleagues were having breakfast, I was drafting and rewriting the papers my team would present at the UN, or I was on the phone talking to people who had the power to influence de Klerk, who could force him to accede to our wishes. My friends worried about my total absorption in my work, my doggedness, my relentless pursuit of my goal. I wanted complete consensus for our demand for the release of Mandela, I told them. I wanted the world to issue a moral imperative to the government of South Africa: the unconditional freedom of all political prisoners. The unconditional end of apartheid. I wanted no loopholes, no chance for compromise.

"You need to relax," they said. "You need to take a break. Socialize."

I socialized. I went to every event at the UN, I attended every cocktail party, every dinner hosted by the embassies of countries useful to our cause. In four evenings I was present at thirty parties, but I went to these events with the single-mindedness of my mission and left the minute I felt I had the agreement of my hosts. I used every technique I had learned in the art of persuasion, every skill I had inherited to make others like me. No one and nothing escaped my attention, my focus on achieving our mission, the mission of all the nations of Africa. At nights I fell on my bed, exhausted. There was no time to dream of Marguerite, no time to wonder whether she would want me, whether she still loved me.

And yet I counted the days. And yet when the fifth day passed, I knew, and on the morning of the sixth, I woke up with only Marguerite on my mind.

Again, she did not answer when I called, but the recording on her phone had been changed and I knew she was back in New York. This time I left her a message. I tried to make it as simple as possible. I tried to remove the emotion from my voice, my anxiety to see her.

"Hello, this is Oufoula. I am in New York and would like to see you. Call me when you can. 555-7398."

I left that message four times on the answering machine in her office at the New School, each time struggling harder and harder to conceal my apprehension, my fear that she did not want to speak to me. Then, on the third day, she called my apartment. I was at the UN. She left her home phone number with my answering service.

I was nervous when I called. What if I was wrong? What if her husband answered the phone? But she was not at home, and the voice on the recording was her voice, not a male voice. She did not give her name, but that fact alone—that the voice on her home phone was hers, not her husband's—was enough to fan the hope in my heart, to confirm what I had suspected: she no longer lived with her husband. She no longer was married to him.

She called me back that same night. "I'm so sorry it took so long for you to reach me. I was at a conference at the University of the West Indies in Jamaica."

I could hear in her voice the same confidence, the same optimism I remembered when she had turned to me in the restaurant, a lifetime ago, and said, *"This is my work."* My heart raced. "A conference?" I asked her.

"I was invited to show slides of my work."

"You're painting again."

"Yes." She laughed. It was a happy laugh.

"It's good to hear you laugh." But I was uneasy.

She laughed again.

"You sound happy." *What if she had another lover?*

"I am."

I took a deep breath. "Can I see you?"

"Of course."

"When?"

"I have a class at the New School tomorrow night."

"Then tomorrow night?"

"Yes, that would be fine. After my class. Say, ten o'clock?"

My hands were shaking when I put down the phone.

A day never passed as slowly. Ten o'clock never took so long to come. I left the UN at five. By eight o'clock I had looked at every news program on the television and was now staring blankly at the screen, calculating for the umpteenth time how long it would take me by taxi to get from Forty-fifth Street to Knickerbocker's on University Place and Ninth Street, where we had agreed to meet. By nine-fifteen I decided to walk the thirty-six blocks to Knickerbocker's thinking to dissipate the nervous energy that had made it difficult for me to concentrate on my work all day. I arrived at Knickerbocker's sweating in the warm September night air, panting for breath, my shirt plastered to my chest, my tie choking my neck.

"You didn't change your suit."

Marguerite's face burst through the bodies that had jostled past me—the eccentricities of the streets near Washington Square: young men with purple hair, rings pierced through their ears, their noses, their eyebrows; girls who could pass for boys; university students with their backpacks and raucous voices; men and women in business suits; tourists who came to gawk. Her face shone through them all.

"The uniform. Always the diplomatic uniform." She stood on tiptoes and stretched up to kiss me. I bent down to her. Her lips grazed my cheek.

"You are perspiring." Her smile lit up her eyes.

I would not have recognized her if she had not come up directly to me. She seemed so young, so different from the woman in the long skirt I had seen fifteen years ago, the mother of a nine-year-old boy, the wife of a politician, the teacher, the homemaker. Time had receded for her, stood still at that summer when I first met her. Her hair was long again. She wore it in a single plait behind her head, hardly different from the ponytail I remembered. She was slim again, her hips narrow again, her breasts tiny again. She was wearing an ivory blazer cropped at the waist and a short narrow tan skirt. It exposed the legs I loved—the curves of her calves, the smooth skin above her knees.

"You haven't changed," I said.

Suddenly I felt old.

"Come. Take off your jacket."

Suddenly, I was the old man cheating on his wife with a woman half his age, the man Ibrahim Musima had urged me to become. And yet Marguerite was not half my age. She was fifty, a mere six years younger than me.

"Loosen your tie."

I undid the top button of my shirt and slid my arms out of the sleeves of my jacket. I felt worn out, stuffy in my wool suit.

"That's better." She helped me out of my jacket.

"You look beautiful," I said.

"You always knew how to flatter me."

"No, I mean it. I did not expect you to look like this."

"Like what?"

"You look younger than when I last saw you."

"I use a good hair dye."

"No. It's your face. Your skin."

We were standing near the entrance to the restaurant. People were passing around us to get to the door. She touched my arm. "Let's go in," she said.

She stepped back when I opened the door, and her hair brushed against my chest. It took all my willpower not to wrap my arms around her, not to turn around and embrace her.

In the darkened dining room of the restaurant I saw the circles under her eyes, the flesh that had loosened around her mouth and eyes with the years, and yet there was not a wrinkle on her face, not a line, not an indentation. Her skin was as smooth as a river-washed pebble. Her eyes shone with the brightness—the confidence, the optimism—that usually dulled with age.

She was four years younger than Nerida. No one would have believed it. Nerida's waist had long thickened, her hips had spread, and the muscles in her breasts and stomach had slackened with five pregnancies. Any optimism that remained in her eyes was the hope she had for her children. Nerida had long ceased to set goals for her personal fulfillment, but in Marguerite's eyes I saw the excitement, the anticipation of the young, of a life yet to be realized.

"This was my friend's favorite restaurant." She smiled broadly. The smile spread across her face and widened the gap I felt yawning between us—the stodginess I seemed to personify, the youthfulness that exuded from her. "She was a writer. She introduced me to Knickerbocker's." She stretched out her arm, taking in the room around us. "Isn't this a great place?"

There was a bar, close to the door. People were cluttered around it, drinks in their hands, applauding and cheering a baseball game on the huge television screen that hung from the ceiling. It reinforced my discomfort. It made me feel out of place, out of time, out of sync, and I wanted to be in sync with Marguerite. I wanted to be light and gay as she seemed to be—to be the man who could seem young as she seemed young, the man who could smile and talk as if he were young, as if life had never burdened him with disappointment, with loss; as if the weight of responsibility for his children, his family, his country, his mission now for South Africa had not lain heavily on him.

I found myself taking comfort in the staidness of the dining room. It was like the dining rooms I had been accustomed to in hotels—solid and formal—linens on the table, china, stemmed glass, brass reflecting candlelight, wood-paneled walls. In the corner I saw a black baby grand piano. I latched onto it. I turned it into a symbol of the world I knew, the world in which I exercised power, in which I was in control. The world in which I had a place.

"Does anyone play the piano?" I asked Marguerite.

"Sometimes." She seemed puzzled by my question.

"Tonight?"

"No, not tonight."

I pulled the bottom of my tie and tightened the knot at my neck.

"There's a baseball game tonight," she said.

I was aware she was watching me.

"Oh." I spread my fingers on the table, unwilling to put an end to the attention she was giving me.

"Does the TV bother you?"

I did not answer her.

"We could go to another restaurant," she said.

The first time we met I had behaved this way. But then I was a young man preening with the pretensions of my office. I wore a suit—the diplomat's uniform, as Marguerite had called it—to signal my status, even to the woman I had planned to seduce. She wore leggings and a loose shirt and shamed me. She shamed me now again. There was nothing wrong with the restaurant. There was something wrong with me.

"No," I said.

"The bar is too noisy?"

I wilted when those trusting eyes were fastened on me, for it was insecurity that had made me so peevish. "It's fine," I said.

"If you don't—"

I stopped her. I reached for the courage that had abandoned me. "It's a great place, Marguerite. A really great place."

"Are you sure? Because if you're not, we could—"

"It's fine, Marguerite."

"You're certain?"

"It's fine. I like the bar with the television. It makes the room less formal."

Her smile returned, the one I had removed with my schoolboy petulance. She leaned back in her chair. "That's why my friend liked it. Doris was her name. DorisJean, as she preferred to be called. You know, like it was one name—DorisJean. She liked the bar especially."

The room grew noisier. People were slapping high fives at each other, yelling and shouting.

"It's the playoffs for the World Series. The New York Yankees are up."

I looked up at the TV. The man who had slid into first base was covered in dirt all along the sides of his pants and up his shirt-sleeves. Baseball was not a game I liked. Tennis was my game. The diplomat's sport.

"They seem to be winning," I said.

"For now," she said, but she was not looking at me. Her eyes were on the TV.

"Do you follow it?" I asked her. I did not want changes I could not identify with, could not relate to, could not understand. I did not want any changes at all. When I knew her she never talked about baseball.

"DorisJean got me involved in it, but I don't follow it much." She turned back to me.

"Ah, your friend." I relaxed. I had thought it was the American husband who had taught her to like this sport.

"I used to think that's why she came here. To watch baseball. Then I caught her drinking here."

She bent her head to one side and tucked a loose strand of her hair behind her ear. I wanted to pull it out again. I wanted to be the one to smooth it back into place.

"When she came to my house for dinner, she always refused the wine," she was saying to me. "Then, one day, it was her last birthday, I decided to take her to dinner here at her favorite restaurant. I got here late, I can't remember why. But when I arrived she was at the bar, plastered. I didn't talk to her for months after that for lying to me. Everybody knew she drank, except me. And I was one of her best friends. Then she died suddenly and I regretted those months I did not talk to her. I come here often now. This place reminds me of her."

"Maybe we should go someplace else," I said. "I don't want you to be sad."

"No, I'm not sad when I come here. I'm happy."

The waiter approached us. "Sparkling water," she said. "What about you?"

"Water is good for me, too."

"Not wine?"

"I don't drink."

"Not even socially?"

"Never. Have you forgotten?" How easily the jealousy returned. How easily it slipped back in again after I thought I had righted myself, banished my insecurities.

"No, but that was a long time ago."

"I haven't changed. I still do not drink. I'm still a bore at parties."

She dismissed me with a wave of her hand.

"I like coming here because I like remembering DorisJean," she said.

But I wanted her to tell me that she was glad I was still a bore at parties. That I had not changed. That I was still the Oufoula she remembered. The Oufoula she loved.

"Do you remember me?" I asked her.

She laughed at me. "Same old Oufoula," she said.

The tone of voice was not what I wanted, the words not what I wished she had said. I sat back heavily in my chair. "Old," I said, "but not the same."

"You're not old. You look great. The years were good to you. You haven't put on an ounce of fat."

I patted my stomach. "Except here."

"Where? I can't see it."

"It's there. I see it every day. And my hair. Don't you see how gray it is?"

"You haven't lost it. Most men your age are bald or they've lost at least half their hair. Look at you. You just have a sprinkling of gray hair and it makes you look great. Like a famous, distinguished ambassador."

"I am none of those. Famous or distinguished."

"False modesty will get you everywhere."

The waiter brought us the water she ordered. I let her choose my dinner. She did so without looking at the menu.

"I've memorized it by now," she said, not missing the eyebrows I raised. "I told you I came here often. With DorisJean, of course," she added as if I had asked. *The old Marguerite. Still solicitous, still careful of my feelings.* "So," she asked, crossing her arms over the table, "why are you here?"

I told her.

"Then you *are* famous and distinguished."

"I'm just a part of a team. Tell me about you. Tell me about your trip to Jamaica."

"I was invited by the University of the West Indies. A conference on postcolonial art. I hadn't realized how much Edna Manley had influenced art in Jamaica. The people there are doing extraordinary work."

"Then you're painting again?"

"I began in earnest about five years ago. After I left my husband. I'm divorced, you know."

"I guessed as much from the message on your phone. I'm sorry," I said. The words came out bland, dry, devoid of emotion, of any genuine compassion.

"Don't be. It was the best thing that happened to me. I don't think I would be painting today if I'd stayed in my marriage. To tell you the truth I like coming to this restaurant not so much because I want to remember DorisJean as because it is here that I realized what a false life I had been living for years. I thought I could have given up my art for my son. I was Miss Super Mother, Miss Super Homemaker, and all the time I was angry inside. That's why Doris-Jean never told me she drank. She didn't want to shatter the Polly-anna image I built around me, the fairy-tale world I pretended to live in. The politician's wife dressed in politician wife's clothes. No wonder you think I look different now. It's the clothes."

She was speaking to me as if the conversation we had had fifteen years ago had never ended, as if it had continued in her mind and she was answering questions I had raised about her marriage to a politician, about her willingness to give up her art.

"It's not just the clothes." I said. "You look young. Your eyes are young."

"I've come back to life."

"I never understood how you could give up painting. It meant so much to you."

"It was easy once I found a way to put it out of my mind. I'm good at that—putting things out of my mind when I need to."

I felt the wound to my heart. It was what she had done when we were young. What I wanted her to do. She had put the things she did not want to know—I did not want her to know—out of her mind. My secret would have destroyed us. She would have stopped seeing me if I had allowed her to expose it. But Marguerite was not thinking of those times. She was talking of the times *after* I had forced her to face the truth, *after* I had given her no choice but to banish me from her life. She was talking about the times when I was no longer in her life, when the people in her life, the people she loved, were her husband, her son.

"I was lying to myself thinking I could stop. Paul said I became a better mother, less nervous and edgy, when I started painting again every day. He told me that it was easier for him to get on with his life when I was happy. He didn't have to spend so much time worry-ing about me. He was a terrible student all through elementary school and high school. His teachers would say the same thing: Paul has the intelligence, the potential, but he won't concentrate, he won't do his work."

She opened her handbag and took out a photograph. "Here's a picture of him."

I took it from her hands. The bar erupted again with shouts and laughter, but Marguerite did not turn to look at the TV. We could have been the only two people in the restaurant, the noise around us mere background.

"Then in his last year in high school, everything changed."

She spoke with the same intimacy I remembered when we were lovers. When I was certain she loved me. When she told me all—all her thoughts, all her feelings—because I was the one she loved, the one she trusted.

"That was when I had decided to leave Harold and I went back to painting again. Paul asked me not to leave until he went to college. He said too many of his friends were living with a single mother. He needed his father in the house until he left home for college. I stayed nine more months for Paul. I don't regret it. Paul knew the marriage was over, but I think it was a relief to him that I had stopped trying so hard. That there was no more tension in the house. We all knew what was happening. Paul knew I did not want his father as a husband, but he still had Harold as his father. I was happier. I was painting. Paul's grades made a complete turnaround. Now he's in graduate school. Happy and doing well."

I looked at the photograph she had given me, fighting my guilt, struggling with my jealousy. Her son was a handsome young man but he looked nothing like her. He was tall, darker than she was, his lips thicker, his nose broader. The thought crossed my mind that he could have been mine. It was a foolish thought, yet I asked her.

"How soon after we broke up did you get married?"

She looked straight into my eyes. "He's not your child," she said.

Still, I persisted. Still, I did not want to give up the illusion that there had been no quarrel between us. That through the years of not seeing each other, something still held us together, linked us.

Like a child. Like a son. Like a child conceived out of our passion, our love.

"He looks like an African," I said.

"His father is African American."

Just the barest hint of anger flashed across her eyes but it was enough to stop me. "It was a foolish thing for me to suggest." I did not want her upset with me. Not now. Not on the first day after fifteen years. Not ever. She reached for the photograph in my hand and I handed it back to her. "I was hoping," I said.

"I would have told you."

"I wished—"

She cut me off. "Do you have pictures of your children?"

"Marguerite—"

"Let me see them." She stretched out her hand.

I reached for my wallet. "They are grown up now."

She took the photographs from me and studied them, shifting them over and over between her fingers. "And your wife, do you have a picture of her?"

I lied to her. I did not know why. Embarrassment? Loyalty to Nerida? I could not show her a photograph of Nerida, a photograph of a woman who looked twice her age.

"I don't have one with me," I said. She didn't ask for an explanation.

By the time the waiter brought our dinner, her mood had shifted completely from the lightheartedness with which she had greeted me. She seemed older now, more mature. But it was a maturity that still retained its youthfulness, a youthfulness I did not find disconcerting. We talked some more about our children. We avoided the precipice of my marriage, the possibility that she had a lover. I skirted that dangerous tumble downwards to the rocks from the solid ground on which we stood. I asked her to tell me more about Paul. She said he was working on a Ph.D. in urban planning at Howard University. Besides being smart, he was a loving son to her, kind and compassionate.

"When he was twelve and I saw him leaning toward the wrong

crowd, I bribed him into doing some social work. I thought if I could teach him to care for someone other than himself, he wouldn't join the 'me' generation, he wouldn't become like too many of the self-ish, self-centered young people I see today. There was a senior center near me. I arranged for Paul to be an assistant to a counselor there. Of course, there was no such position for someone as young as Paul, but I asked them to do me a favor. I gave them the money to pay Paul for working there ten hours a week in the summer. It was the best thing I did. Paul went there only for the money at first, but soon he was rushing out of the house, telling me that one of the seniors was expecting him to take her for a walk, or something like that. He learned the importance of being reliable. He discovered that other people needed him and he had to be responsible."

"Like you were," I said. "Like how he was able to rely on you."

She looked down at her hands.

"Paul's a compliment to you," I said.

"I didn't mean it that way," she murmured.

"You shouldn't be embarrassed. When children turn out well, it's because their parents paid attention to them. Because their parents were reliable and responsible."

"And your children?"

"Like your son. Good students. Good human beings."

"Then you were a good father."

I told her the truth. "Their mother was a good mother. Still is. I was always away, or I came home too late."

"You have a good wife, then?"

"Yes," I said.

An awkwardness grew between us with my response. It gave me hope. If all she wanted from me was friendship, she would not have grown quiet. She would have asked more questions about my wife. There would be no tension between us as there was now.

"We're lucky," I said, breaking the silence. "Not all parents are so lucky."

When our dessert came, we were still talking about our children, about our good luck, still avoiding any mention of my wife, any mention of a man she may be seeing. I told her I had friends whose sons had dropped out of school in spite of their parents' money. Some were on drugs.

"Even in Africa?" She was surprised.

"Television," I said, "is the new colonizer. We're in an age of cultural imperialism. Western television beams into our living rooms all over Africa. It invades our lives. Our children imitate what they see. In our cities it's pornography and drugs. Some of the old ways of respect for the elders are dying."

"Then you know how hard it is here."

"That's why you should be proud of yourself for the way your son turned out."

This time she accepted the compliment. My comment did not seem to make her uncomfortable. She smiled. "There's going to be a little reception tomorrow at an art gallery in Brooklyn for the opening of an exhibit on Caribbean art. Would you like to come?"

"An exhibit of your work?"

"Just three of my paintings are included."

"So you're the one who's famous!"

"It's a small gallery."

"Well, well."

"Just three paintings. Will you come?"

"Of course I'll come. I want to come."

"Here's the address." She handed me a card. "The reception is at six."

She kissed me on my cheek again when we parted, but there was a difference. It was not the warm, cheerful gesture of affection between friends she had extended to me outside the restaurant. This time she touched my arm when she raised her head to kiss me. Her fingers pressed my flesh. I could feel them through my jacket as if she had touched my bare arm. I put my arms around her. She leaned her head against my chest. It was only for a moment, but a moment was all I needed to hear her heartbeat race with mine. A moment was all I needed to know she had not forgotten me, that she had not expelled me from her heart.

23

In the many times I had been to New York I had never been to Brooklyn. Marguerite had told me much about Brooklyn that summer when I first met her, in those days when I was not so foolish as to think I was more important to her, or even just as important to her, as her art. When she would not take a full-time job because it would interfere with the time she needed for her art. She told me she would know her work was good when people in Brooklyn bought it.

"Brooklyn is the West Indian mecca," she had said. "The first port of call for West Indians in America, and for most, the last. There are more West Indians in Brooklyn than in any other place outside the Caribbean. That's why Sparrow says, 'Brooklyn is my home.'"

The Mighty Sparrow. He was the reigning calypso monarch from Trinidad and Tobago. Even in Africa we had heard of him.

"Come Labor Day, Eastern Parkway is a sea of West Indians. They bring carnival to Brooklyn—the costumes, the steel band, the calypsos. They have to close down Eastern Parkway. The Americans call it the West Indian parade, but it's not a parade, it's a jump

up. Just like back home with people dancing and winin' their bodies in the streets. I'll take you to it."

But Marguerite and I parted before Labor Day and I never got
the chance. Now I was driving down that same parkway she had
described to me. It reminded me of the boulevards of Paris. There
were shades of an elegance that once must have been there but
now could only be guessed at from the wide avenue and the cobble-
stone pavements that came between the avenue and the narrow
streets on either side. Trees lined the avenue and there were park
benches and lanterns on the pavements, but these were recent re-
placements, the frustrated effort of some city planner to recover a
past that had foolishly slipped through the fingers of the white people who once lived there, who took flight when the Jews descended
from Harlem, the Jews who themselves ran to Long Island when
the West Indians arrived.

"Soon there'll be no place for white people to go but in the sea.
Then they'll come back to Brooklyn."

Marguerite had predicted this to me in 1968, and in 1989 the
evidence was before my eyes. Park benches had been repaired,
painted, and welded onto iron platforms lodged into the cement,
but that did not spare them from the graffiti that was looped across
the fresh green paint. Maple saplings were wired to the ground,
but paper swirled around the roots, garbage carelessly discarded
there by people who seemed indifferent—hostile, even—to the at-
tempts at urban renewal that surely they knew were not being
made for their sake. So they let their dogs defecate on the sidewalks,
and threw empty beer bottles and soda cans on the cordoned-off
areas around the newly planted trees. Too disillusioned, Marguerite told me later, to have hope. Too poor to care.

There were places along Eastern Parkway where the stone facades
of apartment buildings had been sandblasted and bright new awn-
ings shaded oak doorways, but these seemed incongruous, even to
my eyes, to the rest of the buildings, with their torn window shades
and dirty entranceways. Young mothers sat with their babies on front
stoops, young men leaned against walls unsuccessfully camouflaging

the beer cans in their hands with brown paper bags. These were the daughters and sons of black immigrants who must have had great hopes when they crossed the Atlantic, some dream, now lost, of getting their piece of the American pie. These were the unemployed, the neglected, the poor.

Past the wide roundabout, the grand Soldiers' and Sailors' Memorial Arch with its bronze statues of the triumphant Winged Victory, Lincoln, Grant and the soldiers and sailors of the Civil War, past the stone walls of the Brooklyn Public Library, past the Doric columns of the Brooklyn Museum with its freshly cut front lawn, Eastern Parkway seemed unconquerable, irreclaimable, the home indeed of West Indians. But further down, a few streets beyond Nostrand Avenue where the art gallery was, where I was going to meet Marguerite, a new wave of Jewish immigrants was pushing its way westward. The Hasidim. In a very short time, they would clash in the infamous Crown Heights riots—the West Indians refusing to yield in their march eastward, the Hasidic Jews determined to reclaim territory abandoned by their predecessors of another clan.

In those days, and still today, the West Indian hold on Nostrand Avenue was firm. Unshakable. All along the street I saw bakeries, restaurants, video shops, beauty parlors, pharmacies, travel agencies, all touting West Indian names. West Indians were everywhere. I recognized them by their characteristic way of talking with their hands, their animated gestures. My driver was forced to bring the car to a crawl, sometimes to stop abruptly in the street when the car in front of him braked suddenly for the driver to hail someone he knew or for a gypsy cab to discharge passengers. It reminded me of Africa. The inefficiency and inconvenience that disturbed me less than the efficiency and convenience of the developed countries where the heart did not count, where nothing mattered more than how much money was made, how much lost.

The art gallery was three blocks south of a college named for an African American civil rights martyr, Medgar Evers. But the founders of the college had underestimated the tenacity of the West Indians, their persistence and determination. In 1989, almost all the students were first- and second-generation West Indian Americans and the college was finding itself forced to adjust to a new music, a different rhythm, and an ambition focused less on breaking down the barriers of race than on removing the obstacles of class.

Marguerite came to the door to greet me. She was wearing a pale green fitted short-sleeved jacket over a long black-and-tan-print sarong not unlike the ones women in my home village wore. She looked lovely. I told her so. She smiled, took my hand, and led me inside.

It was a small place, the studio of an art framer that had been divided into two rooms: the front, where he received his clients, and the back, where he did his framing. That evening the countertop in the front room served as a bar and a table for hors d'oeuvres. People were huddled around it leaving a small corridor that led to the room where the paintings were exhibited. I saw Marguerite's work immediately. It was not difficult to identify. There were three framed drawings, all in black and white. One was of a man, the other two of women. Light and shadows played across their faces and bodies, giving them an emotional poignancy that was startling in its realism.

"Do you like them?" Marguerite studied my face.

She had perfected the technique she was working on when I first met her, that she had told me was called chiaroscuro. "It looks like me." I pointed to the drawing of the man.

"It is you. I started it years ago and finished it recently. I had to touch it up."

It was me as I was twenty-five years ago, my skin firm, taut. No gray hair, none of the puffiness that had developed with age under my chin. But my eyes were sad. An old man's eyes.

"Did I seem that unhappy when you knew me?"

"When I saw you again fifteen years ago. I never forgot the expression in your eyes when you told me about the accident."

"The accident?" But in that instant I knew what she meant.

"I saw the pain in your eyes."

"You cried with me."

"I saw your courage, your pride. Your commitment, your decency."

"You give me more credit than I'm due."

"Oh, you're due it. You're due it."

"I thought you had forgotten me."

I had not intended to weaken so soon, to let her know so soon how anxious I was to be with her.

"An artist never forgets an image that makes an impression on her," she said.

"An image? That's all I was?" I spoke like an adolescent.

We had been standing in front of her drawing of me. A small group of people had collected behind us. She pulled me aside. "Go see the other work," she said. She pointed to the wall behind me and, before I could respond, she walked away in the opposite direction.

For the rest of the evening she ignored me. Once I caught her eye and she smiled at me, but most of the time I saw only glimpses of her back as she stopped to talk to the people who had come to see her work. A young couple, assuming from the way I was dressed that I was an African of some stature, engaged me in a discussion about South Africa that became somewhat heated when some of their friends joined in. I was grateful for the distraction, but I felt abandoned by Marguerite, rejected, and it was only later, when the crowd thinned, and the couple had left with their friends, that, finding myself once again face-to-face with the portrait she had done of me, I allowed myself to take comfort in the evidence that she had not forgotten me, that even if all I was to her was an image for her art, she had not wiped me out of her mind.

Toward the end of the evening, just when I thought I would not get the chance to say good-bye to her before I left, she suddenly reappeared. She could give me a ride to my apartment, she said, if I could wait fifteen minutes longer. She lived in Long Island now, in a tiny house on the water. She could take the Midtown Tunnel on Thirty-fourth Street. It would be no trouble to drop me off.

It was the first sign she had given me all evening that she wanted to be with me. I sent my driver away and waited for her.

In the car we talked about her art. Her work was being exhibited more, she said. Even in Manhattan, though only in small galleries. But it was a beginning. I told her I wanted to buy the portrait she had done of me.

"I would never sell it to you," she said. "I would give it to you. But I can't right now. I need a collection. When I have enough of a collection I will give it to you."

She spoke to me as if we were discussing a business transaction. She explained that there were advantages to having a number of works to show potential buyers. She did not want to seem like a Johnny-come-lately. It inspired confidence in the buyer if an artist had a collection, she said. She wanted to keep her best work until there was a demand for it in the market. Then, she informed me, it would fetch the price she wanted.

Nothing in her voice suggested any lingering romantic feelings that may have still remained in her heart, but yet I did not lose hope. I remembered the pressure of her fingers on my arm. I remembered that she had leaned her head on my chest when I had embraced her the night before. I did not despair.

When she stopped the car to let me out, I reached to kiss her. She resisted. She turned her lips away from my mouth and pushed me away from her, but I held her tightly in my arms and sought her lips again. She struggled, pushed me away again, but I kissed her again. And so we did three times—I kissing her, she pushing me away—until suddenly, when I least expected it, she yielded to me, her kiss so intense, I was taken aback, surprised, momentarily stunned. My lips froze, my heart raced, my knees turned to liquid. It was seconds before I recovered, before my lips thawed, before my mind accepted that she had kissed me, and when it did, I returned her kisses with the longing of twenty-five years, with the passion of a man who had tried to forget, who for twenty-five years had made a futile effort to blot out memory; who, no matter what he did, how much he had used work, family, friends to forget her, still remembered her, still loved her, still desired her.

With my mouth on hers, I reached feverishly for the buttons on her jacket. She let me spread my fingers over her breasts; she let me hold them, caress them. She stopped me only when I slid my hand through the slit in her skirt searching for her thighs.

"Not here. Not now." She clamped her fingers over my wrists.

But she was still yielding to me, still twisting her body away from the steering wheel toward me.

"Calm down. Calm down."

I remembered the words we said to each other that first time.

"Calm down. Calm down."

The words did not reach my lips.

We were parked on the street near the corner of Thirty-eighth Street and Fifth Avenue. Cars slowed down past us to stop at the traffic light, people walked inches next to us. I did not care if they saw us.

I was a man who had grown accustomed to the caution of the diplomatic world. When I traveled outside of my country, I made it a point not to eat in the same place twice, not to enter my hotel at a predictable time. I was always aware of the people around me. I knew who stood at my side, at my back. In the years since I first met Marguerite, I had learned how to measure my words, my actions. I left no tracks to be traced, nothing for the blackmailer. Nothing for the person who could twist my words for his purposes, who could find the skeletons in my closet where I had buried them. Yet here I was, former ambassador, member of a prestigious African delegation sent on a mission to the UN for the liberation of Mandela, the overthrow of apartheid; here I was, husband of a faithful wife for twenty-eight years, admired father, role model. Here I was sitting in a car at a busy intersection in Manhattan, off Fifth Avenue, my mouth on the breast of a woman who was not my wife, my hand between her thighs, desperately clinging to her as if my life depended on her—on her love, on her desire for me.

Marguerite would say afterwards, she had experienced an epiphany. "A sudden clarity of feelings I must have denied for years. I knew at that moment that it was you I first loved. You I always loved. You I will love forever. I yielded to that realization. I did not fight it."

But she did not come up to my apartment that night though I

begged her to, though I promised that we would not make love unless she wanted to.

She needed to go home, she said. She needed to catch her breath, to breathe before she drowned, before she lost herself irrevocably in me again. It had come too quickly, too suddenly. But she would not refuse me. Ever again.

"Come, spend the weekend with me," she said. "You win."

24

I took the train to Long Island. Marguerite picked me up at her station. I brought her red roses. I would bring her red roses the next time I saw her. One week later, when she was sure I knew she loved me, she asked me not to bring her red roses again.

"It makes me feel like a courtesan. Your mistress. I am more to you than a mistress."

We had been together again for just seven days and she knew that already.

But that first time when I brought her red roses, I had taken a risk for her that was more than the risk a man takes for a woman with whom he knows he would have only an affair, a temporary arrangement, sexual and nothing more.

I had had a meeting that afternoon with the UN ambassador from the United States. It was a meeting that my team had planned for weeks. We wanted a clear understanding of the extent of the U.S. commitment to the unconditional suffrage of all black people in South Africa. We were aware of the fears of the white world. We knew of the nightmares that terrorized even their waking hours: the specter of the masses of black people free at last. Liberated. *Armed.*

For decades white South Africa had unleashed indescribable cruelties upon its black fellow citizens—insufferable oppression, torture, humiliation. Now white South Africans were terrified. They knew that that kind of suffering demanded not simply justice, but revenge. This was not America. This was not England. Black people in South Africa were not in the minority. Only brute force, they believed, guns—weapons blacks could not afford—had been able to stop them from massacring their torturers. White South Africa was afraid to shut its eyes, afraid to sleep. What if the locks to the prisons where they had penned black people were removed? What if their passes were destroyed? The ones they had created to herd black people into slums, to rope them out of the areas where they had built their sprawling houses? Where their children played? They had let black people in, of course, to work in their kitchens, to dig their ditches, to empty their garbage, their refuse, but what if? *What if?*

We had met with the American ambassador as much to calm the nerves of white Americans, Europeans, white South Africans as to reassure ourselves that the West would not retreat from its position of outrage at the injustices that had been inflicted on black people in South Africa. I was prepared for this meeting. I had spent weeks rehearsing what I would say, anticipating objections, preparing rebuttals, and yet that afternoon, all I could think of was Marguerite, my mind unable to fix itself on anything else but her.

My teammates told me that I had looked at my watch three times. Brilliant strategy, they said. We let the Americans know that we were the ones running out of time. If they did not use their power immediately to force de Klerk into complying completely with our demands, we could not be responsible for what would happen in South Africa. We could not guarantee that white women would be safe. Who knows what could happen when the people get their hands on the white man's guns? On his money?

But it was not a strategy I had intended, and one man, the oldest on the team, suspected me. He was the brother of the president of my country. Bala Keye, my wife's uncle, a man I never liked, a man who never liked me. At the last minute my president had sent him to join the team.

"In case something happens to you, Oufoula. Like you're sick one day and we find ourselves in the unfortunate position where our country is not represented."

It was not an unusual arrangement for my president to make— to provide a contingency plan in case of an emergency. The only unusual part of it was that he had chosen his brother to be second in command on our team to the UN.

Bala Keye was the youngest son of the president's father. He was a man with more ambition than talent and even less presence, and his brother knew it. Of the men who claimed they admired me but who I knew wished me misfortune, Bala Keye wished the worst for me.

I say he was the oldest man on the team, but not many years lay between us. Less than ten, enough that it seemed reasonable that he should be convinced that he had seniority over me and thus was entitled to more privileges than me, and yet sufficiently slight that he could consider me a peer, a contemporary, a competitor with whom he saw himself in contest for prizes he always lost. It was that precarious difference between our ages that was the cause of his resentment of me. That, and the fact that though the president was his brother, he had chosen me over him to be his first ambassador to Ghana.

Bala Keye carried this resentment like an albatross around his neck. Even when he laughed it was easy to mistake the quivers that ran through his body and the tears that rolled down his eyes as expressions of rage rather than joy. I did not know what caused the president to change his mind and send him on this mission to the UN. Perhaps Bala Keye begged him and the president did not have the heart or the will to refuse him. The president was past seventy-five. There were many who said he was becoming soft, docile.

It was Bala Keye who pressed me to join the team for dinner that night. We were more certain than we had ever been of Mandela's release. My team wanted to celebrate. I said I was tired. I said I had a headache. The others were sympathetic. I had worked hard, they said. Harder than any of them. But Bala Keye was insistent.

It was five-thirty before I could get him to surrender. I was running out of the florist carrying the red roses I bought for Marguerite on my arm like a bridal bouquet when I saw him. Our eyes locked in one terrible moment before he turned away.

It was the gesture of an amateur diplomat, but he had put me on notice. He had an advantage over me, his eyes told me. He could trade on it whenever he wished.

I had made two mistakes that day, because of my desire for Marguerite. I, who had been known to be meticulous, a man whose appearance was that of a happy man, a contented family man. A man whose insouciance put the enemy at ease, who concealed his anger, his rage, his hatred, a man who did not wear his heart on his sleeve, who did not leave trails to the thoughts on his mind. Yet I had looked at my watch three times at a meeting with the UN ambassador from the United States. I had run like a lovesick puppy to the florist shop. I was seen cradling a bouquet of red roses on my arm rushing to the six o'clock train to Long Island. Rushing to Marguerite.

But these two were not the first mistakes I had made since I met Marguerite again. I had kissed her in the car on the corner of Thirty-eighth Street and Fifth Avenue. I had put my hand under her blouse and cupped her breasts. I had slid my fingers up her thighs and would have done more. Would have pressed her back against the car seat and made love to her there, in her car, had she not stopped me, had she not promised the weekend.

I would have done that though I was aware, though part of my brain was aware that I was in a car parked on the street in the middle of Manhattan. That I could be seen. That in this city, in this country where fortunes are made by the humiliation of public figures, where a president can be brought down low, hauled into a court of senators, exposed before a nation for a single indiscretion, say, fondling the breasts of one of those willing sycophants intoxicated by the mere proximity to power, I could have tainted the reputation of my teammates, undermined the seriousness of our commitment to our mission, a mission that had consequences not only for the liberation of South Africa but for the liberation of all of

Africa—the liberation from stereotypes that still persisted though
Tarzan had been unmasked for what he was: a myth to quiet the
white man's fears of the power of Africa.

Had I been asked to tell the principle that guided my life up to that
moment, up through all the years to that moment, I would have said,
as I believed then—as I believed that day when I tore up Catherine's
letter, the letter that gave me Marguerite's phone number—one
should not allow one's private affairs to affect one's public affairs. I
had conducted my life according to this standard. I believed chaos
would follow, confusion and disorder, if one's private life spilled into
matters concerning one's public life.

But now disorder engulfed me. Yet I was not afraid, for chaos
had not followed, nor confusion. Never before had I achieved such
clarity of purpose. Never before had any decision of mine, any action I had taken, been so completely untainted by influence other
than my personal desires, my personal needs. I knew what I was
doing. I was choosing to do it, freely, of my own volition.

Up to that moment, for more than half a century, I had carefully
compartmentalized my life. I had put the things that pleased me,
the things that reassured me, in the front parts of my mind where I
could see them, where I could retrieve them. The others—the
things I did not like, the things I did not want to face, or could
not—I had put in boxes and sealed them. I had stored them deep
in the dark enclaves of my soul. And yet they had resurfaced. And
yet always they had filtered through the reality I had orchestrated:
the things I wanted to forget in the daylight—my mother's suicide,
my father's indifference. Mulenga. Margarete, the dark fantasy I
had created from Mulenga. Marguerite of flesh and blood. Marguerite whom I loved, whom I lost. These memories filtered through
my dreams, the lies I told as truths. They did not go away.

My mother must not have been afraid of the chaos I feared up to
this moment. She must have found freedom when her passion for
the man she loved spread over everything, engulfed everything, di-
minished everything—public expectations, public demands, her
reputation, her place in her village community, her security, her future. The son she loved.

She must have been able to think her *own* thoughts then, feel her *own* feelings when the lines blurred, when the barriers came down between the things that ought to have mattered to her and the things that did. She loved me. She loved the man who slit his throat for love of her more than she loved me.

So it was that Marguerite mattered most to me now. At this moment. Not the American ambassador to the UN, not Bala Keye, not the possibility that Bala Keye could blackmail me.

Marguerite's hair was up in a ponytail when she came to meet me, the way she had worn it the first time I saw her in New York. She had on a short black-and-tan-plaid pants skirt, a white T-shirt, and a gray cardigan. She looked younger than she had seemed the night before. I felt old again, uneasy. I wished I had stopped to change my clothes, to take off my gray suit, my white monogrammed shirt, my drab blue striped tie—my old man's uniform—but Bala Keye, my nemesis, with his envious heart, had not allowed me. In seconds, though, my uneasiness dissipated. She was fifty years old. Women less than half her age had desired me. They considered me handsome. They knew I was a wealthy man, a man in a position of great power in my country. If I had not had affairs with them, it was not because I could not, but, rather, because I would not. It was because of my commitment to my family, my dedication to my work.

It was because of my love for Marguerite.

No woman who ever tempted me compared with Marguerite. No woman had been able to make me take the risk of losing my wife, my family, my position, my prestige—all I had.

Still, when Marguerite ran toward me, I broke out in a cold sweat. I was a man looking into a mirror of himself, terrified of the reflection there. A man who seemed to have no fear of what could await him, who did not care how his life could change now that he would have in reality the woman who had consumed his dreams for more than twenty-five years.

Once, passion had made me a prisoner in my room until a fantasy saved me. Once, passion had bereft me of a mother, caused her to take her life. I remembered all this as Marguerite approached me, but I could not turn back. That man in the mirror would keep on walking into that fire before me. Nothing I could say or do would deter him, not even the knowledge that the flames would devour him.

Marguerite reached up and kissed me passionately on my mouth. "I was surprised when you told me you were going to take the train," she said. She took the red roses from my hand as if I had given her a business card. I should have guessed then that the roses had not pleased her. "Where's your driver?"

"I take trains, too, you know."

"A man in your position?" She dug her fingers in my ribs and tickled me.

My tension broke. "Yes, a man in my position." I laughed with her. "But only for you."

"Well, I hope you don't mind driving in a beat-up old car."

I opened the car door for her. "So long as you're my driver," I said.

"And you go where I take you?"

Her smile and her question were the smile and the question of a woman of confidence, a woman who knew she could take me wherever she wanted and I would follow. The man in the mirror did not care. He would go with her willingly, anywhere.

Marguerite lived in a little house with white wood shingles, facing the Great South Bay in a small town on the South Shore of Long Island. She said it was the servants' quarters that was once connected to the dilapidated Victorian house that stood next to hers. It used to be the summer home of some rich Manhattanite, she told me, in the years before they discovered the Hamptons. She had gutted the interior and opened the roof with skylights. There were only three rooms in the house: a small bedroom, a kitchen that faced the street, and a large room in the back that opened to the sea. We had to walk through the kitchen to reach it.

"It's the secret of the South Shore." Marguerite stood next to me at the huge glass sliding door that extended from one end of the large room to the other.

The water surprised me. I would not have guessed it was there. We had driven through a residential area of tiny clapboard houses separated by squares of manicured lawn. The cars parked in the driveways and on the streets were domestic American cars, not the usual boxy foreign cars one associated with the rich, the people who could afford to live near the sea.

"Nobody guesses it either. A lot of streets here lead to the water—to the bay or the canal."

The water in front of us was still. Quiet. Two boats moved slowly across it. In the diaphanous twilight I could make out a dog and a man in one, two children and their parents in the other. "It seems so calm," I said.

"Because it's a bay, not the ocean."

"Does it ever flood?"

"Well, for one, we're built about eight feet above sea level. See the bulwark at the end of the lawn? And for the other, we're protected by that barrier reef in front of us." She pointed to a thin strip of land on the other side of the bay. "It protects us from the Atlantic, though sometimes the ocean breaks through, but not as far west as where we are. More to the east where the rich people have their houses."

"You don't seem to be doing too badly yourself," I said.

"I was lucky. The couple who bought the big house couldn't afford the servants' quarters. They needed the money, so they sold it to me at a bargain. It was a mess when I got it. It cost me more to fix it up than I paid for it. There are always banks that will lend money to someone with a full-time job."

She walked to the kitchen and I followed her.

"So you're still working full-time?"

"I'm tenured. You don't give that up. I teach at night. It still gives me time for my art in the day. Then I have the summers."

She opened a drawer under the kitchen counter and pulled out a tablecloth. "I put this on my drawing table and voilà," she said. "A dining room table."

It was the simple elegance of that ivory linen tablecloth accomplishing just what she wanted it to do that reminded me suddenly of Nerida. For the second time in two days I would find myself noticing how similar they were, and, perhaps, it was that thought more than anything else that calmed my anxieties finally.

There was no likeness, of course, in their physical appearance, but they had the same character—the same values, the same goals for the children. Now, as I could see, the same taste. Gone were the bright colors, the careless scattering of pillows I had found liberating in Marguerite's old apartment. But I was a different man now, with different needs. An older man. I wanted to gather in my nets. I wanted to hold on to the things I had. I wanted to bind to me the people I loved. The muted colors in my home suited me, reflected my mood. The colors in Marguerite's house were muted, too, the furniture sparse and neatly arranged. They pleased me.

Marguerite had folded her easel and stacked it against the wall to the side of the glass front door.

"When I work, I put it in the middle of the room under the skylight," she told me. "That way, I get the light from the sun above me and in back of me."

There was a wooden closet with large doors next to the easel. She told me she stored her tools there and her work. Apart from a striped gray and white couch that faced the bay, and her drawing table with two chairs that stood behind the couch, the only other furniture in the room was a matching pale gray armchair and a pine wood cocktail table on which she had placed a stack of large art books and an antique bronze metal jug filled with sunflowers.

I had noticed the sunflowers immediately when I entered the room. I knew she would not replace them with the roses I had given her. She had put my roses in a glass vase. After she set the table, she placed them on top of the linen tablecloth. They looked garish. Out of place. Vulgar. And yet I would bring her red roses two more times, until she stopped me. Until she told me that red roses were the flowers men brought to their mistresses—the peacock's plumage meant to announce to the peahen the peacock's readiness to straddle her: biology, the animal instinct, set irreversibly in motion.

"I'm not as colorful as I was before," she was saying to me now, as though she sensed my need for an explanation, some way to understand the change in her, to interpret the pale palette of colors before me.

"The sea tamed me. I couldn't compete. Only blend."

She said she kept her work in the closet to prevent it from being bleached by the sun. Most of it she took to her office. She had hung only one in the room. It was a large framed painting of bamboo trees. She had mounted it on the back wall, away from the windows on either side of the room.

"There was a pinkish carpet on the floor. At least I think pink was its original color, not red. Most of it had turned ivory, except in the places where I suppose there was furniture. I ripped it all out and sanded the floors. The wood turned out to be in good shape."

"It looks great," I said.

"I thought of staining it darker so it wouldn't look so raw."

"I like it," I said.

She smiled approvingly at me.

The furnishings in her bedroom were sparse, too—simple: a bed with a plain white spread, a pale green rug on the bare wood floor, a night table covered with a white cloth edged with white embroidery. On the table was a clay pot of purple African lilies and a silver reading lamp next to a stack of books. Opposite the bed, bookshelves, some buckling under the weight of too many books, lined the walls from ceiling to floor. There was no TV in the room. She kept it in the kitchen, she said. It distracted her when she cooked.

"Maybe I shouldn't be distracted." She laughed.

We sat down to eat. She had made poached salmon. It was a fish Nerida knew I loved. She had prepared it the way Nerida knew I enjoyed it.

"I can make this better, I promise you."

"Let me taste it," I said. I put some salmon on my fork and brought it to my mouth. "Perfect. It couldn't be better. Perfect." I touched her hand. "Like you, Marguerite. Like everything about you."

After dinner I searched the bookshelves in her bedroom looking for the books she once wanted me to read.

"Do you remember our quarrel over Achebe?"

She joined me. *"Things Fall Apart."* She pulled it from the shelf.

"You were right, you know." I took it from her hand. "I was a callow fellow. I expected too much from Africa. I was too ready to blame Africa alone for its problems."

"I was also too young, too idealistic. I didn't want to believe that colonialism had done such damage. I didn't want to believe that it affected our minds, that it could distort our thinking. Fanon was right. Though the Europeans have gone, we still have to battle racism. The one we have internalized. Have you read him?"

I nodded. "A Martiniquan gave me a book of his."

"Black Skin, White Masks?"

"Yes, that's the one. But we should be easy on ourselves. We were both young, Marguerite. We didn't know better." I handed her back the Achebe novel.

"Do you still have the books I gave you?" She turned to put it on the shelf.

"They are in my bedroom," I said. "Opposite to my bed on my bookshelves. Like yours are." She was standing in front of me. I put my arms around her waist.

"Do you read them?"

"Sometimes," I said. "The times when I missed you."

She leaned her head against my chest. "Did you miss me?"

"There were times I missed you so much, I could not bear to have anyone around me."

She faced me and put her arms around my neck. "And did you dream of me?"

"More times than I would want to tell you."

She kissed my neck. "I want you to tell me," she whispered. "Tell me how many times you dreamed of me."

"There were nights I could not sleep, waking up from a dream about you."

She kissed my mouth. "For twenty-five years? You dreamed about me for twenty-five years?"

"Twenty-five years. I never forgot you."

She unbuttoned my shirt. "And what did you want to do when you dreamed about me?"

"I wanted to make love to you."

"Like we used to?"

She had taken off my shirt. My fingers were now under her T-shirt, unfastening her bra. She pulled her arms through her sleeves, and I lifted her T-shirt over her head.

"Did you ever dream of me?" I asked her.

"Many times."

"And did you want to make love to me?"

"Many times."

I slid off the band that held up her hair and kissed her behind her ears.

"Even when I was married," she said, "I dreamed of you."

I cannot blame what followed on these words she said to me. I cannot say that because she mentioned her marriage, I was reminded of mine, and because I was reminded of mine, my body refused me. For the truth was I had not forgotten my marriage. I was the son of a long line of men who had had many wives, a man who had come to Christianity after he had passed the age of myth. So Marguerite had often told me before.

So it must have been.

So it was that I felt no guilt when I kissed Marguerite, no guilt when I lay naked next to her. And so it had to be that when my body failed me, when it could not do what my heart, my soul, every fiber of my being desperately pleaded with it to do, I could not say it was because I was married, because Marguerite reminded me that I already had one wife.

"Did this ever happen to you before?"

I could hear the tremors in her voice.

I lay on top of her naked, impotent. "No," I said.

Tears gathered in the corners of her eyes. "It must be me. It must be me, then."

"No. No." I pulled her on top of me and hugged her. "It's not you. It's me."

"It's happened to me before," she said. "Harold . . ."

I put my finger to her lips. "It's not you. You are warm and beautiful and lovely."

"It happened with Harold," she said.

"I am not Harold."

"He said it was me."

"It's not you. How could it be you? Look at you. You're a sensual woman. Your skin is the color of the Sahara. Brown, warm, smooth. Not a blemish, not a mark. You smell like the desert. Like a flower in the desert."

"He said it was me," she repeated.

"Harold was a fool."

"He said I was hard to love."

"Harold was wrong."

"He said—"

"You are lovable, Marguerite. You are easy to love."

"Then why?

"It happens to men, you know. More than we are willing to admit. I'm just nervous. Anxious. It's been too many years. Tomorrow," I said. "You'll see tomorrow. I'll be okay tomorrow."

I had told her the truth. I was anxious and nervous. But it had not happened to me before. Not in twenty-eight years of marriage to Nerida.

This was the fear every man lives with: the day he would lie on top of a beautiful woman and be betrayed by the body that had always served him. And yet I did not think that this was happening to me—the impotence men of my age feared. I knew that the stories we told of our wives' declining libidos were a camouflage to mask our anxieties, our fear of losing our own sexuality, our potency. We sought reassurance from each other. We wanted to convince each other that the end had not come. And I did not think the end had come for me that night. I knew that when my heart had stopped racing, that when with each touch of Marguerite's hand on my body my toes would stop tingling, my spine would stop quivering, I would have control of my body again.

"Let's sleep," I said. "It's too much for one day. After so long."

After so long. Not only with Marguerite, but also with Nerida. But I did not tell her that. That it had been six months since Nerida had let me in her bed. I was overexcited, overstimulated. My desire for her too intense, my mind racing too fast for my body.

Yet I knew that when my body failed me, it was not only because anxiety had reduced me to jelly, not only because I had waited so long, wanted her for so long. Remnants of a hard-learned reticence had returned to plague me. When I lay naked, stretched out on top of her, trying in vain to make love to her, it came back to warn me: this thing I had taught myself to shun. I remembered the passion that took control of me with Mulenga, the passion that had driven me into my room in the mission school, a prisoner of my fantasies. The passion that drove me into my work when Marguerite ordered me to leave her apartment, the passion that sometimes made me a stranger in my house.

The passion that had cost my mother her life.

The passion that made the man who loved her put a razor to his throat.

"You are beautiful," I whispered to Marguerite. "Desirable. Too desirable."

She curled into my arms. "Tomorrow," she said. She kissed the hair on my chest. "I love you," she whispered.

Her words would make me sleep until morning, would make me forget. They allowed me to sleep without dreams that would wake me in a sweat. I had her with me now, the curves of her body locked into mine like the pieces of a puzzle. We were whole again. I was safe. The passion would not undo me.

In the morning I reached for her. The trembling under my skin had subsided, my blood ran warm again through my groin. We made love as we had before when we were young—with the same energy, the same intensity, the same passion. I remembered she liked my tongue in her navel. She remembered I liked hers in my ears. I remembered she loved when I kissed her neck. She remembered I loved when she licked my chest. When the moment came, she stretched out taut beneath me and pushed me away, shouting the same words, "Get off. Get off." They had the same meaning. I braced myself and held on to her until the moan that had begun in the back of her throat rolled out to her lips, gathered force, and she screamed. Screamed with the pleasure of it. Begged me not to stop, not to let go. "Wait. Wait. Not yet. Not yet." And when I joined her, our voices became a symphony of the past restored.

Afterwards, she lay on her side next to me. My hand traveled across the sand dunes of her body, the crest of her breasts, the slope down to her waist, the incline up her hips. I kissed each inch I touched. I buried my face in the basin that cradled her navel.

"I like this," I said. "I like this valley. I could lose myself in this valley."

She kissed the top of my head and turned my face upwards to hers.

"And I love this," she said. She covered my eyes with her mouth, first one eye, then the next, and she ran the tip of her tongue down the spread of my nose and across my lips. "And I love this."

No one had ever kissed me like that. Not Nerida. No one. No one had ever made me *feel* so worthy, so handsome. She said she loved my wide nose, my thick lips, my nappy hair, my blue-black skin. I had a classical face, she said. Like a piece of African art.

"Tell me," I asked her, grateful, wanting to give something back, "tell me your secret. How do you stay so beautiful, so young?"

"I am beautiful and young because you think I am beautiful and young."

"No." I looked into her eyes. "I tell you this objectively. Without bias. A man would have to be blind not to see how young you look, how beautiful."

"I'm short," she said. "Short people seem younger than they are."

"I know short people your age. They don't look as young as you."

"Ah," she said, "you mean menopausal women. You mean women who can no longer have babies. Women whose wombs have dried up."

Discovered, I rubbed my chin across her hip to distract her.

"Ouch," she said. "That hurts."

"My stubble."

"I take a tiny little pink pill every morning." She would not let me off so easily from the slip I had made—Ibrahim Musima's theories that had penetrated my defenses even as I rejected them.

"A what?"

"To keep me young."

"A pill?"

"The elixir of life for the menopausal woman. It keeps us vibrant. HRT. Didn't you hear of it? Hormone replacement therapy. It gives us the estrogen we lose after menopause. It makes us young again, our breasts firm. It makes our skin glow. It's bad for us."

"Bad?"

"Yes, bad." She turned on her back. "Some say it can cause breast cancer."

"Then why do you take it?"

"Vanity."

"If it's bad for you, throw it away."

"You see this skin you like?" Her fingers brushed her cheek. "It would be dry without it."

"I don't love your skin. I love you."

"All men say that, but we women know it's the image you love."

"Marguerite!" But as my tone of voice admonished her, my heart sank. What else did she know, my Marguerite?

"You can't imagine how terrible a woman feels when she sees the disappointment in a man's eyes that will inevitably be there, later if not sooner. Then she knows for certain that she is not who he has fantasized her to be." Her eyes grew dark.

She was speaking about men in general, but still she frightened me. She had come too close to a truth I had lived. But there could be no comparison between her and my fantasy. She was infinitely more beautiful, her character immeasurably more admirable.

"We are not talking about men and women, Marguerite," I said, and pulled her to me. "We are talking about you and me, and I, Oufoula, say to you, Marguerite, that I love you, not your skin."

She closed her eyes. "Let me get old, Oufoula."

She said it as if begging for something I would willfully withhold from her and, perplexed by this sudden change, the pleading evident in her eyes when she reopened them, I responded quickly, "We will get old together, Marguerite."

But that was not the answer she was looking for. "I don't want to have to make myself young to please you," she said.

"You don't have to. I love you the way you are. Because of who you are." I brushed my lips across her forehead.

"And will you still love the real me when my skin is wrinkled?"

"Oh, Marguerite."

I was about to add more protestations, swearing my love for her, when she sighed and pushed herself away from me. "We play your game," she said. Her lips curved downward, sadly.

"Game?"

"We wear the makeup, the fancy clothes. We diet. We let doctors cut us up. I take HRT. But there is always someone younger, firmer, that TV gives men to dream about."

"Marguerite." I pulled her back to me. "I have no interest in someone younger. It is you I love."

"And will you still want me when I am dried up like a prune?"

"I will love you forever." I held her tightly to my chest. "When you are old, when you are gray . . ."

"Grayer."

"When you've lost your teeth. Forever."

She laughed, but she repeated the word after me. "Forever," she said.

We both believed that was true.

25

It was past noon when we got out of bed. Marguerite wanted to show me the swans. They were the same swans, she said, that were there when she moved into the house three years ago. They lived in a bend in the bay near the canal. Her neighbors told her they had been there for years. Ten, at least.

"Swans mate for life. Did you know that?" she asked me.

We were looking at them through the wide glass panes of her living room door. They glided across the bay in front of us, one behind the other. So serene. So tranquil. Who could have guessed the terror they could unleash on the waters?

"For life," Marguerite repeated.

I did not know if she was thinking of my marriage just then, or what she could have been thinking of my marriage. But when she said *for life*, I immediately thought of Nerida. That was how long my commitment was to her. I remembered so without regret.

Marguerite was standing behind me. She wrapped her arms around my waist. "Will you love me for life like the swans?" She pressed her lips to my back.

I clasped my hands over hers. "For life."

I heard her let out her breath and then she laid her cheek against my spine. "Did you ever see them make love?"

"Once," I said.

"It's frightening."

I told her about O'Malley. How when I was a young teacher in my country, an aging Irish farmer quoted Yeats to me and invited me to his house to witness the mating of his swans.

"He said they make love like that because they are angry with God for tricking them into making babies whose sole purpose is to replace their parents when they die."

" 'Thou wast not born for death, immortal Bird!/No hungry generations tread thee down.' "

"Keats," I said.

"We were reading his poem in school when my mother died. I thought I was to blame for her death. I was the hungry generation that had tread her down. She had centered her life on me. Everything for me. I had never stopped to think what it had cost her to send me to the best schools in Jamaica, to buy paint and brushes for me when she hardly had money to buy a dress for herself. All I thought of then was me, me, me. The world was me."

"Teenagers think that way, Marguerite. You were no exception."

"Yes, I know that. In my head, I know that. Not in my heart,"

"Your mother would have been proud of you today. Look what you have made of yourself." I turned her around to face me. "Look at yourself, Marguerite. You've raised a son in college, you have a master's degree, you teach in college, your work is exhibited in an art gallery, you were honored at the university in Jamaica. You are going to be a major art force. Marguerite, the world's greatest artist!"

She laughed and brushed me away. "I didn't mean to sound sorry for myself."

"Everybody needs to feel sorry for themselves every now and then."

"Well," she said, "at least we don't have the problem of the swans. We can make love without rage. My eggs are all used up."

"But not my sperm."

She laughed again. "Your sperm better be if you plan to be with me."

"Poetry. Pure poetry." I grabbed her.

We made love on the floor of the room that was also her studio. It was gentle sex. Lighthearted sex. When my climax came it rippled through me like a babbling stream tumbling across smooth pebbles. It left my body limp, loose, relaxed. Marguerite rolled on top of me and buried her head in my shoulder. We slept that way for more than an hour. I woke with the sun blazing down on my head from the skylight. Refreshed.

"Do you want to see my work?"

Marguerite had woken up before me. She was opening the wooden doors to the closet where she stored her work. She had put on a short white silk kimono and had pulled her hair in a plait behind her head. She seemed to me at that moment child, mother, virgin, lover. An innocence wrapped in the years that had deepened the furrows between her eyes and set an expression around her mouth that spoke of her determination, her tenacity, her endurance. Now in the sunlight, only hours since I had traced the map of her body, traveled across each inch, remembered, I saw lines around her mouth I had not seen before, lines clouded by my excitement in seeing her again, my joy, my ardor for her. Now I saw them and I loved her for them.

She pulled out her paintings and drawings and lined them against the wall, witnesses of her sacrifice. What a toll her marriage had exacted from her art! They were stunning, more beautiful than the ones I had seen in the art gallery. More moving.

"I haven't shown these yet," she said. "I call this collection Memories."

The images in the paintings before me were vivid, sharp, the details drawn out as if they had been in front of her when she painted them. One was of the sea, the beach shaded by sea grape trees and coconut fronds, two of the open market in Kingston. These were the ones that struck me most. I had known such market scenes. Middle-class black women, the new bourgeois of the decolonized countries, their bodies rigid with a newly acquired superiority and an insecurity they could not disguise, standing in front of vendors, the farmers from the countryside, who sat on wood stools, piles of ground provisions and bright colored fruit in front of them, their faces expressionless, blank, devoid of any emotion. These women, face facing face, I had often thought forced the observer to question ordinary notions of freedom and oppression.

"I didn't know you went back so often," I said.

"To Jamaica? Only twice, and the second time was when I returned last week."

"These are so accurate. One would think you painted them there."

She turned her head from one side to the other, reexamining them. "I never forgot those faces," she said.

There were three other paintings, all of women, one older than the other two. Like Marguerite, they all had the same brown skin, the same dark thick hair and high cheekbones, but their eyes were fierce, combative. I remarked as much to Marguerite.

"My mother, my aunt, my grandmother. They were daughters of the Maroons," she said.

I knew what she meant. The Africans of the resistance in Jamaica. The slaves who revolted. The ones who hid in the underground caves and plotted uprisings. But these black women did not look like Africans, not those from the west coast of Africa, where the Europeans made their raids on human flesh. The color of their skin was too light, the curls in their hair too loose.

"They look different," I said.

"My great-grandfather was Portuguese. He married an African."

I turned away abruptly from the paintings when she said that. Later she would rebuke me and I would know she had not missed the coldness that had steeled my eyes. But I had seen the relics of Portuguese brutality in East Africa—in Angola, a country torn apart by civil wars, wasted by greed and selfishness. I did not want to know the woman I loved had Portuguese blood.

"Did your husband see these?" I drew her attention back to the paintings of the market vendors.

"No, none of them. I did them all after I left him."

"He was a stupid man to lose you."

"No, he was quite ordinary. An average man. He thought I worked to augment his income. He saw my art as a ticket to a paycheck. Once I was teaching, once I had a real job, he didn't see any point in my doing any more paintings than were necessary for me not to get fired. He didn't understand that I worked for our food and shelter, yes, but mostly to buy canvases and paint and brushes. Mostly to free myself from worrying about money so I could paint. I am the classic example, I suppose. I teach so I can paint and draw. I don't paint and draw so I can teach. Harold did not understand that. He tried to make me feel guilty. I was inadequate as a wife, he said. A wife would cook dinner, a wife would campaign with her husband, a wife would entertain his friends, a wife would be available. I could do those things some of the time but not all of the time. I was miserable. Eventually I began to resent him."

I was not unsympathetic. I had come close to making the same mistake. More than once I had felt threatened by her devotion to her art, a commitment, I feared, that could replace me in her heart. Still, I judged him.

"He deserved your resentment," I said.

"Maybe not. He didn't ask of me more than another man would."

"He didn't love you," I said.

"In his own way he did."

"It was not enough. A man who loves you wants you to be happy even if it costs him time away from you." I did not have the grace to feel embarrassed by the irony of my words.

"Harold did his best."

"You say that like you feel sorry for him."

"I didn't love him. Maybe I never loved him."

"You married him."

"A man deserves to be loved. Everybody deserves to be loved. Harold knew I didn't love him. I say he resented my art, but I think that if he thought I loved him he would not have resented it as much."

She was sitting on the floor, her legs crossed into each other, looking blankly at the bay.

"You can't blame yourself, Marguerite, for not loving someone," I said.

"No, but I can blame myself for being with someone when I loved someone else."

I put my hand under her chin and turned her face to mine. Her eyes were dripping tears.

"Oh, Marguerite, I'm so sorry. So sorry." I sank my face in the thickness of her hair.

"I married him to forget you. When he touched me, it was you I was thinking of."

I rocked her back and forth against my body.

"At the beginning I could only bear going to bed with him if I thought it was your lips I kissed, your arms that embraced me, your legs wrapped around mine."

In the beginning it had been so for me, too, and even later, in spite of my contentment with Nerida. Many times it was Marguerite I thought of when I made love to Nerida, when I held her.

"I will never leave you, Marguerite. Never. Nothing will ever part me from you. You are my wife now. You were always my wife."

She did not ask me what I meant, nor did I ask myself. It was a statement I made that felt right, that felt good. I did not want to examine it, put it under a microscope to raise doubts, to ask the question, how? How could she be my wife when Nerida was my wife? How could I make her my wife when I was a Christian? How could I remain a Christian when I wanted to keep Nerida as my wife?

I did not probe. I did not analyze. I did not remind myself I had already found the answer to the question that had haunted me from the moment I first fell in love with her—when I was young and she was young. The question that stayed with me until without consciousness, without an awareness that I knew the answer, I pushed her into voicing it for me.

I did not remind myself that in the days after the deaths of my firstborn son, my firstborn daughter, I knew that thousands of years of culture, of a way of life, of a system of beliefs, had not been wiped away, eradicated from my soul. I knew that in spite of the missionaries, I was African, my view of family was African, and as an African I felt no contradiction in my soul, no conflict in having her as my wife and Nerida, too.

I did not remind myself of this because I did not want to remember the consequence of my acceptance of this. I did not want to remember that I believed then that I was to blame for the tragedy that followed. I did not want to remember that I believed it was my ingratitude, my hubris, that caused my son to be killed, my daughter not to be born.

I had tried afterwards to live the Christian life, the monogamous married life, yet still I desired Marguerite. Yet still I loved her. Now I would not probe. I would not analyze. In my dream had not my dead children loved Marguerite? I saw them holding her hand, smiling at her, loving her. Surely our love was not the cause of their deaths. It was their fate, as Marguerite had said to me, to die when they died, for my wife to be crossing the street when she did. I accepted the words that came from my mouth: *You are my wife.* I accepted them as my reality, and so did Marguerite.

We began calling each other husband and wife soon after that. It was not something we had planned, agreed upon beforehand. It happened. And it felt natural. The way it was supposed to be.

We agreed we would see each other as often as we could while I was in New York. She did not ask me when that last day would be. I did not tell her. We established a routine that felt right for us. I would meet her after her classes on Monday and Wednesday nights. We would go out to dinner and she would spend the night with me in the city. On the other days of the week, we called each other twice, in the morning when we woke, and at night before she went to bed. On Friday nights I took the train to her house and stayed the weekends with her. Sometimes on the weekend, while she painted, I sat at her table working on speeches I had been asked to give at rallies that were mushrooming all over New York in support of Mandela and the end of apartheid. Most had been organized by black political groups in Harlem, some by university students. Even the mayor's office called our delegation.

Sometimes I discussed strategy with my teammates on the phone. I did not speak in English when I spoke on the phone. I spoke in Housa or Mossi or in French, eventually only in Housa or Mossi unless I was forced to do otherwise. Marguerite had studied French. She was not fluent, but sometimes she understood. One day she joked that she knew what I had said and she would sell my secrets to the CIA.

"Would you do that to your husband?" I asked her.

"Of course. I'm a loyal naturalized American citizen."

I knew she was not serious. Still, more and more I found myself speaking in Housa or Mossi when I used the phone from her house, not because I thought Marguerite would betray me, but because I was a cautious man, a man who by habit had learned to watch his back. A diplomat by nature, Marguerite would remind me.

Often when I was at Marguerite's we went for long walks along the edge of the bay when the tide was out. I knew that it was safe for me to walk with her there. No one had followed me on the train to Long Island. Bala Keye seemed content to have dinner with me twice a week. Those were the evenings I did not spend with Marguerite. He did not question me about the weekends, and I lulled myself into believing he had plans of his own that did not include me. That I had been mistaken about that long second when his eyes locked into mine as I ran out of the florist shop clutching the red roses I had bought for Marguerite. Such was my desire to be with Marguerite that I let myself think this way.

I convinced my office to give me a cellular phone. That way, I said, I could keep in touch with my colleagues wherever I was. Nobody could tell where you were from a phone call unless they wanted to track you.

I felt safe, secure in Marguerite's home. I held her hand when we took our walks. Often I put my arm around her waist. At times she rested her head against me, her hand draped across my back. I had never walked this way with Nerida, not even when I courted her. I liked the closeness I felt walking with my arm around Marguerite. I liked the intimacy.

One morning, while I was shaving, Marguerite came into the bathroom. She wanted to take a shower but when she saw me, she turned to leave. I pulled her into the shower with me. "That is how it begins," I said.

The second I said those words, I thought of Nerida. It had started this way between Nerida and me five years ago—innocently—with no intention on my part, conscious, that is, never to sleep in the same bedroom with her again. But I was cautious now. I knew now a word, a simple act, could trigger off a habit that could be irreversible. I knew it could take an insignificant thing, such as an inconvenience, a minor discomfort. *A crowded bathroom.* I did not want an inconvenience or a minor discomfort to set in motion a series of actions that could culminate in the day when Marguerite would never want to take a shower with me, hold my hand, let me kiss her on the bone on the back of her neck. I was just beginning to know, just beginning to love these intimacies. I did not want to lose them.

But it was not a habit formed to avoid an inconvenience, a minor discomfort that had led Nerida to refuse me her bed. I had voiced my fear to Ibrahim Musima: Perhaps Nerida had not lost interest in sex, only in sex with me.

I had told myself that I left her bed because I loved her—because I did not want to disturb her, rouse her from her sleep. But it was a dream I had had of Marguerite that had awakened me, that had forced me to consciousness drenched in sweat. And it was Nerida's presence, solicitous, sympathetic, caring, that had driven me away.

Nerida must have seen the revulsion in my eyes, my disgust as I flinched from her touch. Perhaps more. Perhaps she had heard me speak Marguerite's name. She had told me that sometimes I talked in my sleep. Mumbled, she said. She could never discern the words. Perhaps she had discerned this single one. Perhaps Marguerite's name had slipped out of my dreams clear, distinct. Intact.

Nerida was the woman I had married, the woman I loved, the

woman who bore my children, yet I did not want her near me. I did not want to feel her breath on my skin when I was yanked from my dreams of Marguerite. Perhaps this is what she knew. Perhaps she knew I wanted to be alone with my dreams. That it was *she* I did not want.

When I said I would sleep in another room for her sake, she did not oppose me. But afterwards, weeks after I had taught myself to camouflage my revulsion, to hide it with apologies, regrets that I had awakened her, she refused me. Perhaps she refused me because she did not trust me. Because she did not believe I would make love to her with my whole heart, with my soul free to love her. We became partners after that, friends. Parents to our children. It was an arrangement that seemed to suit her. It did not always suit me.

"This is how it begins," I repeated to Marguerite. "It takes only the first time."

I pulled Marguerite into the shower with me. Water cascaded down my head and into my eyes. I shut them. Marguerite teased me.

"Open them, Oufoula. Open them. Didn't you learn how to swim with your eyes open under water?"

26

Marguerite had not come out of her marriage unscathed. She had developed a problem in her stomach that began soon after her divorce. It started with spasms that rippled across her stomach and which, she said, seemed to cut off the supply of blood to her head and leave her feeling as if her head were stuffed with cotton balls.

"The doctor told me that I had developed mechanisms for survival when I was married. After my divorce, when I did not need them anymore, they unraveled. He described my intestines as twisted rubber bands that got tighter and tighter each time I put aside my painting to be the wife Harold wanted me to be. Now the twisted rubber bands are unraveling."

I would not have known about this if one night, when I was at her house, I had not felt her leave the bed and heard her footsteps fade into the kitchen. She came back to bed with a slice of bread in her hand.

"What is it?" I asked her.

"I have to keep something in my stomach at all times," she said. And she told me about her pain. She said that when it got worse, her doctor referred her to a gastroenterologist.

"He told me he had seen a lot of nuns with my problem. It took me a while to realize what he meant. And, of course, what he meant was that I needed to have sex. That's what men think about divorced women. If we had sex—and of course if we had stayed with our husbands in the first place, we would have had lots of sex—our problems would vanish. Maybe he was propositioning me."

I had thought of asking Marguerite if she was involved with anyone after her divorce. I thought the better of asking her now. If she was, it was over. I had to be satisfied with her silence.

The next time I felt her sit on the edge of the bed, I stopped her before she got up.

"I'll go," I said.

She tried to hold me back but I paid no attention to her. She was still protesting when I returned with the bread.

"I could have gotten it. You didn't have to go. I didn't want to wake you up."

I had said the same words to Nerida those nights when I woke from my dream, sweat pouring down my forehead. She did not have to get up. She did not have to mop my brow. She did not have to bring me water.

Now I said to Marguerite, "Do you think it's only women who want to serve the ones they love?"

This was what Nerida wanted. This was what I had denied her. This was why she knew I did not want *her* to comfort me. This was why she knew it was not *her* arms I wanted around me, not *her* lips I wanted on my mouth, not *her* body I wanted next to mine.

Marguerite, I knew, was quite capable of getting out of bed and walking the few feet from her bedroom to her kitchen. But I had served her. I had proven to her I loved her, in her terms. In women's terms.

I looked at the happiness spread across Marguerite's face and understood for the first time that it is the little things that count for women, not the big things. For women, love is expressed through sacrifice, the tiny small inconveniences they willingly put upon themselves for the sake of our happiness: the food they cook for us, the clothes they wash for us. They want us to measure these things not by their intrinsic value but by the sacrifices they entail. They had put our needs, our pleasures, before theirs. It is not the food, the clean clothes, they want us to appreciate. It is they themselves.

I had brought flowers for Marguerite that were not red roses; at other times perfume. Once a gold necklace, then diamond earrings. Nothing counted as much to her as that slice of bread, my willingness to get out of bed for her, to let her rest, to put myself in discomfort for her, to deny myself for her.

Marguerite sank into my arms, the slice of bread clenched between her fingers. I had denied Nerida this joy, the pleasure I now felt in having served Marguerite, in seeing in her eyes her gratitude, the reassurance of her love for me. Nerida must have felt rejected when I refused her offer of love. I must have caused her to doubt my love for her when I did not let her give me comfort, when I turned my back on her and left our bedroom.

There were other times when I experienced this kind of confidence that is only possible when the person you love not only allows you to express your love and devotion to her, but mirrors these same feelings for you in her eyes.

Once, when Marguerite spent the night with me in my apartment in Manhattan, she had to leave early to attend a faculty meeting the next morning. We had both forgotten to set the alarm on the clock the night before, so accustomed were we on such days to leisurely mornings together before I would have to leave for the UN, she for Long Island. It was late when we woke up. Marguerite riffled hastily through her overnight bag, flinging a skirt and blouse on the bed before dashing into the bathroom. I noticed immediately that the blouse was rumpled. I set up the ironing board and plugged in the iron. I was ironing her blouse when she came out of the shower. Marguerite could barely get the words out of her mouth to thank me, so choked was she with emotion.

"No one has ever done something like that for me. *Ever*," she said. "Look at you. My god, if your colleagues from the UN could see the distinguished Mr. Ambassador!" She wrapped her arms around my waist and hugged me tightly to her body as if she never would let go.

I must have looked odd, clad only in my underpants, hunched over the ironing board, all six foot two inches of me concentrating on getting the creases out of her blouse. Perhaps my colleagues would have laughed at me. They would have wondered if I had not gone soft. But I did not care. I was willing to go soft for Marguerite.

It is the little things, too, that count for men, but we do not use the measurements women use. We are territorial. Like the cheetah, we mark the boundaries of our possessions. A look, a touch, a word said unwisely that threatens to intrude, to encroach on the territory we marked is enough to unhinge us, to cause us to pull out our weapons.

I had loved to kiss the back of Marguerite's neck. I had considered it mine, along with the basin her waist made between her hip and her ribcage when she lay on her side next to me, along with the well that cradled her navel. Sometimes when we walked, I would rub my fingers on my spot on her neck, or push her hair aside when it was down and kiss her there. I loved to do that most—to move her hair and kiss my spot, though I loved to kiss it, too, when she wore her hair up in a ponytail or a chignon and bared her neck for me.

One evening, when I met her after her class, she told me that her husband had just touched her there. I did not think she knew the pain she caused me.

"Harold came to see me in my office," she said. "I was on the phone with my back to the door and I felt someone touching me on my shoulder. I waved the person away but I did not look back. I was in the middle of a conversation and I did not want to be disturbed. Then the person touched my neck and I turned around. It was Harold."

Marguerite could never have guessed the fire that flared through me then. I could only contain it with silence, so stony that she was forced to pity me.

"He asked me to have lunch with him," she said. "Of course, I said no. Of course, I did not accept."

It was only her refusal that calmed me, but I began to fear the dreams I would have when I had to leave her, when my mission was over in America and I had to return to Africa. Who would intrude on the territory I had marked?

27

There were times, frantic to lessen the distance that geography had put between us, I wanted to tell Marguerite all. Not of my years with Nerida, but all that had shaped me, all that made me into the man I was, all that had happened to me when I was a boy in Africa. I wanted her to know me, to understand me. I wanted to fuse my soul with hers.

I told her about my mother. I told her that my mother had died for love. She did not think my mother had killed herself. She did not think it was suicide.

"It was grief," she said.

I wondered what grief would cost me, how I would mourn her absence when I had to return to Africa. Would I be the same man I once was? Would my voice betray me? My eyes? Would I find myself remembering her when I sat at the table negotiating contracts for my country? Would my lips tremble, my eyes turn bloodshot red? I, of whom they said he kept his heart in his sleeves, his private self apart from his public self, who kept his personal thoughts, his personal feelings always out of reach of public scrutiny?

Marguerite said my mother's death was not a suicide. She had not killed herself. Grief had killed her. I knew then that the questions that had begun to trouble my sleep were troubling hers. She, too, was beginning to realize that it would not be long before I would be recalled to Africa. She, too, was beginning to fear the price our separation would impose on her. How would she withstand the pain? How would we? Would grief kill her, too? Kill me?

"How many years do you think we'll have left together?" she asked me one night. It was late. We had turned off all the lights. The moon was high in the sky above the bay. It had left a trail of silvery gold shimmering across the water. I was trying to lose myself in the water, in the shimmering light. I was trying to silence the questions in my head. I wanted to drown them, make them go away.

I have noticed this about water, when I am close to a large body of water—the sea, a lake, the river that runs through my country in Africa: it is easy for me to lose myself, to let my spirit drift, to merge myself into a oneness with it. Water is forgiving, compassionate, healing, comforting. Perhaps this is so because it awakens in us a lost memory, a memory we never recall with consciousness but that consoles us all the same. A memory of that first place of safety, of comfort, of forgiveness. Our mother's womb. The amniotic sac, where we swam free of worry, free of concern, protected. Perhaps we remember this, and that other Eden before the Ice Age, before we were forced to crawl on land in search of food. Marguerite had to dig her elbow into my chest to rouse me. I had already curled deep into the maternal arms of the bay in front of me.

"Do you think we have as much time left as we have already lost?"

I did not want to think of it—of parting from her, of returning to Nerida. Of being forced by grief to make choices I did not want to make. I loved Nerida. I loved my children. I loved my life in Africa.

"We will be together forever, Marguerite," I told her. "Forever."

But this time she wanted me to define forever.

"How many years?" she asked me. "Tell me."

I bargained. I told her a story. It distracted her. It diffused for a moment the moment we both knew we would have to face. It bought us time. It gave me a chance to tell her more, to tell her how my reinvention began, my conversion, when the missionaries came to my father's compound and took me. When my father did not stop them.

"I do not know how many years we have," I said to her, "because I do not know how many years old I am."

This was the story I told her. It was the truth. I told her that not only had the missionaries given me their god, they had given me time.

"I was in my second year in the mission school. One day the teacher walked into our class and asked us our age. He was an old Frenchman accustomed to giving orders and having them obeyed. None of us could answer him accurately. All of us were boys from the village. Our parents did not mark time like the Europeans. For them, birth, life, and death were part of the same cycle. They saw no value in recording any part of it.

"I think Europeans invented time to fool themselves into believing they can control time. Time eludes them anyhow. It stops them with death. They do not stop time. The people in our village did not try to stop time, to mark this or that birth as if they could put a fix on time, prevent it from slipping away from them.

"The old Frenchman wanted to know if our parents had stopped time for us, if they had marked our birth, and when we could not answer him, he stopped time for us. The next morning when we came to our class, he divided us into two groups by height. I was in the taller group. The boys in the taller group were given the older age. We were told we were eight, the boys in the other group were seven. Then one by one we were given the month and day of our birth. I was given April. April twenty-fifth, nineteen thirty-four. That is the date on my passport. I do not know the day I was born."

Marguerite did not calculate years after that. She did not try to add and subtract, to compare the years we had lost with years we could have together. But I knew the question still remained in her heart: What would happen to us when I had to leave New York? We did not have the courage to face the answer.

28

There was much else I told Marguerite without telling her of my life with Nerida. She had asked me how I came to be a diplomat. I told her it was an accident of fate. One day I had found myself in the presence of the president of the country when he needed an interpreter. I did not tell her that the president was the father of my wife or that when he gave me my first appointment he made me a present of his daughter.

"Accident or not, it was good that it happened. Diplomats don't get as passionate about causes as you do," she said to me. "They don't get as committed."

I had shared with her the papers I had written about South Africa, about the torture of men like Mandela who fought for freedom. Twice she had come to hear me speak. They were on the days she taught at night. I did not want her to interrupt her time for painting because of me, but she wanted to know more, to know if apartheid was practiced in other parts of Africa.

"Tell me about Angola," she said to me one day.

It was the day I had noticed the prints of my fingers on her hips. I had held her there the night before when we made love.

I was already lying on top of her and could feel my desire for her mounting, but she stopped me. "Stop, stop." She wanted to try another way. She pushed her hands against my chest, pressed her knees into my stomach and turned.

I must have grabbed her hips roughly, squeezed her skin with my fingers when I entered her. I had already arrived at a state where it was too late for me to be gentle.

Yet if I had held Nerida as I had held Marguerite, there would be no marks on Nerida's flesh.

When Marguerite lay beside me I saw the prints my fingers had left on her hips. Her blood had broken through the vessels. It had stained her brown skin red, then blue.

For no reason, except for the fact that we had been talking of my boyhood days in the mission school, I remembered a fight I once had with a French boy there. He was older than I and bigger, and he had started the fight. I had thrown him some blows, but he had beaten me viciously. I bled profusely where he had struck me. He was only bruised. Yet in the places where I had struck him, his skin turned red. The next day it was blue and I was the one who was punished.

When I saw the marks I had left on Marguerite's skin, I remembered this, and I remembered at the same time that Marguerite had told me her great-grandfather was Portuguese.

"Tell me about Angola," she said.

Her head was lying on my chest. I was thinking of the strokes the headmaster had cut across my back. I was cruel. "Your people," I said, "were among the most vicious. They have put their claws into Angola like crabs and ripped the country to shreds."

Her head barely escaped striking the metal edge of the bed rail when I pushed her off me.

Marguerite told me later that she had not missed the coldness that crossed my eyes when she first told me her great-grandfather was Portuguese. She said I had turned my back on the portraits of her mother, her aunt, and her grandmother as if they had offended me.

"My great-grandfather married an African," she said. "What does that make her? What does that make me?"

Marguerite would ask me more questions like these. She would stretch my world. She would teach me that life is complex: the serpent never leaves the Garden. Or the apple. Each choice we make contains its antithesis—something we hate, detest. Something that chafes against our smug view of ourselves.

I loved Marguerite. I would have to accept that I loved a woman through whose veins ran the blood of a people whose cruelty I abhorred.

I wanted Marguerite. I would have to accept that in wanting her, loving her, I was not who I was thought to be: a man to be admired for his fidelity to his wife, his Christian adherence to monogamy. A man whose reputation for honesty and loyalty was built in no small part on this: He could not be seduced no matter the temptress.

I did not want to leave Nerida. I would have to accept that in staying with her, I compromised myself, I compromised Marguerite. I compromised all that was good in the passion that bound us, in the passion that liberated us.

29

Our mission was going well. There were rumors that de Klerk would free Mandela and declare the end of apartheid by Christmas. We had good reason to believe that these were more than rumors. In October, de Klerk ordered the release of Walter Sisulu and seven political prisoners who had been imprisoned with Mandela on Robben Island for their involvement in the outlawed African National Congress that had fought so valiantly for the liberation of South Africa. Not long after that, de Klerk opened the beaches that had been banned for black South Africans and put an end to the humiliating Reservation of Separate Amenities Act that had imposed the same kind of segregation that Jim Crow had legalized in the southern states in America. My team rejoiced. I did, too, but my heart was heavy with the knowledge that my time in New York was coming to an end.

I spent most of my days and nights now with Marguerite, canceling any appointment that was not directly related to my work for South Africa. I stayed with Marguerite even on those days she had set aside for her art, telling myself she would have time enough when I was gone. She did not object. Though we had yet to speak of that time when I would leave, she, too, had heard the good news about South Africa. She, too, knew our time was short.

The men on my team said I seemed distracted. That my mind strayed. Once, in the middle of a discussion, I left the room abruptly. I had remembered that Marguerite told me she liked cashews. I wanted to bring her cashews when I came to her house that night. I wanted to get them before I left the UN. I did not want to miss the train to Long Island. I did not want to be late.

I felt Bala Keye's eyes on me when I came back to the room, a brown paper bag clutched in my hand.

Be careful, Oufoula, his eyes seemed to say to me. I know your secret.

It was that evening, the evening I brought cashews for Marguerite, that she told me that she had spoken to Catherine.

"What? Here in New York?"

"She's moved to Canada," she said.

"Why didn't you tell me?"

"Catherine said she wasn't sure you liked her."

I was sitting opposite Marguerite at the table. She had made dinner for me. Steak. It was the red meat I most enjoyed. She had bought it at the butcher shop, not at the supermarket. I saw the plain white paper wrapping stuffed in the kitchen garbage can. I had walked out of an important meeting to get cashews for her. She had put aside her paintings to go to the butcher for me.

Private lives spilling into public lives: we had allowed personal feelings to affect the work we did, the work we had to do. We did not care. It did not matter to us that we had abandoned the safeguards we had constructed to protect ourselves. That I had abandoned the safeguard I had constructed after Mulenga, the caution I practiced after I understood the power of the passion that had taken my mother's life. Her lover's life. I was in love. We were in love. Love did not allow us to see much beyond ourselves. Love colored everything beyond ourselves so that we accepted the delusion: we could work, we could love each other. Our love would not hurt our work.

"Well, do you like her?" she asked me.

I could see tiny quivers gathering in the corners of her mouth. I did not know why they were there.

"Yes," I said. "Of course," I said.

"She does not think so. She said you did not answer her letter."

The time we had left together was too short for lies. I knew what letter she was talking about. It was a long time ago, but I remembered.

"Her husband was a brutal man," I said. "I did not know what he would do to her if he knew she had asked me for help. If he knew she had told me about him."

Marguerite studied my face. "Catherine warned me that there were cultural differences between us that I could never patch together. You are a macho man. Both of you are macho men."

"I didn't think you'd buy that stereotype." I said it with a sneer.

"Stereotype? I am calling you what you are."

"Am I a macho man? Have I treated you like a macho man? Can you compare me with Catherine's husband?"

She was too angry to answer me. She got up from the table and walked toward the kitchen.

"It would have made no difference if I had spoken to him," I said to her retreating back, already regretting my sneer, my foolhardy harshness. "I could have made things worse between them."

"How much worse than losing her child?" She turned and faced me. There was no love for me in her eyes. She knew what she had said. She knew it would hurt me. She knew she would trigger memories of the children I had lost—my children who had died.

"Catherine said you were an ambitious man. A cautious man. You weighed the consequences of all you did. Even the friendships you made."

"Do you believe that, Marguerite?"

"She said you made no enemies. She said people like you because you make it your business to make them like you. You cultivate them like plants. You water them. You court them."

"And you believe her?"

"Did you court me, too, Oufoula? Was I a plant you nurtured, too, Oufoula?"

"Think about what you're saying, Marguerite. Words count. They poison the air."

"Was I R and R to you?"

"R and R?"

"Rest and recreation. Did you need someone to screw when you came to New York? Is that why you looked me up?"

"Stop this, Marguerite. What has got into you?"

"Well, did you?"

"Look in your heart, Marguerite. Does your heart tell you that what you're saying is true? I love you, Marguerite. I am in love with you. I have been in love with you from the very first moment I saw you. I have never stopped loving you."

She sat down. The quivers around her mouth intensified. Tears welled in her eyes.

"You know what I said is true. With your head, your heart, and your soul, you know that." I came close to her.

"Catherine said that if you were Adam you would never have taken the apple from Eve." She wiped away a tear that had dripped silently down her cheek. "She said you would have saved the whole human race from sin." She laughed. It was a bitter laugh.

"I would have taken the apple if you had given it to me," I said.

I think it was the seriousness of my tone that stopped her, that changed the colors in her eyes, that took the edge off her anger.

"Catherine said when you go back to Africa, you'll be a diplomat again."

Those were the words we had avoided, the words we had not wanted to speak. *When you go back to Africa.* We were afraid of what would happen to us when my time in New York was up.

I could not look at her. "I do not know what I will do when I go back to Africa," I said.

That night we did not make love. We hardly slept. We lay quiet in each other's arms, shutting out the words we did not want to hear, stilling them on our tongues.

"I didn't mean to hurt you," she said.

"I know."

"I know you loved your children."

"I know."

"I know you miss them."

"I know."

But she would become angry with me again. Again, she would say words to me she would regret. She would accuse me of not loving her. She would know as she said those words that all she said was false. But she did not have the courage yet to say the words she wanted to say, the words I feared.

"Do you think that what we are doing is a sin?"

This was the first question Marguerite asked me when we woke up that morning. I was not ready for it.

"Oh, Marguerite," I said, and pulled her to me.

"Well, do you?"

"Marguerite, please."

She pushed my arms away and swung her legs off the bed. I shut my eyes and turned to the other side. I could hear her shuffling the papers in the large bag she carried to her classes.

"It says here in the Bible, 'Thou shalt not commit adultery.'"

She climbed back on the bed and hovered over me. "Do you see it? Did you read it? Here. Here in the Bible."

I opened my eyes. Her face was clouded, dark. Her breasts hung inches above my face. I wanted to touch them, to caress them, to lick my tongue on the dark circles around her nipples. These were the breasts I had loved, I had kissed. I had drunk from these chalices, I had received her sacrament of love. Now these breasts were my accusers, pointing their fleshy globules at me, condemning me.

She straddled me. She dug her knees into the mattress on either side of me. She waved the Bible above me. It grazed my nose.

"Are we sinners? Tell me, Oufoula, are we sinners?"

I grabbed her wrists, held them still, bound them in one hand,

and with the other I took the Bible away from her. "This is not the place," I said.

"Why isn't it the place?" She struggled with me.

I reached past her. "Leave it there, Marguerite." I put the Bible on the table next to the bed and loosened my hold on her.

She lurched for the Bible again. "Why can't I have it?"

I pulled her back to the bed with me.

"Give it to me." She flung out her arms and struck me. "Give it back to me, Oufoula." She struck me again.

"Stop, Marguerite." I bound her hands again.

"Because it's too holy? Is that it? It's too holy to be on the bed with us. Tell me, Oufoula, is it too holy to be on the bed with us because we are sinners?"

"Marguerite, stop."

"I want to know what you think, Oufoula."

"What is it you want to know, Marguerite?"

"I want to know if you think what we are doing is a sin."

I released her. "I love you, Marguerite."

"Is it a sin, Oufoula?"

"I adore you, Marguerite." I was kissing her now, clasping her face between my hands, kissing her eyes, her nose, her cheeks, her mouth. "No more. I adore you. I adore you."

She struggled some more. I held her tightly until she was spent and her head fell in the well of my shoulder. "I found the Bible in your apartment," she said. Her words were muffled against my neck. "It was in the drawer of the table next to your bed." She looked up at me. "Do you read it?"

"Yes," I said.

"Do you take it with you wherever you go?"

"When I travel," I said.`

"Do you read it every day?"

"When I get a chance," I said.

It was a habit formed out of gratitude in the mission school when I wanted to please those who had saved me from the rejection of an indifferent father, the shame of a dishonorable mother. I had followed their rituals; their rituals became my rituals, habits not easily shaken. I had become accustomed to sleeping with my Bible next to me. I took it wherever I went. I took it with me to New York.

"But you won't read it before you go to bed with me? Is that it, Oufoula?"

I kissed her again. "No more, Marguerite."

"Because you know you are breaking God's commandment. Is that why you don't read it before you go to bed with me?"

"I am in love with you, Marguerite."

I reached to kiss her mouth again. She turned her head away from me. "Don't you see the contradiction?"

"People in love don't look for contradictions, Marguerite. I had you once and then I lost you. I won't lose you again."

"You have a wife."

"I am in love with you."

"What about your wife?"

"I am in love with you, Marguerite."

I seemed to have convinced her, or perhaps it was simply exhaustion that made her end her fight with me, but I knew this would not be the last time we would have such a quarrel. Our days were becoming fewer. We were frantic. We were desperate. We needed answers. We needed to know what next. *What next, after I left?* We were afraid of what next. She was afraid to ask me more questions about my wife. I did not want to answer questions about my wife.

I had said to her I would be with her forever. I had not wanted to know the consequence. I wanted only the thought of forever with her in my mind—forever, nothing else.

Before she stirred out of my arms again, she whispered to me, "Will we go to Hell?"

I had been taught the answer to that question in my mission school. It did not seem right now. It did not seem possible that what we had done, what we were doing, what I hoped we would continue to do, could displease a merciful God. And yet I knew it was one of His commandments. She was right. I could not read my

Bible when she was in the bed next to me. I could not have it visible, witness to my love for her. I hid it in my drawer. Had habit infiltrated my conscience? But I did not feel we had sinned. Nothing in my soul told me we had sinned.

In the days that followed, Marguerite was tortured by guilt that was brought on by anxiety, our refusal to confront the reality of the diminishing days, the little time we had left together. It gave her no respite, no release.

"I left Harold," she said to me one morning, "because he had an affair."

"You left Harold, you told me, because you did not love him."

"Yes, but I would have stayed with him if he had been faithful to his vows."

"You said you would have stayed with him if you loved him."

"I would have loved him if he had kept his word. I kept mine."

"Marguerite, you did not love him. You could not have made yourself love him."

"Not the way we love each other. But I could have loved him enough for a marriage. Marriage," she said, "is not about passion. It's about love. Security. If he had not broken the contract he had made with me, I could have had that kind of love for him. I wanted to love him when I married him. Lasting love is in the will, not in the heart. I could have willed myself to love him."

She could have been speaking of my marriage to Nerida. I did not love Nerida when I married her. There was no passion between us. There never was. But I came to love her. I loved her kindness to me, her commitment to me, her loyalty. No matter what happened in my life, Nerida was there for me. She was my comfort, my support, the net to hold me if I fell. She had given me children. A family. How could I not love her? Yes, I agreed with Marguerite, marriage is not about passion. It is about the willingness to love. It is about commitment, security. I did not want to lose the security I had with Nerida, the reassurance that the ground would never shift beneath my feet, that nothing would change.

"We had been married only six months when Harold was unfaithful to me," Marguerite was saying to me now. "He admitted it after I found out and confronted him with it. For eighteen years I lived with the pretense I had forgiven him, forgotten about it. But I never did. Sometimes I actually made myself believe the lie that I could not love him because he did not appreciate my art. But that was not the reason I could not love him, I could not bend my will to make myself love him. It took me eighteen years to admit to myself that I never would, that his betrayal of me had shattered our marriage irrevocably.

"Marriage is about fidelity, not just sexual fidelity. It is about trust. It is about believing in the word of your spouse. I give you my word that I will honor the terms of our contract, you give me your word you'll do the same. When that word is broken, the contract is broken, the marriage is broken. You may continue to live together, you may be friends, lovers, parents, but without that word you are not husband and wife.

"If there is any advice I have for my son, it is that no matter what he does, he must be careful not to push Humpty Dumpty over the wall. A woman will take a lot for a man. You can push her close to the edge. But push her over and she cracks, and all the king's horses and all the king's men cannot put her together again. My marriage was cracked. It was cracked for me in the first six months when Harold had his first affair."

Did I crack my marriage, too, with my dreams—the days I sat morose, huddled in my armchair, with the books Marguerite had bought for me, the hours I spoke to no one? Nerida kept the children away from me those days when I wrapped myself in my memories of Marguerite. "Baba is in his mood," she would say. Did it crack then? Or was it when I ran from her bed, my body trembling for Marguerite, my eyes burning with my longing?

Perhaps Marguerite was right. Perhaps the crack I had caused in my marriage was irreparable. Perhaps it was too late to make it whole again, to be a husband to Nerida, not just partner, friend, parent with her of our children.

The simplest of happenings, the most ordinary of events became lessons in morality for Marguerite in those days, allegories that held larger personal meaning for us, revelations we both understood yet discarded.

Soon after Marguerite had turned a child's nursery rhyme into a cautionary tale for my marriage, she would tell me another story and I would tell her another, and our stories would expose our hypocrisy, would reveal our fear of acting on the truth. We spoke the words of things we would not do, could not do, without ending our happiness, without making it impossible for us to remain as we were.

Marguerite had taken her car to the mechanic. She came back with a Sunday sermon for us both, a homily we knew too well, one we had passed on to others. A lesson in integrity and honesty we both professed to practice.

I had already told her my story, the story of an old man from my village who was renowned for his honesty. His job was to calculate the exchange of monies between my country and the one that bordered us. He was a simple man, a man without much schooling, but he had a gift for numbers. He could calculate fifty digits in his head, add and subtract them without paper. He was in charge of the small outpost on the border of my village. One day, when I was no more than twelve, I bought something in his shop. A piece of cloth for my aunt. I had saved the money I had earned from sweeping the floors of the mission school. I was proud to be able to buy this gift for my aunt, but I was prouder of the fact that I was first in my class in math. I excelled not only in arithmetic, but also in geometry and algebra. When I gave the man the French currency I had, I knew exactly how much it was worth in exchange for the currency we used for trading with the neighboring villages. But he gave me more than I thought he should. Principled, full of integrity, I argued with him. He stood his ground. He would not take back the money.

I thought it was his pride. He did not want to look foolish before a schoolboy, but I could do nothing to change his mind. Later, I found out I was wrong. The rate of exchange had gone up that morning. He had known that and he was too honest to cheat me.

Still, I insisted on giving him the money. I wanted to reward him for his honesty. It was a virtue I prized.

I told that story to Marguerite and she shared my awe of the man.

"There should be more people in the world like him," she said.

We both believed we were among those few.

Marguerite's story about her car mechanic was similar to mine. She had paid for the service on her car with her American Express card. When she came home, she realized that the mechanic had made a mistake. He had undercharged her by a hundred dollars. She wanted to return the money.

"He was a white man from the North Shore where the rich people lived. He couldn't believe a black woman was challenging him. I don't know what baffled him more—that I was black and could count better than he could, or I was black and was honest enough to tell him I owed him money.

"I don't think he wanted to see me after that. I offered to bring him the hundred dollars. He refused to accept it. He said he would take the loss. It was his fault, his carelessness."

We were hypocrites, Marguerite and I, full of self-righteousness and pride for our honesty and integrity, but all the time we felt the tension between us, the truth hanging over us like a guillotine. We would have to run to save ourselves. Something had to happen to spare us. If we stayed where we were, the guillotine would fall down on our necks and chop off our heads.

Then something did happen, but it did not spare us. It forced us to confront the truth, to see ourselves as we were: so desperate to be with each other, so terrified that we could lose each other, we were willing to lie to ourselves and to each other, to do anything to avoid the moment, the choice that was always inevitable, that was always unavoidable, that was the consequence of our human condition: We cannot have it all. One or the other. The apple or the Garden.

Ten days before I was scheduled to leave, Nerida phoned me. She wanted to come to New York. She wanted to hear me speak at

a rally. She wanted to be in the thick of the excitement that was
bubbling up in New York. Mandela was going to be free, she was
certain of it. We were certain of it. She wanted to be present in the
making of that great historical moment.

It was Bala Keye who had put those thoughts in her head. I had
no proof, but there was no doubt in my mind. It was he who had
told Nerida to come. He had seen me run to the train with red
roses in my hand. He had seen me bring back a brown paper bag
the day I walked out of a meeting in the middle of an important
discussion. He had seen my eyes stray, lose focus. He had had to
call my name three times once, when we were at dinner, before I
acknowledged him. My soul had drifted to Marguerite.

I did not try to dissuade her. I did not ask her to stay in Africa. I
knew she would guess the truth. She had figured out the truth
when I left her bed. She would know now I did not want her here
with me in New York. No excuse I could make—work, the pressure
to make certain nothing endangered the release of Mandela, the
little time I would have to spend with her—nothing I could say
would fool her, persuade her to believe otherwise.

"I can get a flight in two days," she said. "I called your office. It's
all arranged. Uncle took care of the details."

Bala Keye, the man who had guessed my secret.

I did not tell Marguerite that night that Nerida was coming, that
though there were just a few days left for us to be together, I could
not spend them with her. That she could not come back again,
here, to my apartment. That I could not wake up to see the mornings with her.

On the day Nerida arrived I did a stupid thing, a foolish and an
immature thing. A cowardly thing. My excuse was my desperation,
my fear of losing Marguerite, of losing Nerida.

I was a young boy wanting to bury his head in the sand like an
ostrich. The storm would have passed when I looked up again.
Everything would have settled into place. Nerida would still be my
wife; Marguerite, the woman I loved, the woman I had begun to
call my wife.

234ELIZABETH NUNEZ

So, bargaining for a stay, I thought. So, deluding myself that I could forever postpone a decision I would have to make, I thought.

"Your colleague is here," I said to Marguerite.

I had left her house that morning and had said nothing to her. Nothing about Nerida's imminent arrival. Nothing, not even when we planned I would meet her at the theater that evening.

I was at the UN when I called her.

"My colleague?" she asked me. Unsuspecting Marguerite. Marguerite who did not want to know what I had to tell her.

"Yes, your colleague."

"I don't know any colleague of mine that you know."

"Think, Marguerite."

"A colleague you know?"

"Think."

"Who?"

I heard the question stretch to a pause, and then quietly she acknowledged the truth.

"Your wife?"

Her voice was soft. Gentle. There was no accusation in it, no condemnation.

"She's coming tonight," I said.

"Did you just find out?"

"No," I confessed, shame forcing the truth from me at last. "I've known it for two days."

My words traveled without sound the distance to her heart. When she spoke to me again there was the same compassion, the same forgiveness in her voice as there was when I made her say what I was too much of a coward to say: that it was my wife who had arrived. My wife who was the colleague.

"It must have been hard for you to tell me."

"Marguerite, you must believe me, I love you."

I wanted to tell her that nothing had changed. That everything was the same. I wanted her to know I adored her.

"I know you do," she said, but her voice was sad, lifeless.

"I will call you, Marguerite. Tonight, no matter what. I love you, Marguerite."

No matter what.

When she put down the phone those were the words that drummed in my head. *No matter what.* No matter the inevitable. No matter that I knew what was going to happen. What I could not stop from happening.

I waited for Nerida at the airport, my head pounding with the impossibility of it: of Nerida's head on the pillow where Marguerite had laid hers; of Nerida's body on the bed where Marguerite and I had made love; of Nerida's presence in the apartment that was Marguerite's and mine.

Marguerite had sat on the edge of the bathtub and watched me shave. I had seen her brush her teeth, swab cotton pads across her eyes and mouth, remove makeup from her face. The apartment was our home, our sanctuary. I had said I loved her there. She had said she loved me there. I could not imagine it. I could not make my mind conceive of Nerida in that place.

30

It is odd how strange familiar people can seem—different—as if you had never known them, as if you had never seen their secret parts, seen them after they had removed their clothes, their makeup, the things they did to camouflage their flaws, to disguise the parts of themselves they hid from the world; as if every movement of theirs, every expression, every curve and line of their bodies was not as known to you as your own, as indelibly printed on your memory as your own.

I had woken more than ten thousand mornings with Nerida, slept with her as many nights, and yet at the airport the person who broke away from the stream of passengers herded through the exit corridor from the plane was a stranger to me.

She hurried toward me, this person, wearing the traditional clothes of my country: the blue print sarong I had known Nerida to wear and that I loved, the matching headdress wrapped exquisitely around her head framing a face I knew, a face I loved, the same bright smile I had seen on Nerida's lips, the same graceful stride that was distinctly hers, the same polished black skin, wide eyes, purple-stained mouth. She was as beautiful as I remembered Nerida to be, the fullness of her hips and breasts not unattractive to me.

When Marguerite had asked to see a photograph of Nerida I had
not shown it to her, but it was not because I did not think Nerida
beautiful. It was because I wanted to protect her. Because I loved
her. Because in some foolish way I wanted to spare her the pain
she would feel if she knew that Marguerite was witness to how
time had not been as kind to her. It was because when I saw Marguerite, her body slim and youthful, her face as lovely as it was
when first I saw her, I felt embarrassed for Nerida.

I walked now toward this woman who was smiling at me, opening her arms to me, and I thought: I could not have made love to
this woman and have forgotten. I could not have lain naked next to
her and find it now so impossible to recall.

We talked in the car, this woman and I. We talked about my
work. We talked about Mandela. My lips formed words to answer
questions I barely heard, my mind struggling to quiet my heart, to
remind it that this was my wife, Nerida, the mother of my children,
the woman I loved, the woman who had loved me for more than
twenty-eight years.

I wore pajamas to bed that night. I had not worn pajamas to bed
once since I had been with Marguerite. I wore them now as armor,
as a barrier to separate myself from Nerida. They were still folded
and pressed as Nerida had instructed our housekeeper to do. I un-
folded them and put them on.

Nerida's eyes followed me, but her thoughts, had she guessed
the ones on my mind, remained silent on her tongue. My son had a
new girlfriend, she said. *National Geographic* had approached one
of my twin daughters to publish the photographs she had taken of
the last of the African nomads of the Sahara; my other daughter
was still at the top of her class. My son was, too. Nothing had
changed. My children were good, successful. They were still making us proud.

When I was in Africa, I boasted of my children. I would talk of
them for hours if my listener allowed me. I would tell of their
achievements, I would show off their photographs. Yet except for
that first evening when we had dinner together, neither Marguerite
nor I talked much about our children, though we loved them.

I think now that this is what happens to men like me, men past fifty, men who wake up to mornings that no longer offer the promise of challenge, men for whom the slide down to familiar routes is inexorable, for whom domestic routines have become predictable. We make icons of our children, then. We kneel at their feet and worship them. They give meaning to our meaningless lives, purpose, when we look into the future and darkness beckons us: *Come. There is nothing left to conquer. Your victory days are over.*

We boast of our children, of the future they could give us, when the inevitability of that end terrifies us. We ward off the darkness with the light of their possibilities. We bore others with our incessant talk of them, even of our children who have disappointed us. For they, too, mask the truth we cannot face. They, too, can give us the illusion of vigor, of purpose, of meaning. They, too, can substitute for passion when passion has eluded us.

But I had passion now with Marguerite. I did not need an illusion, a substitute. I could set my children free. I could let them fly. Marguerite gave meaning to my life, purpose to my existence.

I listened to Nerida, thinking this. Thinking that perhaps this was the glue that held our marriage together. Thinking it was our son, it was our daughters. Thinking that this was our end. We had reached it. Thinking that I wanted more. I wanted passion, real passion, not a substitute, not an illusion. Thinking I did not know how I would be able to sleep next to her when it was Marguerite I longed for, how I could bear to have her body touch mine when it was Marguerite I desired, when it was she I wanted in bed with me. Thinking I did not know what I would do if Nerida wanted to make love to me.

But Nerida did not want to make love to me. She did not want me to make love to her. She wanted only what she had wanted in the last few years—my friendship. And she wanted to remind me that we shared a family. She wanted me to know I belonged to her.

Perhaps Bala Keye had advised her to do this—to speak to me about my children, to remind me that she was their mother. She was my wife. I was their father. I was her husband. I was bound to her by family, by tradition, by my love for Africa, by everything that was important to me. Yet my awareness of these ties, these obligations, did not lessen my love for Marguerite. I adored her. I was desperate for her.

I had called Marguerite from my cellular phone at the airport while I waited for Nerida. Our conversation was brief. We did not speak of Nerida. I told her I would take the train to see her the next evening. We both knew I could not stay the night.

But Nerida had plans for me the next evening. She told me of them in the morning. Bala Keye had arranged a dinner party for her. All the African ambassadors to the UN and their wives would be there, she said. She did not seem surprised when I told her that I did not know of these plans.

My life had been so different with Marguerite. In the past six weeks I had grown accustomed to intimate dinners at her home or in small restaurants in Manhattan. I had forgotten these spectacles. I had managed to excuse myself from them except for the cocktail parties, and even those I treated as extensions of my work. I used them for meetings to make connections that would be useful for my work, for my country. I rarely socialized beyond these obligations, and no one made demands on me. But I was now the husband of Nerida, the daughter of a president. There would be expectations.

I called Marguerite to tell her I could not be with her. Her voice was even quieter than it had been on the phone the night before.

"When do you think we can see each other?" she asked me.

"Tomorrow," I said.

Tomorrow was Saturday. I told her I would take the train to her house in the morning.

"I'll make lunch," she said.

But Saturday came and I did not have lunch with her. I could not. Bala Keye had arranged for Nerida and me to go with him to Washington. Jesse Jackson was speaking at a rally for Mandela that day. Nerida wanted to be there. It was impossible to refuse her.

Marguerite did not answer the phone when I called to tell her that I could not meet her for lunch. Like a coward I was grateful. Like a coward I left her the message I was afraid to deliver in person: that I had to go to Washington, that I had to accompany my wife. I did not think I could bear to hear the sadness in her voice, the doubt that was surely growing in her heart.

Answering machines have this usefulness. They give us reprieve when we lack the courage to face the response we know will bring us discomfort; worse, will cause us pain: sighs, tears we are responsible for, accusations we deserve. But there would be no tears from Marguerite, no accusations, only acceptance, an acknowledgment of the unspoken truth: that I could not go to lunch with her because I was with my wife and my wife had asked me to go with her to Washington.

The night I came back from Washington my dream of Marguerite returned again. I woke up with a start, my heart bounding in my chest.

"What? What?" Nerida sat up on the bed and put her arms around me.

I flinched from her touch.

"I have to get some air," I said.

Before she lay back down again, she asked me, "Is it the same dream, Oufoula?"

She did not wait for my answer. She shut her eyes and pulled the blanket over her head.

But it was not the same dream. I dreamt of Marguerite but I dreamt of her as she was with me now. I was holding her in my arms. She had raised her head to kiss me, but the moment our lips met she began to fade. Frantic, I tried to bind her to me, to hold her, but her body passed through my arms like a ghost and then vanished altogether. I woke up in terror.

I called Marguerite from the street, huddled against the wind in the marble doorway of a store on Fifth Avenue. It was two o'clock in the morning. I had on a pair of black slacks and a gray sweater. Over these, I wore my navy trench coat. I could have been a drug dealer with the phone on my ear, my back to the street, a thief or a common criminal. The police had profiles on men who looked like me, black men with dark skin seen in places they were not expected to be, at times that would have brought them there for one reason alone. No one would have believed I was an ambassador, that in parts of Africa I was a valuable man, that I was the head of a distinguished delegation of Africans who had come to the UN to secure the freedom of Mandela, the freedom of Black South Africa. But my safety and my reputation were insignificant to me now next to my need to speak to Marguerite, to hear her voice, to know she was alive. To know she was still mine.

Five weeks ago I would not have taken that chance. I would not have gone out late at night without my driver. But five weeks ago I had not fallen in love again with Marguerite. Five weeks ago I had been able to live without her. Now I could not imagine how I could.

"Oufoula. Where are you?" Despair tinged her voice, anxiety giving way to loss of hope.

"In Manhattan. In the street outside my apartment."

I heard her sigh.

"I woke up from a dream of you," I said. "I could not go back to sleep until I talked to you."

"I haven't been sleeping either," she said.

"I am miserable without you."

"I am suffering, too."

"I have to see you."

"Don't make any promises," she said, her voice breaking my heart.

"I couldn't do anything about today. Did you hear my message?"

"I was here when you called."

"Why didn't you pick up the phone?"

"It would have made no difference. You were still going to Washington."

"There were plans made I could not change."

"We had plans, too."

"Oh, Marguerite."

"I understand, Oufoula. I understood from the beginning. I knew the situation I was in. I knew how things would go."

"I'll be there tomorrow."

"Let's not make plans."

"I'll take the eight o'clock train."

"If you can."

"I'll be on it."

"I don't want to hope, Oufoula."

"I'll be there."

"I'm painting tomorrow. If you come, you come. If not, it won't matter."

But it mattered. It mattered to me and I knew it mattered to her. Her surrender frightened me. The sudden plunge my heart took to the pit of my stomach frightened me.

"Tomorrow," I said to her again. "Tomorrow."

31

Bala Keye had new plans for Nerida and me the next day. This time I did not let his plans interfere with mine. It was Sunday. I told Nerida I had important business to take care of. My mind was not calm enough to compose an excuse that would give the appearance of truth, that could quiet the questions I saw looming in her eyes: *Why Sunday? What is so important for you to leave me in the apartment alone Sunday?* I told her firmly I had to go and I left before her uncle arrived, before Bala Keye could unravel me with his eyes, with my duty, my obligations, my responsibilities.

Marguerite picked me up at the train station. In the car we did not speak. I did not touch her. Inside the house we ravished each other. I sucked her lips into my mouth. With one hand, I reached under her shirt for her breasts, and with the other, I slid my fingers into the waistband of her skirt. She fell to her knees on the floor.

There, in that narrow corridor between her kitchen and her bedroom, I ground myself into her. She cried out but she did not stop me. She raised her hips to me and pressed her hands into the small of my back. When my final shudders died, I lay on top of her, spent, drained, exhausted.

"Nobody needs to know," Marguerite murmured into my chest. "It is a sin only if she knows. If she gets hurt."

We began, then, to weave an intricate web of deceit, a web we designed because it made us feel good, made us feel righteous, because it assuaged our consciences, because we could use it to protect ourselves from the daggers that pricked our souls, the guilt that tortured us.

I offered her the salve we diplomats used when the truths we concealed did not allow us to sleep at nights. "Discretion," I said to her, "is the better part of valor."

She seized it and made us heroes.

"It takes courage to do what we are doing," she said. "Sacrifice, also. I want to let the world know I love you. I want to shout it out in the streets. But I won't. We won't. For her sake, we won't."

When I got ready to leave her house she examined me, searched my clothes for strands of her hair, smelled the back of my neck for the scent of her body. But she had been careful. She had made me take a shower. She had given me a bar of Ivory soap.

"It's unscented," she said. "My soap will leave perfume on you. We have to be responsible."

I did not make it to the front door. Before I could, we fell into each other's arms, desire—perhaps it was fear—propelling us to make love again, to hold on to each other again. But she set the alarm on the clock, and when it rang, she prepared me for Nerida again: the shower, the inspection for loose strands of her hair, the scent of her perfume, the odor of her skin on mine.

"You'll still be on time for dinner," she said.

I left her house at four.

On the train, I made myself believe it could be done—that I could still remain married to Nerida and keep Marguerite as my other wife. All it would take would be valor, the strength of character to be discreet.

I could not deny it: I had broken the sixth commandment. The Old Testament would have condemned me. But what was sin in those dark days but public chaos, anarchy, that resulted when private ambitions, greed, desires broke free from their moorings and spread a tidal wave of destruction across quarreling tribes earnestly trying to be a nation? There had to be laws and punishments inflicted so that treaties could be drawn, peace made. Contained. *Thou shalt not kill thy neighbor; Thou shalt not covet thy neighbor's goods.* Thy neighbor's goods were also his wife.

Marguerite and I would cause no such rift in the solidity of my marriage. We would keep our love contained within its private moorings. Nobody needs to know, she said. It would be a sin only if *she* knows.

I was so buoyed by the logic of this argument that in a giddy fit of self-delusion I leapt to a more fantastical one; one, paradoxically, more real because I had built it on a logic that required Nerida's complicity. When the train pulled into Penn Station I had formulated it, sanctimonious now: Yes, one may be pardoned and retain the offense if the offense is not really an offense. If it hurts no one.

It was Nerida, I reasoned, who had never abandoned our traditional beliefs. It was she who believed our dead children had joined the ancestors, that their spirits lived with us.

Nerida had become a Christian for my sake. When we swore before the Christian priest that we would be faithful to each other, we had not made an oath before *her* priest. My Christian beliefs were not *her* beliefs. She was the daughter of her father's third wife. Her mother lived in a house next to the houses of her father's two other wives.

I reminded myself that we no longer slept in the same bedroom, that sex had become a burden to her, that she endured it only for my sake. Had Ibrahim Musima not explained the reason to me? I was skeptical then. Later, I felt guilty. Later, I believed I was to blame. Later, I knew Nerida had discovered that I was not free to love her with my whole heart, with my whole soul.

But now I wanted to believe Ibrahim Musima. I chose to believe Ibrahim Musima. It would be a relief to Nerida if I had another wife. Perhaps this is what she expected, what she was saying when she closed her doors to me: We were friends, partners. She was the first wife. She already had that honor. It was enough for her. She was tired. She would be happy to have me take a second wife.

I would tell her, I said to myself, that I loved Marguerite, that I wanted to make Marguerite my wife, that I would not leave her, that she would remain my wife, my first wife.

I felt righteousness. I felt guiltless. In the taxi to the apartment I told myself that I would say this to Nerida the moment I saw her, but even before I saw her, in the street outside the apartment building where I lived, where Nerida was waiting for me, the truth was stripping away the lies and half-truths I had used to delude myself, and in the hallway of the building I found myself face-to-face with the horror of the realization that Catherine's prophecy for me had been fulfilled: *When you lie, you'll believe you're telling the truth. From the core of your being, you'll think you haven't lied.* It had come to pass that night. I had arrived at that state she had predicted for me. I had told myself lies and believed I had spoken the truth. My heart raced in fear of the person I had become.

I saw Bala Keye immediately when I opened the door to my apartment, and relief washed over me. He was there to rescue me.

"You look tired. Worn out." Nerida was at the door to let me in.

I turned from her and hurried to the bedroom.

Behind the closed bedroom door I looked into the mirror. The face I saw there was the face of a man who had been snatched from the jaws of death. The pupils in the eyes were dilated, the skin ashen, the lips dry. I was a man who had been saved from suicide, a man who had been spared the fatal consequences of my mother's tragic choice.

"Is it the meetings, Oufoula?" Bala Keye knocked on the bedroom door.

I rubbed life into my eyes. I prepared myself to enter my world, the world I inhabited with Nerida, the world that would not demand my life, that would not ask for my soul.

"Oufoula seems to be bored with us," he said the moment I came out of the bedroom and he was sure I would hear him. "Maybe we are not sophisticated enough or educated enough."

I tried to distract him. "Did you have dinner?"

But his eyes stayed on me. "We were waiting for you."

"Uncle told me I should wait," said Nerida. "He said you would be back soon."

"Yes. I imagine it did not take long, Oufoula, that business I gave you to do?" He stood close to me and winked.

I knew what he was doing. He was turning Marguerite into a dirty secret. He was lumping her with his concubines, the women who were no more to him than vessels for his lust. Yet I did not stop him. I allowed him to tell this lie for me. I allowed him to save me. I did not let shame draw me back down to my mother's world, where I would have lost all—my reputation, my honor, the respect I had as a family man, a devoted husband, a committed father.

"Did you finish it?" he asked me.

I nodded my head.

"Good. Good." He turned to Nerida. "Oufoula was so bored with us at our meeting last week, he couldn't wait for me to answer a question Awani asked me. He got up and walked right out of the room. What was it, Oufoula? Were we that boring?" He was smiling at me, an oily smile that sickened me. "Where did you have to go that was so important?"

"I had heard your answer to that question already," I said. I looked away from him in Nerida's direction. "Will dinner be ready soon?" I asked her.

"Of course." She touched her uncle's arm. "He's hungry, Uncle. Can't you see that? We'll talk at dinner." She walked into the kitchen.

"I think he went to the store," Bala Keye answered his own question. "What was it that couldn't wait until the meeting ended? What did you have to buy, Oufoula?"

He followed me when I went to the other side of the room.

"He came back with a brown paper bag in his hand." He raised his voice. I knew Nerida heard him, but she did not respond. He bent toward me. "What was in that paper bag, Oufoula?" He whispered the question in my ear.

I called out to Nerida. "How much longer? Do I have time for a shower?"

"You have to be more careful, Oufoula." Bala Keye was still hovering at my shoulders.

Nerida saved me. "No," she answered my question, "we are going to eat now. Enough about business." She handed me a steaming dish of rice. "Can't this wait, Uncle?"

But Nerida knew it was not business that had caused Bala Keye to stand close to me, that had made my face turn ashen. She had become a diplomat. She had learned, perhaps from me, to be discreet.

At the table Bala Keye threw his last punches at me. I ducked but they landed on me all the same.

"You have a humble husband, Nerida. A man who does not ask for much."

I smiled at him. "I do not need much," I said.

"My brother says you show the world that Africa can come out of the bush. He says he made the right choice when he took you out of the bush."

He was threatening me. It was a threat that carried no weight except for the weight of my debt to his brother, the gratitude I owed him for taking me out of the mission school, for opening doors for me to the life I now lived.

"I owe my good fortune to your brother," I said.

"He says you represent the possibilities of Africa. My brother does things the old way, the way we used to." He shook his head in mock regret. "Not that I think having many wives is wrong." He cut into the meat on his plate. "I myself have three wives. I wouldn't want to give up any of them." He looked up at Nerida. "And you, niece," he said, "you wouldn't be here at all if my brother had not had a third wife."

I knew where he was heading before he would make it plain for me.

"My brother may not be a modern man, but he wants the world to see him as a modern leader of a modern Africa. You and Oufoula, you do that for him. You, especially, Oufoula." He pointed his fork at me. "You show the world that Africa is ready for the twenty-first century. Africa can be modern like you."

He was calling in his chips. He was saying to me that I could not embarrass his brother. I could not betray him. I could not be so ungrateful to him. I was the modern African. I had one wife. I followed a European religion. It was said I understood the European logic. I was proof that there was a generation of new Africans ready to lead the world. We did not know that that time would come soon. We did not know that Mandela would become the president of South Africa, that four years before the decade would end, a Ghanian would be head of the United Nations.

After dinner, he draped his arm across my shoulder. "We all bear a burden for Africa," he said, certain I had understood the message behind his compliments to me. "Yours is a light one." His body quivered with satisfaction.

I did not know if Nerida read between his words and guessed the truth, but when she asked me to go with her to the museum the next day, I did not protest. I did not object, either, when she said we had to go to a reception at the UN that afternoon. It was only when I returned to the apartment late that night that I remembered it was Monday. On Mondays I met Marguerite after class at the New School. On Mondays Marguerite and I had dinner at Knickerbocker's.

32

I knew you would not come. All yesterday I had this feeling. I was distracted in my class. Twice I had to leave the room to go to the bathroom to compose myself. I'm not like that, Oufoula. I am a woman who has control over her feelings. You are unraveling me."

I was out in the street before dawn to call her. When I remembered it was Monday, I was already in my pajamas. I did not wait to take them off. I pulled my pants over them and threw on my jacket. I told Nerida I needed to leave a message with the doorman for one of the men on my team who would be coming early in the morning to get it. Four times I called Marguerite before midnight, but she did not answer. I returned to my room and, unable to sleep, I waited for the dawn.

At four in the morning I was still sitting at the desk working on a paper on Mandela. Once, Nerida turned in her bed and asked me what I was doing. I told her the truth. It was that truth that made my lie in the morning convincing when I said to her that I needed to add something more to the message I had left with the doorman for Sangu last night.

"I called you four times," I said to Marguerite.

"When?"

"When I called you the last time it was close to midnight."

"I didn't get home until one in the morning. I waited for you. I thought you had a meeting. Something. I thought you'd be late. I kept hoping you'd still come. When I didn't see you at the school, I went to Knickerbocker's. I thought you'd get there. Eventually."

"Marguerite, I didn't know . . ."

"I think the waiter felt sorry for me. He said he didn't mind serving my table twice. He said I could order without you and he would come back again. But I couldn't eat."

"Oh, Marguerite." They were the only words that came out of my mouth.

"I'm not that kind of person, Oufoula. Not now. Not since my divorce. I do not let men take over my life."

"Marguerite, I will come tonight."

"No. It doesn't make sense. What will you say to her?"

"Leave that to me. Let me deal with that."

"I like to know things. I like to plan. I don't want another day of waiting."

"I'll come today."

"No."

"Why not, Marguerite?" I was begging her.

"You don't know what plans they may have for you today."

She said *they*, but we both knew whom she meant.

"I'll change them."

"Come on Saturday. You have your work. I don't want to interfere with your work. I'll have the time to do mine. You'll do yours and then we'll meet on Saturday. I don't want to spend my time waiting and hoping."

"Marguerite, I could work it out."

"No. Let's make it Saturday. I don't want you to have to make too many excuses for my sake. I don't want to cause you to raise suspicions. It would be better this way. We would both be calmer."

How easily we had spoken of discretion. How easily we believed that when we clothed it in flesh and blood, the abstract could still be real. Marguerite had wanted me to be careful. She would make the sacrifice, she said. *We* would. Everything would be okay so long as we kept our secret from Nerida, so long as we did not hurt her. Now she was beginning to understand the cost of our discretion. Now I wondered if she would find the price too high.

33

W hy did you step out of your marriage?"

Marguerite and I had just made love on the rug on the floor of her living room when she asked me that question. I had come to her house on Saturday. It had not been difficult to get away. Nerida was happy to have me leave. I had spent the week with her doing what she wanted: going shopping, going to the movies, going to museums. Only once had I balked at one of her requests. She had asked me to take her to an art gallery.

"Why there?" I answered her swiftly, desperate to smother the memories that suddenly surfaced. "There are more interesting things we could do."

But she insisted: "Didn't you used to like visiting art galleries when we lived in Washington?"

It was positive proof that Bala Keye's addition to our mission had not been accidental, that it was not the frivolous decision of a president who had gone soft in the head or in the heart. Our very first quarrel in those early years of our marriage had been over an art gallery, my insistence that we visit one, though that day not just she, but I, too, was exhausted from shopping. Such was my need for Marguerite, for something, anything that would connect me to her.

Nerida excused me in the evenings when I joined my team for dinner with influential Africans, the ones with money who owned uranium mines and oil wells in Africa and who could threaten the pockets of powerful Americans and make them see the profit in bringing an end to apartheid. Work saved me then as it had saved me before. It distracted me, helped me suppress my longings for Marguerite, the doubts and fears that plagued me when she refused me, when she asked me to wait until Saturday, five days, before I could see her. It saved me, too, from Bala Keye. He knew that I spent my days with Nerida, my nights with him. It was difficult for him to fan suspicions, which he may have already planted in Nerida's head, and which had caused her to demand my attention in ways she had long ago abandoned in Africa: the cocktail parties, the visits to museums, shopping. The trip to an art gallery. She still had not wanted me to make love to her and for that I was grateful.

On Saturday Nerida said she was tired. She did not want to go out. I told her I couldn't stay with her because I had to meet with a group of students in Long Island who wanted to join our struggle to free Mandela. I was a man habituated to caution and the habit of caution led me instinctively to prepare this alibi in case I was seen, as I once was seen by Bala Keye, taking the train to Long Island.

It was a cool fall day, but the sun blazed through the glass sliding doors in Marguerite's house and made us warm. We lay there naked, her head on my shoulders, facing the silken bay. A lone fisherman was making circles with his boat in front of us, prodding the bottom of the water with a long stick. He was looking for his crab baskets, Marguerite had told me. When she asked her question, I was watching him silently, letting the sun and the water and the reassurance of his single-mindedness lull me into a forgetfulness, into pretending that everything was the same as before, as before Nerida had come, before she had disturbed our Eden. Now Marguerite wanted me to answer her.

"I want to know," she said. "Why did you step out of your marriage?"

I sat up, bracing myself for the beginning of another drop down the seesaw.

"I didn't step out," I said.

"What do you think you did, then?" She sat up, too, and faced me.

"We . . . this does not have anything to do with my marriage," I said.

"What's happening between us has everything to do with your marriage. Why did you step out of it?"

"I don't know what you mean," I said. But I knew where she wanted to take me.

"It's I who don't know what you mean. You are making love to me. I am not your wife. To me that means you have stepped out of your marriage."

"I don't see it that way," I said.

"What way do you see it?" She brought her face close to mine. "You are married. You are supposed to make love to one woman, your wife. And here you are with me."

"I am with you, but being with you is unrelated to being with my wife."

I was going down with her, down to that place where more and more often we were finding ourselves—the place where I feared I would lose her, where she would force me to make a choice, a choice I could not make, a choice I was not prepared to make.

"Unrelated? How can you say unrelated?"

"You are two different people," I said.

"You want to trap me with your words. I am asking you a simple question. Why? What went wrong? You told me she was a good mother. You told me she was a good wife. So why are you with me?"

"Because I never stopped loving you," I said.

"You want me to believe you love two women. It is as simple as that, is it? Well, good. Fine. I believe you. I believe that it is possible for a person to love two people at the same time. But what I want to know is, why did you act on it?"

"Act on it?"

"Yes, act on it. You could have kept on loving me. You didn't have to make love to me. Why did you cross that line?"

She was draining me, wearing me out. I answered her without subterfuge.

"I don't see the lines you see, Marguerite. I don't see the difference you make between loving you and making love to you. If there is a line, I crossed it the minute I fell in love with you. I did not feel that I had done something wrong when I fell in love with you and I do not feel so now. I had not planned to fall in love with you. It was not my intention. It happened."

"But you *plan* now to make love to me? Isn't it your *intention* to make love to me?"

"Making love to you is the expression of my love for you. To me it is only wrong if it is also wrong to love you."

"What about your vow of fidelity to your wife?"

She had returned to the question she had asked me before, the one I had not answered when she wanted to know if I thought that making love to her was a sin. I still had no answer to give her. I was a Christian, but the obsession the missionaries had with the evils of sex always eluded me. As a boy I was fascinated with their god who rose from the dead. Their mystery of an incarnate spirit was not so removed from the beliefs of my people. But it had never made sense to me that this God would create such pleasure for us only to forbid us to enjoy it. I did not agree with O'Malley's cynical theory about God's duplicitous intentions, that God had given us desire for sex so that we could destroy ourselves, but it was easier to accept that than to believe that sexual intercourse between two people who loved each other was sinful.

"I was faithful to my love for you," I said to Marguerite.

She stood up. "You're playing games with me, Oufoula."

"No, Marguerite," I said. She forced me to look up at her, like a boy in the confessional.

"Then answer my question."

"What is it you want to know?"

"What was wrong with your marriage? I do not care what you

say, you would not have acted on your love for me if nothing was wrong with your marriage. Why did you step out of it?"

It was then I told her that Nerida and I no longer slept in the same bedroom, but even as I told her that, I did not think it was the truthful answer to her question. I had never stepped out of my marriage to Nerida. I was not stepping out of it now. I felt as married to Nerida as I did the day I took her as a wife. True, there was no passion between us but there was everything else, everything by which I found my place in the world, by which I defined myself. With Nerida I was husband, father, head of a family—roles that gave confidence to those who assigned me other roles: spokesman for my country, arbitrator for other countries, head of a team of Africans on a mission to save South Africa. Marguerite would not understand that though I was unaware of the truth I spoke to her when I was a young man, when I was desperately in love with her, I still wanted Nerida as my wife, and I also wanted her as my other wife.

"What went wrong?" Marguerite was asking me again.

I told her that Nerida had lost interest in sex with me.

"Why?" She sat back down on the floor next to me, the rigidity in her face softening.

I gave her the answer Ibrahim Musima had given me, the answer I no longer believed. It was the easier answer to give her.

"Menopause," I said.

"Menopause?"

"It made her lose interest," I said.

She laughed at me.

"Where did you get that foolish idea?" she asked me. "I'm in menopause. I have not lost interest in sex."

"You take those pills," I said.

"You think it's the pills?"

"That HRT, whatever," I said.

"It has nothing to do with it. And I have stopped taking them. There. I stopped taking them after we talked."

"You stopped taking them?"

"You said you'll love me, you said you'll want me even when my teeth fall out."

"You did that for me?"

"I threw them away. I wasn't sure of them anyhow."

I kissed her on the mouth. She pushed me away. "Why did she leave your bed, Oufoula?" She was not finished with me.

I removed my arms from around her shoulders. "I was the one who left," I said.

"Why?"

"I was dreaming of you."

She was not ready for my answer. She was not prepared for her part in the answer to the question she had asked me. All her defiance left her when I implicated her in the erosion of my marriage. She leaned against me.

"We must be careful, Oufoula," she said. Her voice was sad, her eyes misty. "We have to be cautious. We cannot let her know."

Marguerite asked me no more questions that day but she would change places again on that seesaw when I spoke to her the next night. Before I left her house, I had made a call to my son. We spoke in French. Marguerite was sitting next to me on the sofa when I called him. She got up after we had spoken a few words to each other. I made no special note of her leaving. She had walked to the kitchen, I thought, to prepare dinner, but the next night when I called her, she would let me know why she had left, and the reason she gave me would cause a painful argument between us and lead us to that place of no return, that fork in the road that would demand that I go one way or the other, that I choose her or the life I had with Nerida.

34

What is the meaning of *petite femme?*" Marguerite asked me soon after she answered the phone.

I sensed the danger immediately in her question.

"You know what it means." I approached her cautiously.

"Does it mean 'mistress'?"

"It could. But it is also a term of endearment."

"But when a man says *ma petite femme,* he means his mistress, doesn't he?"

"He could, but he could also mean his wife."

"I am not your mistress, Oufoula." Her voice was tense, strained. "I am too old to be your mistress. Too proud. I've worked too hard to be any man's mistress."

"What is it, Marguerite? What is wrong? Who said you were my mistress?"

"I heard you yesterday on the phone. I didn't understand everything you said, but I heard you say *'ma petite femme.'* You were telling your buddies you were at your mistress's house. I am not your mistress."

I could hear that her words came through clenched teeth.

"Marguerite, you are mistaken. You don't understand. I would not tell anybody about you. Not the people here with me. If I told anybody about you, it would be my friends back home."

"I am not your mistress," she repeated.

"I was talking to my son."

"Your son?"

"I was speaking about his mother. Sometimes that is how I address her to him. Sometimes I say *'ma petite femme'* and I am speaking about his mother."

"You call his mother your mistress?"

"My little wife."

I knew when I translated the words I had made matters worse, not better.

Marguerite began to cry. "This is not going to work, Oufoula. I don't think I can handle this. I'm lying to myself. I'm a hypocrite. I can't stand the lies I tell myself."

"Marguerite, wait, wait till I come to your house. We can talk then. We can sort this out."

"No. I have to say it now or I won't get the courage to say it ever."

She breathed in hard. Her voice was steady again when she spoke.

"I support women, Oufoula. I draw women. I paint women. Do you remember that time I told you that I believe women would have power when they stopped sleeping with other women's men? I still believe that. I am sleeping with another woman's man and I can't live with myself and do that."

"You are doing nothing wrong, Marguerite. You can't help yourself for loving me."

"I put myself in your wife's place and I see how she would see me. I don't want to cause another woman grief," she said.

"She doesn't know. She'll never know."

"I knew when Harold was cheating on me. Your wife knows, or she will know soon."

Catherine had said that to me. *A woman knows.* John tried to deceive her in the open, at a cocktail party. He thought because he spoke to the woman's husband in her presence that Catherine would not know. But Catherine knew already. She knew that John and the man's wife were lovers.

"I love you, Marguerite."

"This has to stop. We have to stop lying to each other and to her. I can't face myself in the mirror."

"I'll come over tomorrow. We'll talk."

"No. I don't see the point in your coming. It's no use. It won't make a difference no matter what we say. You said you'll love me forever. Now I know it won't be forever."

"I will love you forever, Marguerite," I said.

"I am a backdoor woman, the woman you hide from your family, the woman you keep away from decent people. I told you not to bring me red roses, but I was lying to myself. I *am* your mistress. I will grow old alone. You will grow old with your wife."

"You will not grow old alone," I said, but she did not believe me.

"I am the same woman, Oufoula, that you met many years ago. I thought I could do this, but I can't. I am ashamed to be a mistress. I am ashamed to know I am deceiving another woman. I still can't have an affair with a married man."

"We are not having an affair."

"We are not married," she said.

"What about you? Your feelings?"

"She found you first. She has rights. I don't."

"You are talking about yourself as if you are not human. You are human. Rights or who came first has nothing to do with your feelings."

"Then it's my feelings, too, I'm talking about, Oufoula. I don't like deceiving your wife, but I can't bear the thought of you touching her either. The worst part of that is that I have no right to think this way."

"That's not what is happening, Marguerite."

"You live in the same house."

"But not in the same bedroom."

"You can't tell me that you never, *ever* sleep with her."

I did not answer her.

"That is what I mean," she said. "When your wife was not here it was easy to pretend. I came to your apartment, you came to my house, and we spent the night together. We woke up in the morning together. If you were married, we would not have been able to do that. But your wife is here now and I can't spend the night with you, and I can't call you at your apartment. I can't pretend anymore. I have to face the fact that you are married, and I find I can't live with that fact. I can't be at peace with myself. I pick fights with you, I am always angry. I cry myself to sleep. I am miserable."

"Marguerite."

"I don't want to be miserable again. I don't want to be angry. I have paid dearly not to be miserable anymore, not to be angry. Nineteen years and a costly divorce."

"Marguerite, I—"

"You would be miserable, too, if I were in your place and I were living with my husband, whether I was having sex with him or not."

It was then I told her how I felt when she said to me that her ex-husband had touched the back of her neck, my special place, the spot on her body that was mine.

"I felt such violence rise up in me, I would have hit him if he were near to me. I don't know what I would have done if you had gone to lunch with him. It was only when you said you hadn't that I began to calm down."

"Then you understand."

"I've always understood, Marguerite. I didn't think it was fair, but I loved you and you loved me."

"Then you know we can't see each other again."

"If that will make you happy, Marguerite."

"It will make me suffer less. I have my art, my work. I was content with it before you came back. I'll be content again."

We put down the phone, but in less than five minutes I was calling her again.

"I can't leave us like this," I said. "I have to see you."

"I won't make love to you anymore," she said.

"This is too abrupt. We have to go slower."

"I won't change my mind."

"If I love you, I cannot make you suffer. But we have to do this slowly. You have to give us time to make the transition."

"I won't sleep with you again."

"I am not asking you to sleep with me. We need to talk. I want us to talk face-to-face. I am coming to see you."

"When?"

"Now. I'll take the next train."

"What will you tell your wife?"

"I must see you."

"What will you say when she asks you where you are going?"

"Please, Maguerite."

I was a man drowning.

"Now. Let me come now."

She pitied me.

35

When the door closed behind us we fell into each other's arms.

"Just this one last time," I whispered in her ear.

I did not have to convince her.

We undressed each other slowly. We did not make a sound. No words passed our lips. She lifted her arms and I eased her sweater across her shoulders, over her head, and up the length of her arms. I undid the buttons of her blouse one by one down the front of her chest and at her wrists. I took off her blouse and kissed the spot on the back of her neck where the bone protruded.

I unfastened the hooks of her bra and knelt down before her. I let my tongue linger on the edges of the dark flesh that circled her nipples.

She held my head, pushed her fingers deep into the thick nap of my hair to my scalp, and drew me closer.

She had worn pants. I undid the button at the waist, pulled down the zipper, and put my hands between her panties and her skin and slid them down her legs.

She was standing before me naked now, I on my knees still fully dressed. I wrapped my arms around her waist. I fought back the tears welling in the corners of my eyes.

"I wish there had been nobody but you. I wish you were the first, the only one," she murmured above my head.

I sunk my face into the softness of her belly.

Her fingers searched my neck for the collar of my shirt. I lifted my head and she unbuttoned it. I stood up and she undressed me.

We moved toward each other with the grace of dancers: arms, legs, hips rising and falling to a rhythm we had memorized, a slow dance we had rehearsed to perfection. We moved without effort, my body sinking into hers, hers yielding to mine, neither of us willing to give way when the moment came, holding ourselves back as if we thought to surrender was to say good-bye.

Afterwards I lay next to her, my hands caressing places, it seemed, I had loved for an eternity, places I thought I would never touch again.

I fought against that reality.

"When we are old we will be together," I said. "We will live by the sea in a house in the islands."

"Jamaica?" She entered my dream.

"No. Somewhere in the Caribbean where you have not been and I have not been. Somewhere we both do not know. We will see it for the first time together. We'll build the same memories. We'll make our own history."

"When I'm how old? Eighty?"

"Long before that, Marguerite. Long before that."

Our bodies were warm with the love we had given to each other. We were holding on to the hours we knew were slipping away, stretching ourselves across the years we did not want to lose.

I made one last desperate attempt to change her mind, to convince her that we did not have to part.

"It could be like having a husband who traveled. I could come to you or you could come to me where I am."

"And what about the in between? I would still know you were with your wife."

"Marguerite, can't you try?"

But the dream was over. Finished. "This is the end, Oufoula." She pressed her face against my heart.

. . .

I could not stay in New York and know she was there. Every minute of the train ride taking me away from her was torture for me. I wanted to get off, to turn back and tell her I could not be parted from her. She could not be parted from me. But what could I tell her? I had never thought of leaving Nerida. I would not do it now. I could not imagine a life where I was not an admired husband, admired father, respected ambassador, a man praised by his president, a man in demand for his talents, a man honored in Africa.

A man about whom a griot sings.

There was nothing I had to offer Marguerite, nothing I could say to justify asking her not to leave me. Nerida would not accept my marriage to a second wife. Marguerite would not accept my having a wife.

I wanted to leave New York that day. I wanted to return to my country, where there would be no reminders of Marguerite. I told myself that when I got there I would destroy her books, take down her portrait from my bedroom wall. I would bury her deep in my heart, in my soul. I would try to forget her.

Bala Keye oozed sympathy for me. He would arrange for me to go back to Africa the next day, he said. He did not argue with me when I told him I was no longer essential to the team. We had the world on our side now, he said. It would not be long before Mandela was freed, apartheid come to an end.

He had waited years for this moment to see the lights put out of my eyes. He would assist me, he said.

"It is for the best. It is the right thing to do for you and Nerida. The strength of our country is in the family. You have a good marriage, a loving wife. Successful children. You are an example to our people. You make our ancestors proud. You do not break your connection to them."

He chose his weapons well. He used history, tradition, continuity to blind me. He knew I would fall face forward on the tips of those swords willingly.

"Your grandchildren will look back and see this thing you have done today. They will know of your sacrifice. They will learn to be Africans. They will be grateful to you."

He spoke as my loyal confidant. He would keep my secret, he said. He did not name it. He did not need to name it. I knew he had found out about my love for Marguerite. His body trembled with the pleasure he took in turning my words against me, the speeches I had given on loyalty to Mother Africa in spite of the inconveniences, the inefficiencies I claimed to love. He said he had told Nerida many times that no matter how far I traveled or for how long, she had nothing to worry about. There was nothing outside of Africa—*no one*—that could pull me away from Africa or from her.

I wanted to return to Africa alone. I told him that Nerida could follow me later.

"Yes," he said. "You need the time to clear your head. To clean your spirit. I will tell her there was an emergency at home. I will tell her my brother needs you. I will arrange it."

I called Marguerite from the airport.

"I'll phone you when I get to Africa," I said.

"Don't," she said.

"I must call you."

"Don't call me. *Ever.*"

"Ever?"

"I don't want to wait by the phone. I don't want to think every time it rings that it could be you. I don't want to have expectations."

"But I must hear your voice."

"It will be a living death for me. I prefer to know it's completely over now. I could mourn and move on."

"I could never move on," I said to her.

"You will in time."

"I didn't for twenty-five years."

She lowered her voice to a whisper. "I want you to suffer." Her passion was searing.

"You do not mean that, Marguerite."

"I mean it with all my heart. I want you to suffer. I want you to hurt so hard, you won't be able to sleep nights, you won't be able to eat. You'll walk around like a zombie, missing me."

"Oh, Marguerite."

"I will suffer. I want to know that when I am suffering you are suffering, too. I want to know you'll feel the same pain I will feel. It will give me comfort knowing that. Knowing I am not alone. It won't be so hard for me if I know that."

"Marguerite." My voice cracked.

"There will be nobody after you, Oufoula. You were the first and you are the last man I will love."

"We will be together again, Marguerite. I know it."

Her laughter cascaded over her tears. "Yes," she said.

The image of the female swan on O'Malley's lake flashed through my head at that moment. I saw her beating her wings in the still air, twisting her long neck, tremors erupting through her body. But the male swan had planted his seed in her. Nothing she could do would expel it from her loins. She would carry him with her wherever she went.

36

It is six months now since I have seen Marguerite. I am in my house. I am in Africa. In Africa I am a crab scuttling backwards, a man past his prime trying to teach himself the lessons of his youth. A man trying to accept the wisdom of the decision that was made for him, trying to convince himself he has escaped the chaos, the confusion, the destruction of all he had worked for, all he would have lost, all that would never have been his again, had he let his private life seep into his public life, had he chanced eruption there.

I am Oufoula who wants to make himself believe that parting from Marguerite was the right thing to do.

I have taken her portrait off my wall. I have given away her books, but everywhere I turn I see her—her small body, her smiling eyes, the mouth I want to kiss.

I know when I put my head on my pillow tonight I will dream of her. I have not ceased to dream of her. I do not want to stop those dreams. I want to see her. I want to talk to her. I fear, yet I welcome the pain that will come when I wake in the morning and know she is not with me. That pain has become my friend. It makes her real to me. It makes me know I have not imagined her.

Nerida called our children home from the university when she returned from New York. She said I walked through the house as if I saw ghosts. She said my children would bring me to life again. But I was already in the land of the living dead, the land where my mother lived before she walked to freedom, and it was not my children I wanted. It was Marguerite. It is she alone who can bring me to life again.

When the days are drier, I go to my house in the country, the house I had built on the lands my ancestors had won in the wars. My father is dead now. Years ago his wives moved to the south to plant sorghum on the arable lands they inherited there. I had razed my father's concrete barracks and cleared the ground where his houses once stood. I had swept them away as so much rubbish, the way he had swept any feelings he may have had for me. But my need is such now, my suffering so intense that I look for wisdom in the indifference my father had shown to me, in the coldhearted, callous way he had dismissed my mother's unhappiness, her fatal desperation.

Perhaps my father was right not to protest when my mother left him, not to interfere when I was taken from him. He opened the palms of his hands. He let go of her, he let go of me. "What will be, will be," he said.

My father's spirit rises from the earth and circles me in this place where he once lived. He loved my mother, he loved me, he tells me, he lies to me, but he understood the dangers of holding on to what he had already lost. He understood the futility. He avoided the torment.

I let myself be comforted by this thought, this lie. I had done the right thing not to fight for Marguerite, not to try harder to persuade her to stay with me. Now, I must try to do as my father had done with me. I must try to let go. I must try to free myself of the futility of longing for Marguerite, of the torment of hoping for a future with her.

I find other solace, other reassurance, on these lands where I have built my country house, that place where my mother had obeyed her father, where she married a man she did not love, where she wept for the man she did love. I tell myself another lie that brings me false solace, false reassurance: My mother could have found happiness here, at least contentment. She was the one who brought sorrow to herself by holding on to a past she could not regain, by not letting go. She caused her own death when she left my father, when she turned her back on her home, on her family, on her son. When she walked away.

I make myself remember this. I let my mother's life serve as a lesson to me, a warning. There would have been death for me, too, had I turned my back on Nerida, on my home, on my children— confusion, failure, as my mother's life had been a failure.

History roots us, I remind myself. I teach myself again. History gives us sustenance, our sense of place, of time, of position in the world. Without history we are set adrift. We are lost. We cannot know who we are, where we came from, what we will become.

Nerida gives me history. I can look back into the years and find the person I am in the places we have been together, in the things we have done. In the children we have raised.

I can find myself in the bricks of my house, in the wood slats of my floor. These, too, bind me to Nerida: the trees I planted where my father's house once stood. Nerida was with me then. She had watched when I dug the ground. The trees, the ground, the bricks in my house fuse me to Nerida, connect me to my father, to my mother, to my ancestors. To my children.

I come here to my country house where my griot sings of the past of my people and I find my place here. I know there is much here I love, much I cannot leave, much I cannot give up.

"Who else in Africa is more blessed?" my griot sings of me.

I return to Nerida refreshed, her husband again. We do not sleep in the same room, but still there are nights she admits me to her bed. I am grateful for those nights, for in the city I am afraid to be alone. Even in the daytime I seek the companionship of friends who believe I am a happy man, a contented man, a man to be envied. They—Nerida, too—are buffers between me and the pain I know awaits me at daybreak.

I go to church often now, seeking affirmation, comfort, reassurance. I hold close to my heart a sermon the minister once gave on the Book of Genesis.

"God so loved us, He gave us free will, the will to choose God or to choose evil. Which of us is so foolish as to follow Adam? Which of us would lose Eden again for an apple?"

On the holidays, when my children are gathered together around Nerida and me, I tremble for the choice I could have made, the things I could have lost, the life I would not have if I had chosen the apple, if I had not chosen Nerida, if I had walked away from her.

Nerida talks now of grandchildren. She prods our daughters and our son to marry, to fulfill her dream for them, for us. She speaks to them of the importance of history, tradition, continuity. She tells them we know who we are because we have kept our traditions, because we did not sever our links to the past.

I try to avoid the lie in her words, the contradiction. I try to ignore the hypocrisy so rampant among the élite in Africa, among the educated, among the wealthy, the powerful. They, too, like Nerida, speak of history, tradition, continuity, yet they embrace Christianity, the white man's religion. They—we the élite condemn polygyny. We speak sanctimoniously about monogamy. But I have seen the consequences to those we once honored: first wives, mothers of the firstborn. They are now discarded, rendered useless, set out to pasture, like barren cows, to graze on brown grass. For we know, I know, that as long as we limit ourselves to one wife—*one wife at a time*—we have the blessings of Christians, we have their approval, we can be trusted by investors from the West. For we prove ourselves to be modern Africans. We prove we are not hostage to the past, to impenetrable traditions that could bind us, that could affect the decisions we make, the way we see the world.

I think this way and my cynicism engulfs me; it spreads through me like an infectious disease. Contagious. Its sickness drips over all I see, all I love. I question everything then. I doubt everything then. I put everything under scrutiny, even Nerida.

Innocent Nerida, I had once thought her, always in the dark about the truth behind the lies I told her. Now I wonder. Now I question. Now I remember that when she first came to me, she came with a lie intended to deceive me. She knew there was a chance I would not marry her if I discovered that she had been to the university, if I knew she had a degree.

Now I remember other things: how when we were first married, when we lived in Washington, I believed she had decorated the apartment for me, to remind me of Africa; how later, in Africa, it was plain to me that the colors she had chosen were her colors, the furnishings her taste; how when she persuaded her father to restrict my work to Washington, she wanted me to believe it was my health she was worried about—the fatigue I suffered after each trip I took to New York; how now it was obvious to me it was not me she had been thinking of, but herself; it was not concern for me, rather distrust of my motives that had sent her to her father petitioning for my release; how, though I had thought I had hidden my dreams of Marguerite from her, she had known all along the truth of the nightmares that had woken me up in a sweat; how, now, though twenty-five years had passed, she could still recall an insignificant detail: a quarrel over a visit to an art gallery.

She had sent Bala Keye to spy on me. I am certain of that now. It brings clarity to the puzzle that had troubled me: Why had the president sent Bala Keye on our mission to the UN when he knew his brother disliked me, when he himself had little or no respect for him?

But the president could not refuse his daughter, he could not deny her the favor she asked of him.

Bala Keye had told Nerida about the roses, about my distraction at meetings. About my weekends away from my apartment. She had decided to come to New York to set me straight again, to put me on her course again.

She knew she would win. She believed she knew me. She knew her talk of history, tradition, continuity would rein me in, bring me back, put an end to my juvenile wanderings.

But late at night, when only the stars light the sky, when I am alone, when Nerida is deep in sleep, I ache for Marguerite, I long for Marguerite. I want to merge myself into the darkness of the night and go to her. I want her arms around my neck, her kisses on my lips. I face the truth Nerida wants to hide from me. I am not afraid to let myself know that though humans may live without love, they cannot live without passion. That without passion, we only exist. We merely pass through life as would an animal.

On those nights I am not consoled by history, by tradition, by continuity. I am my mother's son. I am a man first before I am an African. I am an individual, unique, before I am a husband, before I am a father.

My mother was a woman first before she was an African, before she was a wife, before she was a mother.

I am Oufoula. I have needs, I have desires. I want my needs, my desires fulfilled. I want personal happiness. I think neither history nor tradition nor continuity is worth the sacrifice of my person. I tell myself that to sacrifice my happiness is to spit in the face of God.

I do not blaspheme. There are men in the Bible whom God condemns for wasting their talent, for throwing it to the wind, for casting it on stony ground. I do not want to throw my life to the wind. I do not want to sacrifice my happiness.

On nights like these I become Faust. I would exchange all I have for Marguerite, for the feel of her breath on my neck. I would cut the bonds that have sustained me. I would set myself adrift in her arms.

Willingly I admit I had first pursued her to satisfy prurient desires. What man alive does not have traces of darkness lurking within him? Call this darkness moral turpitude; its common manifestation is almost always sexual. This darkness lurked within me, too. But my search for the incarnation of a fantasy I had created to protect myself from a woman who had spurned me did not lead me to damnation. It led me to Marguerite. It led me to the light.

I have done as Marguerite has asked me. I have obeyed her wishes. I have not contacted her. But, once, when a man I knew was going to New York, I asked him to inquire of her for me. He returned with a brochure filled with pictures of her work. He had found it in a gallery in SoHo. He was not looking for her then. He just happened to come upon a painting of a man with such a likeness of me, he knew it was by the artist I had asked him to find.

He read a review of her work to me: *An exceptional talent. An artist who sees into the souls of men.*

She had seen into mine. She would know, if she saw me now, I am a crab scuttling backwards.

Yet life does not give this reprieve. We take the present with us when we go backwards. We must endure, too, the past beyond the past we want to retrieve. I did not want to retrieve the past before Marguerite, nor the past when I longed for her. I wanted only the past of those last weeks we had spent loving each other.

I had believed my private life would destroy my public life. Now I have lived to know the reverse. For marriage belongs to our public life. Passion, the flame that ignites the private self, endangers the public life, puts it at risk. I had been afraid to lose my public self. Now I pay for that fear with the loss of joy in my private self.

On the surface where the public can witness, my marriage is good, even perfect. My life is good, even perfect. I am wealthy. I have power. The griot still sings for me. On the inside where I really live, I am hollow. I live the life of the living dead, the life my mother refused.

Marguerite feared she would grow old alone. I fear to grow old without her.

Nerida does not give me the illusion of permanence. Once I believed it was marriage that offered this consolation, but I was young, afraid of change, afraid of what Mulenga had done to me, what passion had done to my mother. Now I know the illusion marriage offers can be a hollow one, transparent, its source often fear, cowardice, desperation. Habit.

Each day I stay with Nerida I am aware of the passing of time, of the ending of another day without Marguerite. Does this mean I do not love Nerida? I want to love Nerida. She is my wife.

But I do not feel immortal with Nerida. I felt immortal with Marguerite. From that first time we made love, when I remembered the swans on O'Malley's lake and felt no rage, no shame in loving her, I believed our love would never die. That we would last forever.

More and more I dream of Marguerite. I dream of what was. What could have been. I do not know how long I can live this way with dreams, with the emptiness. I do not know how many more breaths will flow through my lungs, how much longer I can exist without her.

The nights are more frequent now when I shout into the wind: "Marguerite, I am suffering."

I hear her answer me. "So am I, Oufoula. So am I."

Her answer brings me comfort.